For All We Know

D1024626

SANDRA KITT
For All We Know

ARABESQUE®

FOR ALL WE KNOW

An Arabesque novel

ISBN-13: 978-0-373-83104-3
ISBN-10:   0-373-83104-8

www.kimanipress.com

Printed in U.S.A.

Dear Reader,

You are about to enjoy some of our most extraordinary romantic fiction in a new series called Novels of Love & Hope, written by two of Arabesque's best-loved authors. In this series—which includes *For All We Know* by Sandra Kitt and *What Matters Most* by Gwynne Forster—great romance combines with heartwarming, compelling stories that help raise awareness about health issues that affect our community. In partnering with St. Jude Children's Research Hospital for this series, we hope to enlighten as well as provide insight into the research and medicine practiced at this preeminent research facility.

The first book in the series, *For All We Know,* tells the heartfelt story of two people whose love is tested as they care for an HIV-infected teenager. The next novel, *What Matters Most,* is a story of romance that defies family tradition and reveals what it truly means to be committed to improving health care for the poor. Both books offer messages of love and hope in the face of tremendous struggles. Indeed, Arabesque is proud to be a part of this campaign launched by St. Jude, and we trust that it will spark interest and awareness among our readers.

All the best,

Evette Porter
Editor
Arabesque/Kimani Press

For the extraordinary legacy of Danny Thomas, St. Jude Children's Research Hospital in Memphis, and for the hospital's dedication and caring in working to save children's lives. Most importantly, this is for the children and their future.

Acknowledgments

It was exciting and challenging to write a book on behalf of St. Jude Children's Research Hospital, while also giving my readers a great love story. But much of this book could not have been possible without the cooperation of the staff at St. Jude and their generous willingness to be interviewed. In particular I want to acknowledge the medical information and details I received from doctors and nurses on staff, notably Dr. Nehali Patel, Infectious Diseases, and Sandra Jones, TTU clinic manager. I'm grateful for the time spent with Nikia Johnson, director for multicultural marketing, who helped to nurture this project from its inception, and those who work with and for her: Keia Johnson, Tiffany Strange and Judith Black. Also, thanks to Glenn Keesee, senior director for marketing (and his lovely sense of humor). I'm very pleased that Linda Gill, general manager of Kimani Press at Harlequin, was immediately enthusiastic about the idea of my writing a story with St. Jude as part of the setting, and thrilled that the CEO of Harlequin, Donna Hayes, so willingly came on board with the offer to publish *For All We Know*. Some of the heart of this story is also due to the insights gained from Elder Pastor John B. Smith of Rosemark Church in Tennessee. I was very impressed and moved by information from Dr. Jesse T. Williams, II, of Convent Avenue Baptist Church in New York City. He's my hero! Finally, many, many, many thanks to my incredibly supportive agent, Lisa Erbach Vance.

Chapter 1

Michaela Landry gripped the steering wheel of the Camry and frowned as she looked out the windshield and tried to read the road signs. Nothing looked familiar. She couldn't find any of the landmarks her godmother had described to help her find her way back from the Memphis International Airport. Was she even going in the right direction?

She sucked her teeth, annoyed with her own ignorance, and blaming Memphis for having streets not being laid out in a more logical way.

She found herself crossing a street called Flicker. She'd seen that before…but then she made a turn. Wrong move. Michaela had no idea where she was.

Just then her cell phone, which she'd placed on top of her purse on the passenger seat, began to trill a musical ring tone. She reached over and pressed the speakerphone button.

"Hello?"

"Where are you?"

Michaela exhaled in relief when she recognized her godmother's voice.

"I'm on my way back to the house, Aunt Alice," she answered as if she knew what she was doing.

Alice Underwood laughed. "Girl, you are lost. Admit it. You should have been back to the house a half hour ago. Ben and I don't live but twenty minutes from the airport. I've been calling the house and getting no answer. You had us worried. What happened?"

Michaela squinted as she passed another unknown street name and confessed that she didn't know where she was. She described her location. Guiding her by phone, her godmother got her pointed in the right direction.

"I would have figured it out," Michaela said defensively. Already she was seeing businesses and buildings she recognized.

"Yeah, but by then you would have been in Mississippi." Alice chuckled.

"Is your flight delayed?"

"No. As a matter of fact they just announced we'll be boarding in a few minutes. I just want to make sure you'll be okay by yourself. Call me if you need information…or if you get lost again."

"I don't plan on having to call you for anything. This is a special trip for you and Ben."

She was feeling confident as she drove along the avenue that would lead back to her godparents' home in the neighborhood known as Chickasaw Gardens.

The wide avenues were clean and orderly, bordered on either side by the occasional high brick wall, or formal entrances indicating gated communities. The trees were tall and leafy and very old, forming an arbor overhead. They shaded the road, with sunlight dappling through the branches.

"You're too proud and stubborn for your own good. Men don't like that in a woman, you know."

"I'm not interested in any man who can't let me be who I am."

Michaela couldn't help responding to her god-mother's reference to her tendency to square off with the opposite sex, and not back down when she felt she was right about something. According to Alice Underwood, that's what had contributed to her persistent single state.

"Anyway, how do you know I wasn't driving around exploring, and getting better acquainted with the University District?"

"*Umph.* 'Cause you can't fool me. You city folk think you know everything. I remember when you and your sister used to come to stay with us when you were kids, how you'd carry on about the bugs and the heat and the strange sounds at night. You weren't curious. You were scared."

"I loved coming to see you." Michaela smiled at the memory, making the last turn on the approach to her godparents' home. "I wanted to live in your house forever."

"Well, now's your chance to find out if you'd really like living in a small city in the South. Memphis isn't like D.C."

"That's why I accepted your invitation to stay by myself while you and Uncle Ben are away on your second honeymoon. I needed a break."

Alice laughed, her voice laced with skepticism. "All right now. We'll see. I told Jefferson to keep an eye on you."

"Your neighbor? I don't believe he even exists. You keep talking about him, but I haven't seen him since I got here. I don't need a babysitter, Aunt Alice. I have Lady for company."

"That fool cat don't like nobody but Ben. She turns up her nose at me."

"If she's not nice to me she won't eat."

Alice Underwood laughed merrily. "Honey, if there's a showdown I'm still betting on Lady to come out ahead. She's got eight more lives than you have."

"Oh, I'm here, Aunt Alice! I just turned into the gate."

"Good. I have to go myself. Ben is signaling me to get off the phone and get in line for boarding."

"Have a wonderful time in Paris. What a romantic place to spend your anniversary."

"Thank you, dear. You enjoy yourself, too."

Michaela finished the call. She pressed the remote, clipped to the sun visor, to open the electronic garage door. When she drove in, the front right side of the car hit something and pushed it along the cement floor. She turned off the engine she got out to investigate. She found a recycled shipping carton in front of the bumper. It was partially filled with articles of clothing, and she guessed that Ben had apparently forgotten to move it when he loaded the luggage into the car earlier. Michaela put it aside, not sure if the clothing were rags, Ben's working-around-the-house clothes, or things to be given to charity.

She closed the garage door and headed to the back door of the house that would let her into the kitchen. There was no question that it felt eerie to be there by herself. She could hear the ticking of the wall clock over the kitchen door, the refrigerator motor, a bird outside in one of the trees. There was a soft ca-thump from the laundry room and Lady, the Underwoods' aging, fat, long-haired cat, came sauntering in from one of her favorite sleeping places on top of the clothing dryer. Lady looked up at Michaela with her wide, gray eyes, meowed tentatively and strolled past her and into the living room.

"It's you and me, babe," Michaela murmured.

Suddenly she started. She heard a hard scraping sound that seemed to be coming from the backyard. Michaela turned around to lean over the sink and peered out the window. She could see almost the entire yard, but it was empty and still. Just visible was an edge of the flagstone patio and a lounge chair. She frowned at it, sure that the day before the chair had been in a different place. Or had it?

She started again. This time it was because of the front doorbell. She hurried to find out who was there, chastising herself for letting her imagination get the better of her. There was no peephole, such as she had on her apartment door in the building where she lived in D.C. Weren't folks here worried about being bludgeoned to death by a stranger they couldn't see?

Michaela opened the door.

Standing before her was a tall, broad-shouldered man with medium-brown skin. He was clean-shaven, but wore wireless rimmed glasses that seemed almost invisible on his chiseled, square face. He was dressed in summer business attire: brown slacks, a white short-sleeved shirt and a smart but conservative tie.

"Can I help you?" she asked.

He inclined his head toward her, askance. "Good afternoon. Are you Michaela? I'm Jefferson McNeill. I live three houses that way." He pointed with a sideward nod of his head.

She quickly gathered her wits. Aunt Alice had neglected to mention that Jefferson McNeill was a good-looking man with an erect, sturdy build. To Michaela he had the demeanor and presence of, perhaps, a lawyer, or college professor...someone who looked like he'd played varsity football. The woman in her did a quick mental survey of her own appearance and decided that what Mr. McNeill was seeing should be equally appealing. She smiled pleasantly at him.

"Yes, I'm Michaela. My godparents mentioned you." She decided against offering Mr. McNeill her hand. That seemed too businesslike and formal. "Would you like to come in?"

"Just for a quick minute, if I'm not interrupting," he responded, stepping past her into the house. "I wanted to officially welcome you to Chickasaw Gardens. I'm going to pretend that you just moved here and don't know anyone."

"Well, that's kind of true, especially with my god-parents gone."

"Did they get off okay this morning? Ben's not big on the travel part. He just wants to be there."

"I know what you mean," she said, leading him into the living room. The kitchen seemed too cozy, and the backyard too informal. She didn't know anything about Mr. McNeill, yet. "Aunt Alice called a few minutes ago. They were about to board the plane. I just got back from taking them to the airport."

Jefferson pursed his lips and looked at his watch. "I was kind of keeping a lookout for you. I thought you'd be back here an hour ago."

Michaela indicated the sofa where he was to sit, while she sat in her godmother's favorite easy chair, curling her long, thin body comfortably.

She watched as Lady suddenly appeared and walked over to check out the visitor. The cat sprang onto the arm support of the sofa, nearest Jefferson. He reached out to stroke the cat's head, but she sniffed at his hand for a moment before gracefully retreating and jumping to the floor and sashaying away.

"I made a few stops," she fibbed smoothly as Jefferson turned his attention to her.

He stared right at her. "You got lost."

She couldn't help but laugh at his unexpected conclusion. "I'm never going to live that down, I see."

"I don't mean to put you on the spot, and there's nothing wrong with getting lost. You learn from mistakes. That's what I tell my girls."

"Yes, you have twins, right?"

"Kimika and Kyla. They're thirteen. They're looking forward to meeting you ever since Alice mentioned that you work at Howard University in D.C.," he said.

"Any particular reason that impressed them?" Michaela asked him.

"Their mother, my late wife, went to Howard."

"Oh…" she murmured awkwardly.

"I came over to introduce myself. Since this is your first night alone I also thought you'd like to join me, and the girls, for dinner. Nothing fancy, but we'd love to have you."

"That's very nice of you," Michaela said, automatically searching for a reason to say no.

"Your eyes are an unusual color," he suddenly observed. "Like ginger beer."

"If that was a compliment, thank you."

"I'm sure you've heard that before."

Michaela merely smiled politely.

She wasn't ready for this kind of socialization yet, and she had a feeling that Aunt Alice had put Jefferson up to the invitation. She also wouldn't put it past her godmother to try and play matchmaker. Michaela had no idea what Alice Underwood might have told Jefferson McNeill about her…and her other reason for getting out of D.C.…but she'd already been given a rundown on Jefferson and knew he'd been a widower for some five years. But Michaela wasn't having it. Meeting an eligible bachelor was not why she'd come to Memphis.

Besides, she wasn't all that sure that the invitation was sincere. He was saying all the right things, but something was missing. To Michaela it seemed like Jefferson was assessing her with a cool detachment, rather than real interest. He adjusted his rimless glasses, staring at her again.

"Come over about six. We'll have time to get acquainted before we sit down to eat."

"Thank you, but I was thinking of going over to the university tonight for a performance I read about. Would it be okay if I called and let you know in the next hour, after I check to see if tickets are still available?"

"Yes, ma'am, that's fine. You'd be welcome anytime."

Jefferson then told her how it had come about that he was able to find a house and move into Chickasaw Gardens. His boasting reminded Michaela of the way her colleagues and friends in D.C. talked about the "good" neighborhoods they lived in, like Prince George's County in Maryland, as if establishing their pedigree. But Jefferson also admitted that her godparents had been warm and helpful and among the first of his neighbors to welcome him and his daughters to the historic community.

In a way, he was returning the gesture.

"Are you okay here alone?"

"Everyone keeps asking me that. I'm not afraid of the dark and I don't believe in ghosts," Michaela assured him. "Aunt Alice left me a long list of names and numbers, just in case. Yours is on it."

"Good enough. Don't hesitate to use it." He stood to leave. "I have to get back. I'm dropping the girls off for music lessons after lunch, and I need to head back to my office for a few more hours."

"Thank you so much for coming over," Michaela said, escorting him back to the door. "I'll call you about dinner."

"If you decide not to come tonight we'll do dinner some other time. Ben and Alice said you're planning on being here most of the summer."

"That was my original idea, but it depends."

Jefferson stepped outside the door she held open, and turned to regard her. "Stick it out. Memphis is a big small city. We're in transition, but there're a lot of good people here."

Michaela watched Jefferson walk away before closing the door. His visit and invitation was an unexpected surprise, and she felt ambivalent about it. She'd been looking forward to housesitting for her godparents while they were away, and having the space and time to concentrate on whatever she wanted to do…or on nothing at all.

She needed space between herself, D.C., the demands of her job and Spencer…especially since turning down his proposal of marriage. Her own family and friends were still wondering if she'd lost her mind. By escaping to Memphis she'd forestalled having to explain her decision, which was a good thing since Michaela knew she didn't have what could be called a logical reason. She'd said no to her boyfriend of two years based solely on gut instincts.

She headed for the kitchen, searching for the local newspaper where she'd seen the ad for the university program. According to the published schedule it wasn't until the next night. Michaela realized that the day stretched long before her and she really had no hard, fast plans for the afternoon or evening…today, or any other day. But there was a personal project she hoped to make some progress with, and now was as good a time as any to review it.

She retrieved a cardboard manuscript box from the

room she was using during her stay. On the kitchen island counter she spread out the contents, a pile of aged and wrinkled scraps of paper, old index cards and a number of letters. All contained handwritten recipes that had been shared and used by her family for as long as she could remember. According to her mother they dated as far back as her paternal great-great-grandmother. The cooking instructions were fading and becoming hard to read, and sometimes made for guesswork. She'd taken it upon herself to organize the recipes into categories, and then enter them in a Word document file on her laptop. She had a vague idea that maybe one day she'd self-publish the collection of recipes for distribution to all her relatives.

Michaela quickly became absorbed in the preliminary task of sorting. There was no sound around her except for that infernal ticking kitchen clock. The house was otherwise as silent as a tomb. The imagery made her uneasy. Lady eventually joined her, jumping onto the counter to stretch herself out, mostly on Michaela's sorted papers. She was glad for the cat's company, but she still felt oddly isolated, as if she had no connection to the world. She had a sudden sober revelation of just how long the summer days stretched out before her.

Then she heard that noise again. It was a sound that she couldn't identify and that made her jump in fright. She looked out the window once more, but the spacious backyard was empty and the garage door was down.

Was she being too skittish? Overreacting? Hearing things?

Michaela looked at the time. It was a little after one

o'clock. Almost an hour had passed since Jefferson McNeill's visit.

She reached for the phone and called him to accept his invitation to dinner.

"Are you sure I can't do something to help?" Michaela asked for the sixth or seventh time.

"No, ma'am. You're company," the twin named Kyla said seriously with a shake of her head.

"Daddy said that we're not supposed to make company work or sing for their supper," giggled the other twin, Kimika.

Michaela had no choice but to accept the rules of the house after making her offer. The twins worked efficiently together, going in and out of the house with leftover food and dishes. Michaela studied Jefferson as he finished scraping and cleaning the outdoor grill with a stiff wire brush.

He seemed an easygoing father, but it was clear that there were rules and the girls had their part to play in maintaining the harmony of the household. Michaela had learned during the evening that Jefferson was the owner-operator of a cleaning service franchise that was doing so well he was about to open a second facility. The girls were in private school, but he had an extended family support system in place that contributed to helping him with their care.

The twins were identical, favoring their father in complexion and features, but already showing signs of eventually becoming very attractive young women. For now they both wore braces, and suffered from the same allergies. Michaela was surprised when she'd arrived at the McNeill house to find the girls dressed exactly the same, their hair cornrowed into identical ponytails, neat and easy to manage. She wasn't sure if their appearance was a deliberate attempt to confuse her, but Michaela quickly learned to tell them apart. Kyla was quiet and thoughtful. Kimika was chatty and outgoing.

Neither Jefferson nor the girls shied away from talking of their mother, who'd died of breast cancer. But neither had they placed her on a pedestal, their memories of her skewered by adoration and loss. Watching him, Michaela considered that he seemed like a man who was no longer in mourning. But she also didn't get a sense of a man who was on the lookout for a second wife.

"Thank you for inviting me over." Michaela smiled at Jefferson, as he joined her after rolling away the grill.

"Glad to have you. Hope everything was to your liking. Did you have enough to eat?"

"Probably too much," she responded, not wanting to add that the meal was far richer than what she was used to eating.

"Daddy, can Michaela come for dinner again tomorrow?" Kyla asked as she returned to the yard.

"We're having chicken-and-rice casserole," Kimika added, wiping the surface of the table with a damp sponge.

"That's sweet of you, but I have plans for tomorrow," Michaela answered.

Jefferson gave the grill utensils to Kyla to take to the kitchen, and he asked Kimika to put the garbage out.

"You both know better than that. You mean to ask, can *Miss* Landry come again."

"It's okay, Jefferson. Please, let them call me Michaela.

I don't mind at all." She turned to the girls. "Next time you should all come and have dinner with me."

"Can you cook?" Kimika asked brightly.

Michaela laughed. "Probably not as good as you two, but I have some great family recipes."

Jefferson didn't respond directly to her invitation, although his daughters seemed to really like the idea. However, when he asked if she'd like to watch a DVD with them, before the girls went to bed, Michaela decided it was time to leave.

"I'm going to walk Michaela back to the Underwood house," he announced through the kitchen door to his daughters. "Lock the door until I get back. I won't be long."

Both girls quickly appeared on cue to say good-night.

Jefferson and Michaela walked through a wrought-iron gate to a semicircular brick path bordering his property that led to the front of the house.

It was a beautiful night, the air warm and sultry as the two of them walked. There was no one else around.

"The girls seem to like you," Jefferson suddenly murmured.

Michaela pursed her lips, staring at the length of their shadows as they passed a streetlamp. "I like them. They're lively and bright. I enjoyed hearing about their summer plans, and their friends, and what they want for their August birthday, and how they're looking forward to going to visit cousins in Florida next week…"

"They told you all that?" Jefferson asked, sounding shocked as they reached the Underwood house. "I can barely get them to tell me what they're thinking sometimes."

"Telling me was like gossiping and sharing secrets. It's what girls do."

"Mind if I asked what?"

They stopped in front of the door and Michaela faced him.

"Sorry. That would mean giving up trade secrets," she teased, but could see that Jefferson didn't share her sense of humor. "I can promise you it's nothing you have to worry about, Jefferson. Your daughters are getting to the age when they're starting to feel very girlie. They love fashion, for example…like my sandals." She lifted a foot in the air and rotated it at the ankle.

"I'm more concerned that they keep up with their schoolwork, do their chores. Listen in church. There'll be time for those other things when they're in high school."

Michaela didn't respond right away. It seemed to her that he was missing the point. Then again, it wasn't as if she had raised any kids of her own.

"I can share one thing with you. As parents go, your girls seem to think you're a great daddy."

Jefferson seemed surprised by that, and chuckled silently. "I just want to make sure I'm raising them the right way."

Again Michaela refrained from commenting. What was the right way?

"Thanks for walking me back, and thanks again for a nice evening. I enjoyed myself."

"We'll do it again. I'm around if you need anything," Jefferson offered. "Good night."

Michaela frowned at his retreating back, a little thrown by Jefferson's sudden abrupt formality. But she was also relieved that he'd maintained appropriate boundaries. After all, the evening had not been a date.

If the house had seemed too quiet earlier in the day, it was even worse now that it was late evening. Michaela tried watching the flat-screen TV in the family room, but had never been much of a TV watcher. She tried reading, but every little sound distracted her. Finally she showered and prepared for bed, checking the doors to make sure they were locked before climbing the stairs to her room. Lady, who generally ignored her presence, came silently into the room, jumped on the bed and settled herself right in the middle. Lady was there when she fell asleep, and it was Lady who meowed sometime later to wake her up. Her eyes flew open in the pitch-black room at the heavy thud of something falling.

After about a minute, something else crashed. Lady jumped from the bed and left the room. Michaela also got out of bed to follow her, making her way carefully in the dark. In the kitchen she found the cat sitting on the counter next to the sink and staring out into the black night. Michaela thought better of turning on a light.

She searched for the wall phone and began to dial 911. But she changed her mind and hung up. Uncle Ben said that raccoons or possums sometimes came at night to get into the garbage. She would be laughed at if that's all the police found. On the other hand, if it was something else, like someone trying to break in…

She dialed Jefferson's, not hesitating just because it was a little after two in the morning.

"Hello," a groggy voice answered.

"Jefferson, it's Michaela," she said urgently, keeping

her voice low. "I'm so sorry to awaken you but…I hear noises outside the house, and…"

"I'll be right over."

The line went dead.

She quickly pulled on a pair of lightweight linen pants, stuffing the tail of her nightshirt inside. Then she hurried to wait by the front door in her bare feet, hugging herself against the chill of fear. There was a light knock on the door and Michaela opened it without even checking to make sure it was Jefferson.

He stepped in holding a flashlight. Michaela pointed to the kitchen.

"Something's in the yard."

"Stay here," he ordered, leaving her.

No way.

She hurried after him. He was leaning over the sink peering into the yard. It was impossible to see anything.

Jefferson unlocked the door and opened it a crack. "I'm going to check out the yard and the garage," he whispered, stepping into the night. He began walking the perimeter, searching out all the bushes and undergrowth along the base of the fence.

"There's an opening right here," he told her.

Standing across the yard from Jefferson, Michaela heard the breaking and snapping of dry wood.

"The wood is pretty rotted right here. Looks like someone or something's been using this spot to get in and out of the yard." He continued around the fence until he reached the outside wall of the garage. "Over here there's a vent, but it's hanging loose. It's a big enough space to crawl through. I'm going inside to check it out…"

"Wait!" Michaela hissed urgently, but already Jefferson had disappeared. She wasn't about to go in that way. She pressed the remote button mounted next to the garage door. It rattled noisily as it opened.

Jefferson had located one of Ben's high-beam emergency flashlights and turned it on, panning it around the space.

Michaela crept forward on bare feet. She reached Jefferson and stood staring at the scene he'd found. If she'd come across it alone in the day she might not even have noticed or thought it unusual that an old tarp was folded on the floor in a corner, an old moth-eaten blanket on top. What looked to serve as a pillow had been fashioned out of an unopened bag of cat food. There were several opened and emptied cans of tuna fish, condensed soup and a tin of half-eaten mixed nuts. It was evidence that not only had someone gotten into the garage, but that they'd been camping out there, disappearing during the day and quietly returning at night. Jefferson bent to examine a liquid spilled on the floor.

"Looks like windshield-wiper liquid," Michaela whispered behind him.

"I think so. Probably knocked over accidentally, and the top wasn't screwed on tight."

"Yeah, but who knocked it over?"

He flashed the light along the floorboards, into corners, behind stacked boxes and under a table saw. There was a wall unit of open shelves organized with gardening equipment. Jefferson suddenly stopped, aiming his light on the floor beneath the bottom shelf. He held the light in front of him with his left hand, and pulled something out of his pants pocket. Michaela made a sound of surprise when his arm rose up and he pointed his hand straight out. He was holding a small automatic pistol.

"Come on out," he ordered.

Nothing happened. Then, Michaela heard a clicking as he flipped the safety catch. She gasped.

"Don't shoot. I didn't steal nothin'."

The voice was male, young, defiant rather than scared.

"Let me see both your hands, now."

"Okay, okay." A pair of skinny brown arms and hands appeared from below the last shelf. "Don't shoot."

"Jefferson…" Michaela didn't realize the tone of her voice was shocked. "He's just a boy. Please put the gun down."

"He could have a weapon."

"Only a pocketknife. I wasn't going to hurt nobody with it."

Michaela frowned. "He sounds funny."

"Come on out," Jefferson ordered. "Move slowly and keep your hands so I can see them."

"Don't shoot me."

"You don't need the gun," Michaela said again, still stunned that he'd brought one to the house.

She watched as a boy emerged from the space on the floor. He was very thin and not very tall, but she couldn't believe that he'd managed to squeeze himself into such a tight space. He kept his gaze down, refusing to look directly at them. Jefferson finally put the gun away and told the boy to turn around. He did so, but didn't seem steady, shuffling his feet along the cement floor and swaying. She could hear him drawing up his nose as if it was runny because he had a cold.

Jefferson patted the boy down to make sure he didn't have a weapon, and then made him turn around again.

"Boy, don't you know you could've been shot? You're trespassing. What are you doing here?"

"Sleepin'," he muttered.

"Sleeping?" Jefferson repeated, skeptical. "Why here?"

The boy shrugged. "'Cause it's nice."

Then, Michaela was caught off guard when the youngster wavered and suddenly dropped to one knee. She inadvertently took a step toward him. Jefferson grabbed her arm and held her back.

"What's the matter with you?" Jefferson continued to quiz him.

"I don't know. I don't feel so good."

"Jefferson, this boy is not dangerous."

"That's for the police to figure out. Why don't you go inside and call them."

"Can I lay down?"

Without waiting for permission, and before Jefferson could say anything, the boy rolled completely to the floor on his back with his hands pressed hard over his ears. He moaned as if he was in pain. Then he shifted position and turned onto his side, curling completely in a fetal position.

Michaela stared at him, deeply concerned.

"I think he's high on drugs," Jefferson said.

She shook her head. "No. No, he's not on drugs. Look at him. Something's really wrong."

"Then call the police..."

"I'm not calling the police. I want to get him to the

nearest hospital. This boy is not a threat to us. He's not going to attack us. Look at him. He can't even stand up."

"It's none of our business…"

"Are you going to help me or not? I'll take him myself, if I have to."

He frowned at her. "I don't think you should get involved. What do you know about him?"

"I know he's alone. Heaven knows how long he's been sneaking in here for shelter. I know he's sick, and he needs medical attention. I don't need to know any more than that."

They squared off, and Michaela refused to back down under the scowling disapproval in Jefferson's stare.

"I'll go get my car," he muttered, walking around the side of the house to head back toward his own home.

Michaela knelt down beside the boy. His breathing seemed labored. She wasn't sure he was conscious.

"What's your name?" she asked, but got no answer. She cautiously laid her hand against his face. His skin was clammy and cold.

Chapter 2

Michaela stood staring after the gurney as it was wheeled away with the ailing boy. He was accompanied by only one nurse to a triage room. But it had taken nearly an hour to convince the hospital staff to see the unknown boy at all. Conscious but lethargic upon arrival, he refused to give his name or an address to the interviewing nurse. He wouldn't even confirm how old he was and seemed to know nothing of his medical history. He wouldn't say much of anything, appearing not particularly interested in the fact that she was only trying to make sure he got attention. Complicating matters was the fact that she wasn't a relative, or even a legal guardian.

It was only when she seriously asked what would happen if the boy suddenly died while waiting in their emergency room, that the nursing staff relented, and agreed to do a preliminary exam.

Jefferson, after initially making his disapproval

known and still campaigning for calling the authorities, had given in to letting Michaela do what she thought was best. It was very simple, she'd explained: to get the boy proper medical attention, not have him arrested. What good would that do?

"Well, you got what you wanted," he said.

"I had to bully and embarrass them. It shouldn't have come to that. He's sick and he needs help. They're supposed to help sick people. What part of being sick don't they understand?"

"You know it's not that simple. Bottom line, someone has to pay for his care."

"He's a kid," she argued. "That shouldn't even be an issue. Were they really going to just leave him on that gurney all night, or put him out in the street again?"

"Okay, maybe you're right. You still don't know anything about him. I don't want you to think I'm not concerned but I have my own children to watch out for. Right now they're home alone, while I'm here dealing with a kid who probably has a rap sheet."

Michaela nodded, contrite. "I know. I'm so sorry. You didn't have to get involved, but thank you for helping with him."

Jefferson accepted her apology. "I still think we should have reported the break-in to the police. You have to be careful with a boy like that."

"And I still think you didn't have to wave a gun around."

"I'm licensed to carry a gun because of my business. I'm not going to apologize for doing what I have to do. I've been robbed twice, once by a couple of guys no older than he is," he said. "You asked for my help and that's what I was trying to do."

"'Cuse me, miss."

Michaela turned to the nurse who was walking toward her. She met her halfway.

"How's he doing?" she asked.

"We don't know yet. He's not talking much and we're doing the best we can. We're really not supposed to do this without a parent's permission, but we'll run some blood tests to see what shows up. The doctors might send him over to St. Jude, depending on the results."

"St. Jude? How come?"

The night nurse seemed reluctant to answer.

"Poor kids end up having things wrong they and their family don't even know about. Like TB. St. Jude specializes in childhood illness and cancers. A lot of kids who come here first end up at St. Jude for…certain things," the nurse said significantly. "But if that chile' needs treatment, we can't do anything without somebody who's responsible for him saying so. He won't tell us nothing and that just makes it harder to do for him. He's very suspicious of all of us."

"Is it okay if I try again?"

The nurse chortled. "Well, you got this far by getting on our case. Knock yourself out. He's in the last treatment room on the right." She pointed down the hall before walking away to speak with a colleague.

Michaela turned to Jefferson. "I know you really have to go, but could you give me a few more minutes?"

He glanced at his watch. "I was able to get my sister to drive over and watch the girls while we're here. I'm going to call her and let her know I'll be home in half an hour."

"Thank you," she voiced sincerely, before rushing off down the hall.

When she parted the curtains in the treatment room, Michaela found the boy lying on his back. He'd been asked to remove his clothing, and he wore a blue hospital gown. He didn't even look up when she entered, but continued to pick at the edge of a pink Band-Aid that was on the inside of his elbow, covering the area where blood had been drawn.

"Hi," she said. "How are you feeling?"

He shrugged, but said nothing.

She came to stand next to his bed, looking down at him. His hair was kinky and uncombed, and it needed a good cut. His skinny legs and arms, even his face, was dry and ashen. Sleep residue crusted the corners of his eyes. She guessed that he'd probably not had decent food in a long time. Michaela was troubled by evidence that this boy might be neglected. Had he run away? Or had someone just given up on him?

"The nurses are going to run some tests. They're trying to figure out how to make you feel better. I told them you're twelve, but I think you look younger," she said smoothly.

"I ain't no twelve," he said in disgust. "I'm almost fifteen."

"My mistake. Sorry." She thought quickly. "I'm Taurus. What's your sign?"

"I don't have no sign."

"Everybody has a sign for the month when you were born. My birthday is May second, so I'm Taurus the bull. There's a sign for every month. Each sign is represented by stars in the sky."

"I don't know nothin' 'bout stars." After a moment, he looked at her, curious. "What's for November?"

"Sagittarius, I think. It depends on the exact day you were born."

"Twentieth," he quickly answered, interested.

"I'm pretty sure it's Sagittarius. I'm Michaela, by the way."

"I ain't tellin' you my name."

"That's not fair," she coaxed.

"Nothin's fair. That's the way it is."

"You know, I could have you arrested. You broke into private property. You were hiding in my godparents' garage."

"I didn't take nothin'. I was sleeping in there at night, that's all."

"What were you doing during the daytime?"

"I was out making some money so I could eat."

"How'd you make money?"

"I find stuff and sell it. I do odd jobs."

"And you want me to believe you never stole anything to help you get along?"

"Only losers do that. Smith said I was smarter than that, and I can do anything I put my mind to. I was doing okay. It was better than where I was living."

"You were not doing okay. When I found you, you were wearing my godfather's old work clothes. You were so sick you couldn't stand. You couldn't have gone on like that for long. Where's your family? You must have people somewhere."

"I ain't got nobody."

"What about Smith? Who is he?"

"He ain't my family. He's just…"

"What?"

He didn't answer for a while. He turned on his side and lay with his open hand pressed between his cheek and the hospital pillow.

"He talks to me, and tells me stuff. He tries to help, but…"

"What do you think Smith would say if he knew you were here?"

"He'd say 'giving up is not an option.' He's always sayin' stuff like that."

"Do you like him?"

"Yeah. He's pretty for real."

Michaela watched the boy closely. He was falling to sleep.

"Would it be okay if I call him for you? Otherwise, the hospital may have no choice but to turn you over to children's aid. Or maybe send you to St. Jude."

"I know that place. I got a friend that has to go there when they real sick."

"I can call your friend for you. I can come back in the morning, see how you're doing, if that's okay."

"You don't even know me. Why you care what happens to me?"

She grinned. "What would Smith say?"

He sighed. "'Give it a chance before you say no.'"

She leaned closer to the boy. "What's his number?"

Michaela was pushing numbers on her cell phone as she walked back to the nurses' station. Jefferson was pacing, and she realized that he'd pretty much reached his limit with the whole situation. But she had to use the information she'd managed to get out of the young teenager.

She put the phone to her ear, hoping she remembered the number correctly.

"How'd you make out with that boy?" one of the nurses called out.

Michaela silently gestured for something to write with as her call was answered in the middle of the second ring. One of the nursing staff passed her a scrap of paper and a pen. She hastily scribbled the boy's age and birthday.

"Yes, this is Smith," a rich voice answered.

She was so surprised by the unexpected timbre of the voice that she stammered. She held out her note to the nurse.

"Good evening. I mean, good morning. You don't know me…"

"I've been waiting for this call. Is this about Terrance?"

"Terrance?" Michaela repeated blankly. "I…don't know. I'm calling from the medical center about a young boy. He says he's almost fifteen…he gave me your name."

"Yes, yes." The relief was evident in the deep voice. "That sounds like Eugene Terrance. Goes by the nickname of ET."

"He won't tell me his name. But he all but told me you're just about the only human being he feels he can trust."

"What happened to him? What's he doing at the medical center?"

"It's complicated," Michaela said helplessly.

"He's not hurt, is he?"

"No, but he's sick. The staff here will only do blood tests. They need legal consent to authorize anything else. They mentioned sending him over to St. Jude."

"I can be there in fifteen minutes. Can you wait for me?"

The request confused her. There was nothing else she could tell this man that he couldn't learn from the hospital staff, or that he didn't already know about the boy. And she seriously doubted that Jefferson would agree to hang around any longer.

"Yes, I'll be here."

"Who'm I asking for?"

"Michaela. Michaela Landry. You'll recognize me by my…"

"I'll find you," he said confidently before hanging up.

When she got off the phone, the nurses surrounded Michaela, exclaiming over her ability to extract basic information from the boy they were now calling ET. Michaela told them everything she could remember that ET had mentioned that might be of any help to the staff.

"Did you find out if he's ever been sick before, or if he has any preexisting conditions?"

"Sorry. I couldn't think of any clever ways of asking those kinds of questions," Michaela apologized.

"You did great. Maybe this Smith guy knows something more about the boy. Like who his family is and where he lives."

"We'll find out when he gets here. He said he was on his way."

She turned to Jefferson. He looked firm but not totally unsympathetic.

"I really need to get going. It's after four. The last time I was up this late the twins were teething."

Michaela looked contrite.

"That was supposed to be funny."

"I know, but I feel so bad that I've kept you out all night. You never wanted to get involved to begin with."

"Maybe I've earned my place in heaven."

"Maybe," she said, trying to appreciate Jefferson's position, but it was impossible for her to forget that he'd held a gun on a helpless fifteen-year-old.

"Well, it seems like they finally have things under control here. We can leave now."

Michaela didn't move to follow. She called out after him. "I can't go yet."

Jefferson turned, dumbfounded, and more than a little annoyed. "What?"

"I'm sorry, but I can't. If you want to leave without me, I understand. I want to stay a while longer."

"There's no more you can do tonight that won't wait until tomorrow. If you feel that strongly about what happens to this kid, call in the morning."

"I won't be able to sleep anyway."

"I have to go."

"I know."

"I can't leave you here," he said, peeved. "How are you getting back to the house?"

"I'll figure something out."

"I'll make sure she gets back home safely."

Both Michaela and Jefferson turned at the calm voice of a man approaching them from the medical center entrance. He was not quite as tall as Jefferson, but walked with a long stride and graceful ease that reminded her of a predatory animal.

Smith, Michaela told herself.

She felt mesmerized by the dark intense draw of his gaze, and the masculine strength of his face, covered mostly by a close-cut beard. His skin was a touch darker than Jefferson's, but his face was lean and chiseled in masculine grooves. He very much reminded Michaela of a painting she'd once seen of a Black Moor in white desert robe and turban, but for the fact that the man approaching was dressed in black jeans and T-shirt, a fleece hoodie sweater and heavy biker boots. Under his arm he was carrying a huge helmet, the chin straps swinging loose.

She knew she was staring, even as the man looked beyond her to Jefferson, in the way that men do when they size up one another. This was not the least bit hostile, or challenging. The men were not squaring off or staking out a claim, but even she could detect the respect silently exchanged between them.

The man thrust out his hand to Jefferson, who grasped it for the introduction.

"Cooper Townsend...aka Smith."

"Jefferson McNeill."

Cooper Townsend turned his dark gaze to Michaela, holding hers as firmly and effortlessly as if she'd been momentarily hypnotized. A smile curved his well-shaped mouth that she couldn't begin to interpret, but it struck a nerve and reverberated a response in her chest and stomach. Michaela realized she was almost holding her breath.

"Michaela," he said simply. "I'm grateful for everything you did tonight."

"I didn't do it alone," she was quick to add. "Jefferson helped."

"It was the right thing to do," Jefferson said.

Michaela suspected it was costing him to be magnanimous.

"I'd like to hear what happened exactly but I need to check on the boy and speak with the staff. I meant what I said about getting you back to where you need to be," he directed to Michaela.

"I don't think…" Jefferson began.

"I'll be fine, Jefferson. Go," Michaela urged him. "I know you have to get home."

"You'll excuse me?" Smith quietly interjected into the conversation, but he didn't wait for their permission. He spoke briefly with someone at the desk and was pointed in the direction of the triage room where ET had been placed. He went striding off, his boots silent on the tile floor.

"I'll walk you to your car," Michaela offered, turning her attention to Jefferson. She added a smile to show that she truly understood his priorities, and respected him for that.

They were both silent until they reached his black Esplanade.

"I can see what the summer's going to be like."

She frowned at him. "I don't know what you mean."

"I have a feeling there's never going to be another dull moment in Chickasaw Gardens." He unlocked his SUV, but hesitated getting in the driver's seat. "I'm not sure about leaving you like this. If Ben and Alice find out… I guess I could have handled things differently…"

"I'll be fine. I'll call you tomorrow if you want and let you know how everything works out for the boy."

"Yes, ma'am, I'm curious. You should also see about getting that fence repaired. I'll try to find someone for you. And you're sure you're okay with this guy bringing you back home?"

"This is his cell phone number." Michaela recited it to Jefferson. "If you don't see me within the next three days, there's a problem."

He grunted and got into his car.

The goodbye was awkward and quick. Michaela stood and watched as Jefferson drove out of the lot. As she did so, she also realized that the sky was just starting to turn the royal blue that was the prelude to dawn. She turned and retraced her steps back into the waiting area. Smith was nowhere in sight.

One of the nurses, knowing she was looking for him, silently pointed down the corridor and Michaela walked back to find him. As she approached, she thought she heard Smith's voice, very quiet and very low coming from the room, but there was no answering response from the boy. When she reached the curtain she held it back and looked into the space.

ET was sleeping. Smith's back was to her and he stood, just as she had, looking down on the boy. But Smith had taken his concern a step further. His left hand rested gently on ET's head. His head was slightly bowed and Michaela would guess that his eyes were closed. In his compelling voice he was whispering a prayer.

She sat in the waiting room, staring out the glass doors of the entrance as the rosy blush of dawn lightened the sky. She had only one prior experience with an emergency room, when she was about nine, and could clearly remember her pain and fear. Not because of her broken wrist, received in a fall from her bike, but because of the cold, institutional environment of the hospital.

Now, Michaela was openly curious about the number of people who continued to arrive…and sit and wait… their illnesses and complaints not ruled by time of day. Many sat patiently for attention, or dozed in awkward positions in the hard chairs, or muttered to themselves in pain. It became clear to her that the emergency room was their health care.

But part of her attention was continually drawn back to the image of Smith praying over ET. His gesture was so totally hands-on. In her entire life Michaela could not recall ever witnessing anything as unexpected, but…touching. Equally bewildering to her was why this man, Smith, had taken it upon himself to reach out in a way that was not only personal but deeply caring. Where was the boy's family? Why did ET prefer Smith's attention over theirs?

"Sorry I kept you so long."

She blinked at the sound of the deep voice, and looked up. Smith was standing over her, his expression serious. Staring up at him, he seemed momentarily menacing with his probing gaze and the light covering of his beard shadowing his face. But the dark warmth of his eyes reflected something much more thoughtful and sensitive. His whole persona created in Michaela an odd, provocative feeling about him. It was in sharp contrast to the grounded peace and calm he also seemed to exude.

She jumped to her feet. He was still a good three inches taller than her five foot eight.

"Oh, that's… It's fine—no problem," she stammered, covertly studying him.

"To be honest, I'm surprised you're still here. I thought for sure you'd have called someone else to come get you."

"I don't know anyone else. Not in Memphis."

He looked surprised. "Is that right?"

She knew more explanation was probably called for, but she wasn't up to it just then. Michaela took a deep breath, pulling it together. "How's he doing?"

"Asleep."

"Is he okay?"

He hesitated. "I'll wait to hear what the doctors have to say."

"What's going to happen now?"

Smith looked briefly away, shaking his head. "Again, depends on the doctors. If they're thinking of transferring him to another center, then I'm concerned."

"I heard one of the nurses say he might go to St. Jude."

Smith played with the strap of his helmet, snapping it closed and then using it as a handle. "I know," he murmured heavily.

Leaning forward, Michaela regarded him through her lashes. "You don't sound happy about that."

"If the staff here doesn't know what's wrong, or they're not going to talk about what they do know, then that means it could be something more than they can handle. It means they aren't going to treat Terrance. And it means he might have to see a specialist. Whatever is happening to him could be serious."

"Hmmm," she uttered, trying to sort it out. "That doesn't sound like such a bad thing if he gets the right diagnosis, and it can be treated, right?" She absently brushed a strand of loose hair, tickling the back of her neck, back up to the ponytail.

"I know but, it's just something else he has to deal with."

"You mean him and his family," Michaela added.

"All things being equal," Smith murmured cryptically. "How long have you been here exactly?"

"Oh…most of the night." She quickly stifled a yawn.

"I'm sorry. You must be wiped out about now."

"Actually, I'm not. But I'll probably crash around noon."

He chuckled silently and turned to the exit.

"Let's get out of here."

They both thanked the night staff at the desk on their way out. Smith stepped outside into the early morning and glanced east in the direction of the sunrise. He turned to stare at her thoughtfully.

"What?" Michaela asked when he remained silent.

"I'll take you home, like I said, but how do you feel about stopping for breakfast?"

"Breakfast? What time is it?"

"About five-thirty. Too early for you?"

"I guess not. I could use some coffee."

"Good. I'd like to hear about how you met up with Terrance in the first place. Where it happened, what he said to you."

Michaela nodded. "I have a lot of questions, too."

Smith nodded and turned to a metallic cobalt-blue motorcycle. Michaela stopped in her tracks and stared at it.

"You're kidding, right?" she asked, pointing at the bike.

"'Fraid not. I knew it would get me here quicker than my car, and I wasn't expecting to have a passenger. There's no traffic at this hour, and we're not going that far. I know what I'm doing. You'll be safe with me."

Michaela made a skeptical moue with her mouth. "I've never been on a motorcycle in my life."

Cooper's response was to take off his hoodie and hand it to her. "It gets breezy on the ride." He arched a brow and silently regarded her, waiting.

She took the sweater and pulled it on, folding back the cuffs of the long sleeves. She slung the shoulder strap of her bag over her head so her hands would remain free. "Just so long as you get me back in the same condition you found me. You don't want my family to have to track you down."

"Yes, ma'am," he said, amusement evident in the tone of his voice.

He faced her, holding the bulky beanie helmet and visor over her head and slowly pulling it on over her forehead and ears. The gesture was so personal that Michaela was instantly assured she had nothing to be afraid of. If anything, she felt an unexpected rising excitement.

The helmet was not nearly as heavy as it looked, although she felt like it doubled the size of her head. Smith made sure the chin strap was in place and properly tightened.

"Where's your helmet?" she asked.

"I don't have another one. I mostly ride alone."

"But, what if…"

"Let's pray there won't be one. Now, all you have to do is sit close behind me, hold on and keep your knees in. Let your body move right with me. No backseat driving. Ready?"

She nodded and gave a thumbs-up. They each took their place on the bike. Smith turned over the engine and it rumbled to life in a fast but quiet repetitive "put-put" sound. Michaela placed her hands on his waist, clutching the fabric of his shirt. But Smith reached for one of her hands and pulled it around his waist for a better hold. She felt funny touching him in this marked way, but followed his instructions, wrapping her arms around his rib cage. Through the fabric she couldn't help but detect that the surface of his skin felt odd, with a raised and uneven surface. Then Smith took a firm grip of the handlebars.

"Hold on."

When the bike began to slowly roll forward, so did Michaela's stomach. She leaned forward and let her hands press against his chest. Smith lifted his feet to the pedals, and they were off. Immediately she felt a light, clean breeze caressing her face where it was exposed. It made her catch her breath.

Michaela held on tightly, leaning into the firmness of Smith's back, sensing his body warmth radiating through the cotton shirt, feeling the tight sinew of his chest flex under her fingers. The contact felt curiously intimate, yet impersonal at the same time. But this was not about a vicarious turn-on. This was about not getting killed.

Smith steered slowly out of the hospital lot and gently banked to the left onto the street that was still fairly deserted at that hour. As it picked up speed she closed her eyes, reveling in the motion and gentle rolling speed.

Michaela couldn't help it. She broke into a grin at the unadulterated sensation of speed and freedom.

Chapter 3

Smith held the door open as Michaela entered before him into the tiny hole-in-the-wall café. It was located on the edge of a community in flux, going from being poor and working class to becoming gentrified and somewhat trendy. He no longer noticed the shabby interior with its cheap, square Formica-and-aluminum tables, and chairs with vinyl seating, duct-taped where it had begun to crack. The smell of grease hung permanently in the air, and the air conditioner had one setting. Warm. But from the first time he'd wandered in, literally dazed and confused, Miss Faye's had welcomed him, no questions asked. And he'd continued to come back because it gave him far more than just a nourishing hot meal.

Miss Faye's had welcomed him with open arms, so to speak, without any airs and not standing on ceremony. The owner had let him keep his secrets, nurse his pain and offered him a haven of peace and acceptance.

"I was just askin' 'bout you. Where you been?" came a boisterous shout-out from behind the counter. "Ain't seen you 'round here for long time."

"'Morning, Miss Faye." Smith smiled and nodded to the diminutive but rotund woman behind the counter.

Seated at the far end of the counter was the cook, a small, skinny man dressed in a stained white apron and chef's toque, sipping coffee and smoking. He squinted at Smith over his shoulder and raised his cigarette in silent greeting.

"Jake," Smith acknowledged.

"I saved your favorite table. Won't let nobody else sit there." Miss Faye chuckled.

Smith appreciated her sense of humor, given that the small place was virtually empty of paying customers.

He carefully watched Michaela's reaction to the café, wondering belatedly if he shouldn't have taken her to one of the new chain restaurants, just a few blocks away, on the main street. He never went to them himself, but now realized that she might be more comfortable in a more established setting.

Michaela looked around silently and he noticed that her expression was not one of dissatisfaction or unease or disgust, but curiosity. She picked out a table just inside but to the left of the entrance. It was the exact table he would have chosen, and the one Miss Faye referred to as his.

"Hey, Smith," a middle-aged man croaked out. He sat in the back corner of the café with a rumpled newspaper, several days old, spread messily over the table.

"Pete, how you doing?" he answered. He watched Michaela turn to see who'd called out the greeting.

Pete grinned at her, displaying a dark, toothless hole. "How you, pretty lady?" he crooned.

Michaela smiled politely, taking off the hoodie as she sat down. She draped it over the back of her chair. "I'm fine. And you?"

"I can't complain," Pete said.

"I hope this is okay with you," Smith said, taking the seat opposite her.

He was trying very hard not to stare, but he'd felt an unexpected caution from the moment he'd introduced himself to Michaela at the medical center. She'd demonstrated the kind of confidence and poise, a kind of show-me watchfulness that had always led to conflicts for him in the past with women like her. And yet, there was also the fact that what Michaela Landry had done that evening had been pretty selfless. Not to mention her willingness to ride behind him on a motorcycle.

Smith let himself drift back into the experience of Michaela holding on to him, her slender arms circling his rib cage, her hands busy and restless against his chest as she sought a comfortable and secure position. The resulting tension had caught him off guard, but had certainly not been unpleasant.

He now watched covertly as Michaela released a clip that was holding her hair in a ponytail. She began using her hands and fingers to comb it into some semblance of order after being flattened by the cycle helmet. She quickly clipped her hair together again and was done with it, all without excuses…or a mirror. And her eyes…

"I take it you're a regular here," she said.

"Miss Faye's is my favorite place for breakfast."

"So you know what the food and service is like."

"She makes the best grits and eggs I've ever had."

"I'm not a big fan of grits." Michaela grimaced. "Where's the menu?" She looked around at the other tables to see if there was one lying around.

"No menu. Just tell her what you want," Smith said.

"Good to see you, darlin'. How's everything?" Miss Faye herself interrupted.

Smith sat back as she put down two white mugs and filled each with coffee.

"'Mornin', ma'am," Miss Faye said to Michaela. From the small tray she carried she removed a small juice glass, half filled with milk, and a sugar dispenser.

"Good morning," Michaela murmured, absently watching the serving ritual.

"You two up early," Miss Faye commented.

Smith quickly exchanged a glance with Michaela. The raised eyebrows and slight smile told him that she was not offended by the innuendo behind the remark. In his prior life he might have been amused as well, and jumped on the spin with a sly comeback.

"I've been up all night," Michaela said simply.

Miss Faye tilted her head down and regarded Michaela closely. "All night?"

"I had to take care of a small emergency," Smith said calmly. He watched Michaela add milk and sugar to her coffee. "Michaela happened to be there. She was a great help."

"Must be them kids of yours. The Lord sure gonna favor you, all you do."

"I'd prefer if the Lord favored the kids."

"There's enough of His love to go 'round for everyone," Miss Faye said sagely. With Michaela's presence explained to her satisfaction, she turned to her. "What you havin', darlin'?"

"Can I get two scrambled eggs with bacon? And, do you have whole wheat toast?"

"No, ma'am. How 'bout English muffin?"

"That's good, thank you. And a fresh banana if you have any."

"Yes, ma'am. If you don't mind me saying so, you don't need to be trying to lose no weight."

"Thank you. I'm not." Michaela grinned.

Again, Smith observed as Michaela took Miss Faye's bold-faced observations with a grain of salt, and a lot of humor.

"I know what you want." Miss Faye nodded to Smith before walking away, yelling out the order to the cook, who took his time swiveling from the stool and heading back to the kitchen to make their breakfast.

Smith realized that he was absently stroking his hand over his hair-covered jaw. He glanced at Michaela and was somewhat startled to find that she was studying him closely, openly, and without any self-consciousness. He rested his forearms on the table and wrapped his hands around his mug. For a moment he considered that he might not appear very presentable at that hour. But Michaela also looked as if she'd not given any thought to what she was going to wear to a hospital in the middle of the night. He couldn't see anything coy or calculating in the way she studied him, but he found it hard to imagine what, exactly, was going through her mind.

It finally occurred to him, however, that he was sitting opposite a total stranger about to share breakfast. Not just any stranger, but a tall, slender, very attractive woman. He could now focus in on the fact that she was light skinned and had amazing eyes: catlike, and almost yellow. When he'd arrived at the medical center, Michaela's eyes were not the first thing about her that had stood out. Instead, he'd picked up immediately on the level of her concern for ET, and her watchfulness toward himself.

Still, without the crisis that had brought them together, and fifteen-year-old ET as the catalyst, Smith felt at a slight disadvantage with Michaela.

"I'm sorry, you did tell me your full name, but everyone seems to just call you Smith," Michaela said, her head tilted in question.

"Cooper Townsend. Smith is a nickname people call me here in Memphis."

"Why?"

Cooper shrugged. "I think I encouraged it. Smith sounds like an average kind of guy. Easy to know. Not threatening. Years ago someone I'd met couldn't recall my name, so I was called Smith. It stuck. It's okay with me."

"I like Cooper," Michaela said honestly. "Smith sounds so…anonymous."

Her comment took him by surprise. The truth was, few people called him by his first name anymore. That also served a purpose that was known only to himself and he wanted to keep it that way. But he had to admit he was pleased with Michaela Landry's decisive take on him being who he was.

He shifted in his chair. "I coach a lot of team sports, and all the boys have nicknames. None of them use their real names. I think it's a way of protecting themselves."

"Or maybe they're trying to hide, to be someone else," Michaela observed thoughtfully. "Like ET. That's a strange nickname for a young Black boy."

"If you ask ET, he'll say that Eugene Terrance is not so hot."

"Does he know that ET is an alien? Cute, but still from outer space."

Cooper chuckled. "I think the movie was before his time."

"What are you hiding from?" she asked.

He pursed his lips and swirled the coffee in his cup. He was taken aback with how astute the question was. "I try to keep a low profile. When I'm with the guys it's not about me. Smith is just a name I answer to. It's not who I am."

Michaela sipped from her mug, gazing steadily at him over the rim. Then she shook her head and put the mug down.

"I think it's about more than that for ET. Do you know you're the only person he seems to trust? Yours is the only name he would give me to call, and I had to trick him into it. He wouldn't tell me anything about his family. He does have a family, doesn't he?"

Smith hesitated. How much did he need to tell her?

"He's in foster care. He lives with a family that took him in, along with two other boys, about three years ago."

"Oh." Michaela nodded at the explanation. "Well, at

least there are people who take care of him. ET wouldn't even give out their names last night."

"I gave that information to the nursing staff before leaving, but there's a complication," Smith said carefully. "Terrance apparently went AWOL a few days ago. No one knew where to find him until I got your call. He didn't even get in touch with me."

Michaela frowned at the story. "He ran away? Why?"

Cooper spread his hands. "Why does any kid run away? Because they're unhappy. They don't think anyone cares. They're not being treated well."

"Which do you think it is?"

"I don't want to second-guess anyone. I think I'll wait to hear what he and the family have to say first."

"Sorry if I'm being nosy," Michaela said.

She sat back as Jake appeared, carefully balancing several plates. He placed her eggs and bacon before her, and another dish with her English muffin. The plate that Jake placed before Smith made Michaela's jaw drop.

It was actually a small oval platter with a healthy serving of hominy grits taking up a third of the space. A large piece of butter had already melted and created a yellow pool in the center. There were also two eggs over easy, several strips of bacon, two thick sausages, chunky home-fried potatoes with onions and four slices of toast.

"Oh, my God," Michaela murmured.

He was silently amused by her expression, and her comment.

"I'm sorry. That was rude. There's no way I could eat all of that."

"That's because you've never been fed by Miss Faye

before. Didn't your mama ever tell you that breakfast is the most important meal of the day?"

Michaela chuckled and picked up her fork. "Yeah. Something like that."

He pursed his lips as Michaela prepared to dig into her scrambled eggs. He suddenly extended his hands, palms up, to her. He saw the momentary confusion in her eyes before putting her fork down and slowly placing her hands, palms down, on his. He curled his fingers closed, feeling the smooth coolness of her skin. He stared into her eyes and could tell that Michaela had no idea what he was doing, but still she was prepared to go along. Cooper squeezed her hands briefly in reassurance as he closed his eyes. In a quiet voice, he said grace.

"Lord, make us thankful for what we are about to receive…"

He thought he felt Michaela's hand move in his, maybe in surprise or agitation, but not to draw away. But even as he murmured the words he'd learned from his own grandfather, he couldn't help but be aware of Michaela's reaction.

"Amen," he finished, and released her hands.

She repeated in kind, but her voice was low, almost inaudible. Michaela once again picked up her fork. He hazarded a quick glance and found her intently spreading apricot jam on half the English muffin.

Cooper stroked his jaw again. He was conscious of the sudden awkward silence between them and wondered if he'd presumed too much by taking her hands. But he thought better of pursuing it. Instead he used his fork to blend the already melted butter into the grits.

"Everything okay?" Miss Faye called out.

"Yes, thank you," Michaela answered, biting into her muffin.

Smith pushed his plate across the table in her direction. She looked at him, puzzled.

"Go ahead and try some. Complete refund guaranteed if you don't like it."

Michaela chuckled.

It was an unexpected, light sound, but Cooper felt relief. He watched as she shoveled her fork into the edge of the grits, lifting it to her mouth. A furrow formed between her brows, not of dislike but of concentration. Her jaw worked. Her lips rolled together as she savored the texture. He averted his gaze, ridding his mind of the image. He pulled back his plate and began to eat, fascinated nonetheless with the expressiveness of Michaela's face. She wasn't one to hide her feelings, whether or not she was aware of it.

"Hmmm. That's good," she said.

"Told you."

"I'm going to have a serious talk with my mother. Her grits always came out lumpy and stiff. I grew up telling people I was allergic so I wouldn't be forced to eat it."

Cooper grinned, shaking his head in amusement. Michaela certainly had an interesting sense of humor. It was ironic and self-deprecating. Engaging. He covertly stole another long look at her. He'd never met a woman before capable of laughing at herself. The realization quickly sobered him. The past wasn't that far in the past.

Michaela helped herself to another serving of his grits.

"I'm sorry. I hope you don't mind."

"Please," he assented at once.

She glanced at him speculatively. "I shouldn't. I don't even know you."

"Too late to worry about that now. We're practically related."

She giggled.

"You're safe with me," he murmured.

The conversation was back on neutral ground and Smith was careful not to kill the mood. It surprised him that that mattered. For a few minutes they just settled into Miss Faye's generous Southern breakfast.

"You said at the hospital that you don't know anyone here in Memphis. Where are you from?" he asked.

"The D.C. area. I'm just here for the summer."

"Visiting family?"

"Kind of. I'm staying in my godparents' house. They're away for most of the summer. I just arrived three days ago."

"And already you've gotten mixed up in something."

Michaela rolled her eyes, as if to say, *tell me about it.* But again, Cooper didn't detect complaint so much as surprise on her part.

"I thought Memphis was going to be slow and laid-back, and this was going to be a hot, lazy vacation."

"Memphis can be all that, but it's not much different than most places. We have our problems. Folks here all have the same concerns and issues."

Cooper used the edge of his toast to dip into the broken yolk of one of his eggs, carefully considering his next question. "Who was the man with you again?"

"Jefferson McNeill. He lives a few houses down from my godparents."

"Name sounds familiar." He considered thoughtfully. He saw that Michaela had almost finished her breakfast. He lifted his plate and smoothly slid off onto hers a portion of his home-fried potatoes.

"You don't have to do that," Michaela said, but none-theless wasted no time helping herself.

"Enjoy them. So, Jefferson came with you to the hospital?"

"Reluctantly," Michaela confessed. "He was going to call the police because we found ET had gotten onto my godparents' property and into the garage. Jefferson actually had a..."

She stopped abruptly, and Cooper waited. Whatever it was she was going to say, she thought better of it.

"I sort of bullied him into taking me and ET to the medical center."

"Why wasn't he willing to help on his own?"

She shrugged and took her time answering. He had the impression that she didn't want to criticize the man.

"Well, he has two young daughters. He was con-cerned about leaving them alone, I guess."

"I want to thank you," Cooper said to her.

"For what?"

"For thinking of ET first."

It was the arrival of new customers that made Smith aware of the time. He glanced at his watch.

"I have to head out to work, but I'll take you home first," he said as they finished eating.

"Let me pay for this," Michaela said, digging in her bag. "I feel like I owe you for introducing me to good grits."

He waved away her offer. "My treat. It's the least I can do for all the trouble you went through last night."

Michaela stifled a yawn as she stood up, grabbing the hoodie and putting it on again. "I hope ET's going to be okay."

"It could have gone the other way," he said as they walked to the register.

He peeled several bills from a thin, folded wad in the front pocket of his jeans, and handed them to Miss Faye, who was also the cashier.

"I'm curious myself why you didn't call the police. You said ET had broken into the property?"

"Yeah, but it didn't look like he was trying to steal anything. If ET ran away, like you said, I think he only wanted a place to sleep that was safe. If my godparents had found him before I did, they might have called the police."

"I'm still waiting to hear why you didn't," Smith said.

"I didn't see him as a threat, to be honest. He's a kid, and small for his age. He didn't seem dangerous to me, just sick."

Cooper nodded. Then he added another few bills to the money he'd handed to Miss Faye. "For Pete. Give him something to take with him for later."

"Bless you. I sure will," Faye said, smiling affectionately at him. "Y'all have a good day."

They left the café. Memphis was awake, the air filled with the sounds of early-morning activity, and already thickening with the promise of high heat and humidity. Smith led the way to his bike, which he'd parked in the alleyway next to the café. Michaela followed behind him.

Cooper once again handed her the helmet. She stood putting it on as he carefully backed out the motorcycle and turned it toward the street.

Michaela climbed on behind him once more. And, once more, as she leaned into his back and wound her arms around his middle, he experienced a roiling, ticklish sensation coursing through him.

"Where are you staying?" he asked as he turned over the engine.

"Chickasaw Gardens. It's close to the Pink Palace."

He nodded. He knew of the community and was a little surprised. It was considered an upscale, older area that had become integrated over the past few decades.

In a minute they were in traffic, headed toward the University District. The ride out of the neighborhood that housed Miss Faye's did not take long, but there was quickly a world of difference in the surroundings. As soon as he could Cooper turned onto Poplar Avenue, a wide boulevard lined with old trees and stately homes. Doing so was like an automatic reflex. He liked this ride, this road, under a leafy umbrella that seemed protective and peaceful.

Suddenly now, even more than when they'd first started out after leaving the medical center, he was aware of Michaela's presence behind him and the female outline of her against his back. He had not expected that part of the events of the night before would include offering a lift home to someone he'd just met, let alone inviting her out to breakfast. He still wasn't sure what had prompted that.

With each new movement of the bike—banking into a turn, slowing down, or swerving from one lane into another—Cooper felt Michaela's response through the tips of her fingers, and in the pressure points of her elbows and knees. It felt to him less like holding on than hugging.

Soon, Cooper could see the sign at the entrance to Chickasaw Gardens. Slowing down, he turned onto the road that led onto the property. Michaela called out further directions to a specific street, all of which, he noticed, were individually named after American Indian tribes. Finally he was slowing down in front of the house that she indicated to him. He shut off the engine, and a silence descended. He held up a hand above his shoulder, and Michaela used it to help balance herself as she stepped off the bike. He followed suit. This time, it was Cooper's turn to look around in curiosity.

"Nice," he said as his gaze lingered on each house in turn that fronted along the slightly curving roadway. "You say your godparents live here?"

"Yes, for years. My sister and I used to come down during the summer to visit, or sometimes at Christmas. I loved it here."

"I can see why. Beautiful neighborhood. Great architecture. It's quiet…"

"And I never had any chores to do."

Cooper smiled at her caustic comment. "Mind showing me how ET got onto the property?"

He followed Michaela up the driveway and around the side of the house. He noted the nearby houses and different architectural styles like Tudor and Colonial and Cape, as well as the layout of properties with their individualized, planned landscaping.

Michaela opened a wrought-iron gate, and he fol-

lowed her through to a corner of a rectangular enclosed
backyard where the back fence met the side wall of the
garage, hidden behind several bushes.

"He got in behind there," she said as she pointed to
the corner. "I have no idea how he found it, or if he made
the hole himself."

Cooper forced aside the bushes with his hands, and
quickly examined the opening. It was a big enough
space for someone like ET to crawl through. But he had
no idea how the boy had targeted this house, let alone
this particular community. Where ET lived in North
Memphis was a far cry from Chickasaw Gardens in
many ways. He let go of the bush and stepped back,
brushing off his hands down the legs of his black jeans.

"You need to get that fixed. You don't want to leave
it for anyone else, or some animal to find it."

"I know. That's what Jefferson told me," Michaela
readily agreed.

They walked back to the front of the house. Smith
looked at the time again but said nothing as they approached the front door. He caught Michaela covering
another yawn. Her eyes were a little red now from lack
of sleep, and seemed slightly unfocused.

"Please don't thank me again," she said. "I just hope
the doctors can figure out what's wrong and make him
better. End of story."

"We'll have to wait to see," Cooper said. "But nothing for you to worry about. Go on inside and get some
sleep."

"I'm going to," she admitted with a tired smile, un-
locking the door.

When she faced him, there was a moment when

neither knew what else to say. Or do. It wasn't enough to say goodbye and walk away. Somehow, it seemed like the two of them had been through too much together. They now had a history in a very unique way.

"Thanks for breakfast. And the ride home," Michaela finally said.

"Thanks for the company."

She opened the door and turned once more to him. He thought that the look in her eyes matched what he was thinking. Chances were slim to none that they'd see each other again. He opened his mouth to speak, but then she yawned, stepped inside her godparents' house and, with a goodbye wave, closed the door.

He stared at it, absently rubbing his hand against his jaw. The opportunity was gone, so he took it as a signal.

Cooper walked back to his motorcycle. He put on the helmet he'd given Michaela to use. It was warm from her skin and a scent from her still lingered. But the helmet also felt a little different, like it was no longer his. He tugged it firmly over his head and fastened the chin strap. When he turned over the engine, it was a harsh, foreign sound in the still morning air. He idled it down and rolled quietly back to the main street, picking up speed at the corner, but feeling as if he'd left something behind.

Michaela heard a repetitive, vibrating noise and tried to ignore it. It seemed to be right above her head and getting louder. She moaned in the back of her throat, as she was reluctantly forced out of sleep. Lifting a heavy arm over her head, she gently pushed at the warm, furry body camped out on her pillow.

"Lady, go away," she mumbled.

Lady responded by letting out a plaintive meow, and not moving.

It began to penetrate Michaela's brain that it was not early the next morning but very late in the same day, and Lady had not been fed. Full awareness came suddenly. Her first thought, however, was of having had breakfast with a somewhat enigmatic man who went by the name of Smith. That segued into the memory of straddling the back of a motorcycle behind him, and holding on to him in a manner far too close and personal for someone she'd just met.

Michaela's eyes popped open as she also recalled how they'd met; because of Eugene Terrance, a truculent fifteen-year-old kid with a troubled life, and an undisclosed illness.

Lady meowed again and began nibbling on her hair.

Michaela gave up on her reflections and got off her bed. She'd managed to strip off the pants she'd worn over her nightie to the hospital the night before. She'd left it on the floor, along with the hoodie that Cooper had lent her. She'd forgotten to return it to him. But, after getting into the house, she'd fallen asleep across her bed with the bedspread haphazardly pulled over her. She felt wrinkled and a little stiff at the moment, but her mind was now filled with the impressions, sights and sounds of her adventure.

Michaela went to the kitchen, yawning as she glanced at the clock and saw that it was nearly six in the afternoon. The sun was in the western sky and lengthening shadows indicated that, sooner than she realized, it would be night again.

"Sorry I forgot to feed you. Don't take it personally," Michaela said as she crouched down beside the cat. Lady rushed her now refilled bowl. Michaela briefly scratched Lady's neck and then stood up, feeling somewhat disoriented.

She'd lost a whole day.

Well, maybe not lost exactly, Michaela corrected. It's not like she had any particular plans for the day, but she still had a heightened sense of activity, of action, a carryover from the night before.

The question now was, was it worth getting dressed? She had made the decision to take a shower and at least change when the telephone rang. She took the cordless from the wall and sat at the kitchen counter with it.

"Hello?"

"Hey, it's Jefferson. Thought I'd check in on you."

"That's nice of you."

"I was getting concerned. I tried calling you this morning and got no answer. I was wondering if I was going to have to call the police after all."

Michaela grimaced. "I didn't get home until almost eight."

"That late? Don't tell me you got lost again. Didn't that guy give you a ride home like he said he would?"

Michaela thought about how to answer, given Jefferson's tone. It sounded less like concern than disapproval.

"It took a little longer than I thought, but Smith…I mean Cooper Townsend, did bring me home. I've been sleeping most of the day. I just woke up a few minutes ago."

"What about the kid?"

Michaela pursed her lips. But Jefferson's question also reminded her of something else.

"The medical center kept him overnight. I don't know what's going to happen next, and I don't know anything about his family yet."

"They never showed up?"

"Not before I left," Michaela admitted. "I plan to call and get an update."

"I wouldn't bother. We did more than we needed to last night."

Michaela was on the verge of correcting Jefferson's recall, but thought better of it. "Were your daughters okay?"

"Yes, ma'am. Both asleep when I got home, but this morning they had all kinds of questions about where I went off to last night. I told them it wasn't anything for them to worry about."

"Hmmm," Michaela said, noncommittally.

"Look, I feel badly about just leaving you like that. Under different circumstances I would have stayed with you and brought you home."

Michaela got up restlessly and began to pace the kitchen. She leaned against the edge of the sink.

"Don't worry about it. It's all over and I got home safely."

"You probably haven't eaten all day. How do you feel about going out for dinner someplace local?"

Michaela's stomach roiled and rumbled. She was hungry, but she hesitated at the invitation.

"Thanks, Jefferson, but if you don't mind, I think I'll just stay in and call it a day. And I have something I need to take care of. Maybe another night," she added.

"I'll look forward to it," he said. "You know, you made quite an impression on my girls. They'd like to have you over again."

Michaela smiled warmly. "Tell them I said hi. Thanks for calling."

But as soon as she finished her conversation with Jefferson, Michaela called Information for a number to the medical center where she and Jefferson had taken ET. She was disappointed but not surprised to learn that he was no longer a patient.

"Was he released?" Michaela questioned.

"The discharge records say he was transferred over to St. Jude this afternoon."

"Does the record say anything about the test results from last night?"

"Ma'am, are you a family member?"

"Well, no. But I was the one who brought Eugene Terrance in to you."

"I'm sorry, but I can't give out that information. You'll have to get in touch with St. Jude."

"Do you happen to have the number?"

Michaela wrote down the number and immediately tried calling. She finally connected with a department that acknowledged having a patient, Eugene Terrance Dunne, who had been admitted earlier that day.

"I'd like to come and see him," Michaela said in response to the information.

"Are you immediate family?"

"Everyone keeps asking me that. No, I'm not family, but I'm concerned about ET…"

"Who?"

"That's Terrance's nickname. ET."

"I'm sorry, but visiting hours have already ended today. Only family is allowed later hours. You can come tomorrow between two and six o'clock, but call first in case he's scheduled for tests or treatment."

"How is he doing? Do the doctors know anything yet?"

"I can't say…"

"I know, I know. I'm not family," Michaela said dryly. "Is there any way you can get a message to him for me?"

"I'll do what I can but I can't promise. Your name, please?"

Michaela responded, also leaving her phone number. "And your message?"

She started to speak, and then stopped. She suddenly didn't know what she wanted to say that wouldn't sound condescending, patronizing, or just stupid to a fifteen-year-old who'd demonstrated imaginative survival skills. Michaela already had a sense that life so far for Eugene Terrance had been rough and fragmented. She couldn't begin to identify with his existence or circumstances, but there was one thing that she believed to be pretty universal in all kids: a need for attention.

"Tell him…" Michaela began carefully. "Tell him I hope we can be friends."

Chapter 4

From a distance, as Michaela drove the approach to the entrance of St. Jude, everything looked pink. There were a number of buildings beyond the security checkpoint, but the layout seemed random and sprawling. There was evidence of continuing expansion in a few areas where she could see construction equipment. The complex was much bigger and less formal than she thought it would be.

Accepting the pass from the guard, Michaela continued into the parking lot, which was already just about full. Following instructions, she found herself on a path that led to an administrative building. Before reaching the main entrance, she noticed, just opposite, a much smaller, magnificent building that looked like a church or shrine.

Inside the main building was a spacious sitting area

of comfortable chairs and sofas. There was no additional security as far as she could tell, but behind the reception desk a blond woman was seated to meet all visitors.

"Welcome to St. Jude. How can I help you today?" she asked with a friendly smile.

Michaela smiled in return, surprised that there was no ledger she had to sign, no request for photo ID, or to search her purse.

"Yes, I came to see one of your patients. I think he was admitted a few days ago."

She provided ET's full name and age to the receptionist who checked her computer records. In the meantime, Michaela looked around, pleasantly surprised by the bright space with its floor-to-ceiling glass entrance that let in light and provided a scenic view across the grounds of the complex.

There were only a half-dozen people in the waiting area, leafing through magazines, having quiet conversations, staring blankly into space. Her attention was drawn to the sight of a young Asian woman who cradled and gently rocked a young girl, or boy, curled up across her lap and an adjoining chair. In front of the chair was a child's riding wagon shaped like a cartoon car. Michaela could not tell which gender the child was because he or she was bald.

Chemo, she instantly conjectured. Cancer.

She was hit with the realization, and the physical proof, that children can also be afflicted with such a dreadful illness. It was one thing to have learned the statistics and facts from reports, but it was another matter to bear witness to someone so young suffering.

And the fact that Eugene Terrance, ET, had to be

sent here raised all kinds of questions. What had the blood test results shown? What was it that had made him sick enough to be moved here?

"Ma'am, are you related to the patient?"

Michaela turned back to the receptionist. She briefly thought about lying and making herself an instant aunt, but instead shook her head. Anyway, the records would show, as Cooper Townsend had told her, that ET was a foster-care child. There had been no mention of natural family.

"I met him several nights ago. It's a long story, but when I found him he was very sick. I took him to get medical help, and then was told he was transferred here. I just want to see how he's doing."

"I understand, but… Wait a minute. What's your name?"

"Michaela Landry."

"Oh, okay. I see your name on a list of approved visitors."

"Really?"

"Yes, ma'am."

"How did that happen?"

The woman shrugged. "I don't know, but if you'll just have a seat for a minute someone will be right out to talk with you."

While she waited, Michaela looked around what she could see of the facility. The first thing that struck her was that St. Jude did not look like a hospital. It really had the feel of a modern school or even a day-care center. There were pictures on the walls that, from what she could see beyond the reception area, were painted in eye-catching pastel colors. And lots of blown-up photographs of children, some showing the obvious effects of their illness. There were fanciful decals on the floor in the shape of footprints indicating direction through the various corridors. And there were those small wagons, here and there, probably meant for the use of children.

She took another look at the wagon parked near the young woman holding the child. The wagons were meant to be more than just a fun toy for kids. Michaela could guess that it was also a means of getting around the building. If children couldn't pedal themselves, they could be pulled.

Michaela saw an African-American woman wearing a white lab coat turn a corner and walk directly toward her.

"Miss Landry?"

"Yes."

The woman held out her hand. "I'm Marilyn Caldwell. I'm from TTU."

Michaela took the offered hand while also digesting the specific affiliation. She missed Marilyn Caldwell's next words.

"…understand the procedures and the need to protect our patients and their family. Why don't you come with me."

"You mean, I'll get to see Eugene Terrance?" Michaela asked, following Marilyn Caldwell down a hallway and toward a set of elevators.

"It might be possible to arrange that. You still have to get permission from the legal guardian but you came at a good time. His foster mother is here. Would you like to meet her? She knows about how you helped Eugene."

"Yes, I'd like to. If you don't mind me asking, have they found out what's wrong with ET?"

"All the tests are done, but I'm afraid I can't discuss the results with you. It's still considered privileged information. Only the patient himself can tell you, if he wants to."

Michaela nodded. "I understand. I didn't mean to be nosy."

"I'd call it concern, and that's fine. But we have a strict protocol when it comes to information about our patients."

They stepped into an elevator along with a young girl in a wheelchair who was being pushed by another girl who might be an older sibling. Although the girl's head was wrapped in cotton and gauze dressing she was wearing earplugs and playing with the features on her iPod.

"You don't live in Memphis?" Marilyn asked conversationally.

"No, I'm just here for the summer."

"I'm sure you hadn't planned on spending your time in a hospital worrying about a young boy you don't even know."

"That's true, but now that I'm here, I'd really like to know more about St. Jude. And more about Eugene Terrance. No one has been able to tell me anything."

"I know it's been frustrating," Marilyn commented.

"But I just found out I'm on the visitors list."

Marilyn grinned. "You can thank Cooper Townsend for that."

"Cooper? Do you know him?"

"Everyone knows Cooper. The kids all call him Smith. Or the Man in Black. He's got quite a reputation and the kids adore him."

The elevator stopped and Michaela followed Marilyn off.

"I'm confused. Does he work here?"

Marilyn Caldwell smiled vaguely but seemed to be careful in how she responded. "In a voluntary way. He works mostly with adolescents and young teens, especially in sports. Cooper's involved with something similar in a community in North Memphis. He's sort of a big brother, slash therapist, slash teacher, slash father confessor. We could use about ten more like him. And that's only what he does in his spare time."

"Oh," Michaela murmured, feeling somewhat dissatisfied with the answer and more confused than ever. She was hoping to learn something more about him, but Marilyn Caldwell seemed discreet and protective of Cooper.

"Cooper knows that a lot of the families in communities all around Memphis don't have access to a lot of services, including basic health care. But the kids still get sick, sometimes with serious ailments. Some of them end up here for treatment. He's responsible for many kids getting the right attention at the right time, and in a few cases probably saved their lives."

Michaela's head was spinning with this new information. In a way it made sense. In the little bit of time she'd spent with Cooper she'd discerned a man who was attentive, caring and who, she was a little embarrassed to admit to herself, she'd also found to be masculine and…kind of sexy.

She'd lost count of the number of times she'd relived riding on the back of his motorcycle. It was an experience that still made her feel conjoined with Cooper in a peculiar way. It was probably inappropriate, Michaela mused as Marilyn opened an office door, that she'd secretly enjoyed being pressed, by necessity, against his back, holding him around his waist.

"Sorry I kept you waiting, Mrs. Wilson. I was just telling you about Miss Landry when I got a call that she was here to visit with Eugene," Marilyn said, entering the room.

When Michaela walked in, however, the first person she saw was Cooper. He rose immediately from his chair and faced her. Comically the song line "I only have eyes for you" suddenly chimed in her brain. And her stomach did a flip-flop strong enough to startle her.

What was up with that?

It was the same reaction she'd had two nights earlier when they'd first met, and hadn't yet even said hello.

"Hi," Michaela breathed out in genuine surprise.

"Hello again," Cooper smiled calmly.

His rich, deep voice kicked in another flip-flop. And she couldn't be mistaken about the sparkle in his eyes. His reaction at seeing her again matched her own. That pleased her.

He was again wearing a long-sleeved black T-shirt and jeans, but with a tan microfiber aviation jacket that gave him a sporty look. On second sight Michaela concluded that the close-cut facial hair was becoming, delineating the strong lines of his jaw. She saw again, though barely noticeable, that there was a slight discoloration to his skin beneath the hair.

"Please, sit here," Cooper said, stepping aside to give her his chair.

Finally sitting down, Michaela registered the third

person in the room, a middle-aged woman seated in a chair in front of Marilyn's desk. She was of medium height and build, and a bit overweight, dressed casually in jeans and cotton top. Michaela couldn't help also noticing the woman's long, fake vinyl nails with a jazzy top design. Her hair was combed back severely and gathered in a knot or ponytail, with a cluster of synthetic corkscrew curls attached.

Marilyn Caldwell made the introductions.

"It's nice to meet you, Mrs. Wilson," Michaela said, offering the woman her hand. In turn Mrs. Wilson reluctantly accepted, but Michaela found her hand was limp and unresponsive.

"Hello," the woman said flatly.

Marilyn sat behind her desk, and as she gave the practitioner her attention, Michaela was acutely aware that Cooper chose to stand more or less behind her chair. She couldn't see him, but she felt his presence in a way that was both comforting and protective.

Marilyn acted as a go-between, filling in both Michaela and Betty Wilson on each other's connection to fifteen-year-old Eugene Terrance Dunne.

"I hope you don't think I'm interfering," Michaela said directly to Betty Wilson, "but I wanted to find out how Eugene is doing. Do the doctors know what's wrong?"

There was just a long enough pause for Michaela to become aware that her simple question was not well received by Betty Wilson, who drew back into her chair but said nothing. Michaela turned to Marilyn, who was thoughtfully regarding Mrs. Wilson.

"Only the patient and his family can make the decision to discuss the medical finding," Marilyn answered.

"He don't even look like he's sick to me," Mrs. Wilson said.

Michaela was confused by the response, but jumped on the opportunity. "When I first saw Eugene he was sick. He said his ear was hurting, his nose was runny. He fell to the ground in front of me. All of that must mean something," Michaela countered.

"I thought the first place would give him something to take and he'd be fine. Then Smith called after Eugene was found, and said I had to sign some kind of release so they could bring him here. It was the middle of the night," Mrs. Wilson confirmed, aggrieved.

"Smith made a good decision, Betty."

"Is Eugene very sick?" Michaela interjected.

Again, Marilyn looked to Betty Wilson to answer. The woman seemed annoyed again by the questions concerning ET.

"They say he is, but I think that boy is just trying to get attention. He's always complaining about his ear hurting, or it was something else wrong."

"Had you taken him to see a doctor before when he complained?"

"Yeah, but the doctor said it was just a bad cold. He had me buy some pills. Cost a lot of money."

"I should tell you that Eugene never complained to me about not feeling well," Cooper added. "Sometimes he'd sit out a basketball or soccer game and tell me he was tired. And I can only remember two practices he ever missed."

"I'd like to see him. Everyone tells me I need your permission," Michaela said to Mrs. Wilson.

"Why you need to see him?" the woman asked, suspicious.

Michaela was taken aback, and resisted exchanging glances with Marilyn. "Well, I… For one thing, I kind of promised I would. To be honest I'm not sure he'll even remember me."

"Betty, I did tell Marilyn that Miss Landry might pay a visit," Cooper said.

"But he don't even know her," Betty Wilson continued to point out. "And I don't want a stranger knowing my business."

"Being in a hospital is scary for anyone, especially a child. I just thought…"

"Me and my husband are responsible for Eugene. When I took him in, it was 'cause I was trying to do the right thing. But that boy has not been easy to handle. Now he's sick and I don't want nobody saying it's my fault. I can't be running back here all the time to see after him. I have other kids to take care of. How do I know you're not going to report me to Children Services, and say I'm not taking care of him right?"

Mrs. Wilson's tirade filled the office. Michaela was again caught off guard by the outburst that seemed so out of place, and overwrought. And she couldn't help but be aware that Betty Wilson's concerns did not seem to have a lot to do with Eugene's welfare.

"I understand that taking care of kids who otherwise wouldn't have a place to live can be exhausting, Mrs. Wilson. Smith has been great, as always, with getting kids like Eugene involved in sports and other activities at St. Mark's, but Miss Landry's interest might help you as well, and be good for Eugene."

"I don't know," Mrs. Wilson said, in a confused but impatient tone.

Michaela, puzzled and a little shocked, looked at Marilyn for explanation.

"The most important thing right now is making sure Eugene gets all the help he needs. Isn't that right?" Cooper spoke up.

Michaela glanced briefly over her shoulder at Cooper. "I don't want to cause problems. Maybe this isn't a good time, and I don't want to make Mrs. Wilson uncomfortable. I'm a stranger in Memphis. I'm only visiting.

"If it will make a difference, I have a niece and two nephews. I taught high school for five years. There's nothing you can tell me about kids and them getting sick that would surprise me."

Cooper gave her a reassuring look with warmth in his gaze. But still, he appeared to shake his head imperceptibly, as if warning her to not push her point.

"Betty, I don't see a problem with Miss Landry's request to see Eugene. As an administrator and health-care provider, I believe that her interest is sincere," Marilyn said.

"Y'all do what you want. It's in God's hands, anyway."

"It's in our hands as well," Cooper said.

Michaela reached out and put her hand on Cooper's arm. "It's okay, I understand. This is a family matter and I have no right to make myself a part of it."

"I guess you can see him." Betty Wilson finally shrugged. "I have to go anyway. My husband is waiting for me and he has to get on to work."

"Thank you. I'll only stay a few minutes," Michaela promised.

"I'll show Miss Landry where to find him," Cooper offered.

Michaela stood up, thanked Mrs. Wilson again and added a pointed farewell to Marilyn Caldwell.

"Do you know anything about St. Jude?"

"Of course I've heard about it, but I don't know much about the facility."

Marilyn picked a selection of brochures and pamphlets from a display rack on a table next to her desk. She handed them to Michaela.

"Here's some information for you to take with you. And please feel free to call me if you have any questions. If you'd like I can arrange for a tour as well."

"Thanks. I'd like that." She turned to Betty Wilson. "Bye, Mrs. Wilson. I appreciate you letting me see Eugene. I'm sure everything is going to work out fine for everyone."

Once outside the office with Cooper, Michaela turned to him.

"It's serious, isn't it?"

"It could be," he said honestly.

She studied him. "Cooper, I know enough about St. Jude to understand that children aren't brought here for common head colds and earaches."

"And I'm glad you didn't say so in front of Mrs. Wilson. You have to understand that down here some Black folks don't really trust doctors, and they're suspicious of any kind of medicine they're told to take. Yes, I know you're concerned about Eugene, but the staff also has to think about how to deal with the family and make sure their young patients get the treatment they need."

She grimaced. "Was I pushy? Typical Yankee, right?" Cooper laughed quietly. "I hope I didn't create more problems."

"I think you're going to be a blessing in disguise," he said, with a warm sincerity that made her smile in return.

Michaela absently leafed through the handful of pamphlets and brochures that Marilyn Caldwell had given her to take away and read. They all contained information and statistics on the list of pediatric diseases that were researched and treated at St. Jude, as well as background details on the facility itself. The words swam before her eyes. There was no way she could focus on this now, let alone absorb the details. She was still trying to process the encounter with Betty Wilson, and the disturbing sense that ET's foster parent seemed less concerned about finding out the nature of his illness than she was about the inconvenience it would pose to her.

She'd heard about cases of unsuccessful foster-care arrangements. One of her former students had lived with the system nearly her entire young life, and had suffered emotional abuse. And yet, one of her coworkers who had grown up in foster care had nothing but praise and love for the family that nurtured him, put him through college although they had no legal obligation to do so once he'd turned eighteen. They had supported his career goal of becoming a computer technician.

But Michaela didn't want to be unfair to Betty Wilson. After all, her question was fair. Why did she want to see

Eugene Terrance Dunne again? Why wasn't it enough
to know he was getting exemplary care and attention?
Why did she feel the need to make sure, in her own
mind, he was okay?

But ET wasn't the only person who now held her attention. Standing alone with Cooper had given her the
opportunity she'd been waiting for since entering
Marilyn Caldwell's office and finding him there.
Michaela had stared up into his handsome face, trying
to read behind the dark compelling gaze, the steady
voice and sturdy presence.

"Who are you?" she asked.

Cooper chuckled sheepishly, stuffing his hands into the
front pockets of his black jeans. It struck Michaela that,
in contrast to his physical mien, there was something self-
deprecating, almost shy, about him. He didn't like talking
about himself. He didn't necessarily want the attention.

"Just a man trying to help a kid, a family."

"But why?"

"Because it needs to be done," Cooper said, serious
now. "If not me, then who? If not now, when? And why
you? Why are you here? I go back to my question of
the other night—why didn't you just call the police?"

Michaela shook her head. "That's not really an
answer, Cooper, and I have the feeling you're going to
duck giving me a straight one."

"I don't mean to sound…mysterious. I'm not all that
important. What you see is pretty much what you get,"
he said simply.

Michaela found his response odd, and it only heightened her curiosity about him. And she felt slightly miffed
with Cooper and herself that she might be pursuing him

in a way. There was a part of her that wanted to say to him, "Come on...work with me here."

"I know you're here to see ET, but do you have time to meet for coffee afterward?"

She grabbed hold of the opportunity with unseemly haste. "That would be nice."

"Good. There's a public café on the first floor...."

That was as far as he'd gotten before there was a great shouting of his name at the end of a hallway as a door opened.

"Smith! Hi, Smith."

What seemed like a chorus of half a dozen young children, turned out to be only one small boy of seven or eight. He had very thin light brown hair, and bright blue eyes magnified behind a pair of glasses with thick lenses.

Cooper turned at the exuberant greeting and crouched to the level of the oncoming youngster. He was rushing toward them in slippers, bathrobe, pajamas. He propelled himself with such force into Cooper's arms that Michaela feared they both would topple over. But Cooper took the impact and stood up with the child in his arms.

"Hey, big guy. How's it going?"

"Okay," the child wheezed. He hugged Cooper, briefly resting his head on Cooper's shoulder before leaning back to gaze earnestly into his face. "Can you stay with me? I have a new puzzle."

"You have chemo today?" Cooper asked.

Michaela stood aside, watching the interaction, surprised with the open and casual way Cooper asked about the boy's treatment, and the equally casual way the child acknowledged it by nodding his head. But she was also aware that, for that moment, the little boy had Cooper's complete and undivided attention.

The boy placed his small, pale hands on Cooper's cheeks and rubbed gently against the facial hair.

"I didn't feel so good yesterday so I have it today. Can you stay with me?"

"When do you get started?"

"Right now," another voice said, that of a young aide who'd finally caught up to her ward. "It shouldn't take long. Three hours at most."

"Tell you what, Kenny. I'll stay for a little bit and we'll get started on the puzzle. But I have to get back to work, so we may have to finish another day. Okay?"

"Okay." Kenny nodded.

"Then, let's go."

With that, Cooper agilely shifted the boy, swinging him over his head so that the child could sit on his shoulders, his skinny arms and hands wrapped under Cooper's chin. Cooper held him securely by his ankles. He turned to Michaela, poised to apologize.

"Another time," she said simply, suddenly moved by the picture Cooper and the boy made together.

"I look forward to it. I'm glad you came today. I think you're going to be good for ET."

"How do you know that? Are you now a sage or clairvoyant?"

"Sometimes," he said.

Cooper walked away down the hall, putting just enough bounce in his step to make Kenny bob up and down on his perch. The child's giggling laughter could be heard as the door to the treatment room closed behind them....

"Who are you waiting for?"

Michaela's reflections vanished as she looked up at a male attendant standing in front of her. She came to her feet.

"Eugene Terrance—"

"ET," he interrupted with a nod. He pointed toward the bank of elevators. "Go down to the first floor. He should be back from his test. Take a look in the teen room. That's where all the kids his age hang out."

She stuffed the information booklets into her bag and followed the attendant's instructions.

She couldn't miss the designated room. The glass windows made it easy to see who was inside and what was going on. There was a young Black girl attached to an IV stand sitting cross-legged on a sofa leafing through several fashion magazines. There was an empty wheelchair nearby that Michaela presumed was for the girl. Another teen was watching TV. Then, Michaela spotted ET. He was dressed in what looked like pajama bottoms and a T-shirt with the logo for Rocawear printed across the front and back. His hair had been cornrowed from the overgrown unkempt hair he'd had when she'd first seen him. He and another boy about his age were playing chess.

She knocked softly on the door. The teen watching TV called out.

"It's okay to come in."

Michaela entered the room but no one paid any attention to her presence.

"Ahhh, man! That was bogus."

She turned at the exclamation from ET's chess partner. Michaela only remembered the basics of the game.

Spencer had taught her once how to play, although she'd always thought he'd taken unnecessary pleasure in beating her, and that had been all the time.

"You not paying attention to your queen." ET shrugged. "She gonna get snatched."

The other player cackled. "That is wack," he said, taking one of ET's men and moving his onto the space.

"No, it ain't. Check," ET said calmly, responding with a counter move.

"What!"

Finally ET noticed Michaela. He looked at her, and then back to the board. "Hurry up, man. Your move."

"Hi," she said, taken aback by his indifference. "Go on and finish. I can wait."

"I bet she's from Social Service," the other boy said loud enough for her to hear. He made another move.

"No, she ain't," ET corrected. "Check," he said again, taking another game piece from his opponent.

The other boy sucked his teeth and slid down into his chair. "I told you I don't play that good."

"The game ain't over yet. You could still beat me," ET said impatiently.

The boy frowned at the board, made to move one piece, changed his mind and moved another.

"Checkmate," ET declared.

But Michaela noticed that there was no sense of elation or victory in his declaration.

Muttering a profanity, ET's opponent pushed away from the table, knocking over his chair.

"You gotta commit and then you gotta stay focused," ET said wisely as he got up. He glanced at Michaela.

"That sounds like Smith talking again," Michaela quipped. "Remember me?"

"Yeah, I remember you. Why you here?"

"I came to visit and see how you're doing. I said I would." She could tell from his expression that he was surprised by the concept of visitors.

"That don't mean nothing." ET shrugged. "You could just been saying that."

"Fooled you. Here I am."

He made a skeptical moue with his mouth, walked around her and out of the room. Michaela followed him.

"Are you busy right now or can we talk? I won't stay long."

He didn't answer and continued to walk until they reached a secluded corner with a large panoramic window overlooking a playground. There were chairs along an adjacent wall and he sprawled in one.

"What do you want to talk about?"

"You. You're looking a lot better than the last time I saw you. How are you feeling? How long are they keeping you here? I met your foster mother. She gave me permission to see you."

He looked at her and held up his index finger. "Why do you care?" Up went a second finger. "I don't know." And a third. "So what?"

This is not going well, she thought.

"You had gorilla biscuits for breakfast, eh?"

ET shifted in his chair and moistened his lips. She had the satisfaction, and relief, of seeing that he was trying to hide his amusement.

"That's cold." He shook his head and shook off her sarcastic comment.

"Anyway, I bet it's more comfortable here than sleeping in a garage and eating canned tuna, right?"

"That was still better than some other places I been in."

Betty Wilson came to mind, but Michaela discounted ET's reference. The woman had, at least, willingly taken ET into her home. Maybe she was right and he was a problem child. But what if she didn't, or couldn't, go that extra step to care about him because he wasn't her own? What if she had provided for him because the state was paying her to? What if he knew that? Not exactly the foundations for a happy home, she considered.

She sat in the chair opposite him. He seemed even smaller than she recalled from that night. "I saw Smith a little while ago. Everybody seems to know him around here. I thought he was a doctor."

ET remained silent, staring out the window and not taking her bait this time.

"I think he made it possible for me to even be here. He told the staff and Mrs. Wilson I was okay."

"That don't mean you're okay with me. I didn't ax you to come," he responded, petulantly. His knee was bouncing up and down nervously. He shot a sideward glance at her. "What did Mrs. Wilson tell you 'bout me? She tell you why I'm here?"

"No. Nobody will. I don't think they're supposed to without your say-so, so I understand. It's not like I'm a part of your family, or a good friend like Smith."

"He knows. Why you didn't ask him?"

She shook her head slowly. "It's not his place to say anything, either, ET. It's up to you."

Michaela began digging around inside her bag. She was aware that ET referred to Betty Wilson in a very formal and distant way. He definitely did not see her as his mother.

She pulled a brightly colored gift bag from her tote and silently handed it to ET.

"What's that?" he asked, suspicious, not making a move to accept the offering.

"A little something to cheer you up. Maybe."

"Not," he came back with a snicker, and then caught himself. He took the bag, peering inside. "What's this?"

"Wouldn't be a surprise if I told you."

"How come you bring me stuff?"

Michaela relaxed. Now he was the inquisitive kid instead of the stoic teen who saw himself alone in the world.

"Because it's no fun being sick, and it's no fun having to stay in a hospital. Someone's always putting a thermometer in your mouth or a needle in your arm."

He chortled, pulling the first item out of the bag and turning it over, squinting at the title on the cover of the paperback book.

"You can read, can't you?" Michaela asked.

He shot her a look of disgust. "Yeah, I can read."

"Remember I told you your birth sign was Sagittarius? Well, this book will tell you all about your sign. It's fun. Then you can go outside and try to find your stars in the sky."

"There ain't no stars in the sky," he scoffed. "You can't see nothing but the sun and the moon."

He briefly flipped through the book before putting it aside. Next, he took a box out of the bag.

"This is cool," he approved, examining the portable DVD player. "I been wanting one of these. Only problem is, no DVDs."

Michaela silently pointed to the bag. ET extracted the last items: two DVD jewel cases and a pack of batteries.

"Ah, man. This movie is off the hook," he said, indicating the first DVD case. After reading everything on the back of the box, he examined the second film case. "*E.T.?* It got my name on it." He squinted at the box, making a face. "What is that?"

"*E.T.* is the story of an alien whose spaceship crashes to earth. He's found by a little boy who hides him from his parents until he can figure out how to get E.T. back home."

"Sounds dumb. Man, he's one ugly little dude."

Michaela laughed. "The movie was a big hit when it came out. Everyone loved E.T. Little kids thought he was cute."

"I might have to change my name. I ain't no monster from outer space," ET said.

"There's no resemblance," she assured him. She stood up. "I better get going. I'm glad I got to see you. You're a good chess player. Who taught you?"

"Smith."

"Why am I not surprised?" she said dryly. She waved and turned to go.

"What's your name again?"

She looked over her shoulder at him, and stopped to face him once more. "Michaela."

He made a face as he repeated it. He was small for his age, but nonetheless had a certain confidence that was both touching and forceful. There didn't seem to be much that ET was afraid of. He had old eyes, but Michaela knew he still had the heart and yearnings of a child.

She was surprised, however, when ET held the bag out to her, returning the contents.

"No, it's for you. Why are you giving it back?"

"It's okay. I don't need nothin'."

"It's a gift, ET."

ET leaned forward and put the bag on the floor by her chair. "I can't take it."

"I don't understand. Why?"

"'Cause Mrs. Wilson will get mad if I do."

Michaela decided not to insist, although she was mystified and disappointed. She was hoping that he'd be happy and surprised by the gifts. She'd arrogantly forgotten that children in ET's situation have a great deal of personal pride, even if they don't have control over their lives.

"Is there something else you would like instead?"

"Don't matter. I ain't never going to get it."

"Whatever it is, you can't be so sure. Anyway, I hope you don't have to stay here too long."

"You coming again?"

Michaela raised her brows in surprise. "Would you like me to?"

He shrugged, again cool and indifferent. "Don't matter. I'm gonna die."

Chapter 5

For the fourth time in the last half hour Michaela stood in front of the three-quarter-length mirror that Alice Underwood had mounted on the inside of the hall closet door. It was meant as the final checkpoint and review of how someone looked in their clothes before leaving the house. She'd already changed her outfit twice, anxious and ambivalent about the current protocol of how Southern women dress for church. She knew that slacks were not an option. In any case, Michaela knew that she would never have considered wearing them even though nearly everywhere, at the office or at the theater, the dress code had relaxed considerably over the years. Going to worship on Sunday was a different and sacred matter.

She'd been surprised when Kimika and Kyla had come over the day before to invite her to join them and their father for church and had wondered if the invitation had been theirs or Jefferson's. But she'd said yes, and the timing was right.

She felt the need to offer up a prayer or two for ET.

When she was growing up there had been a set ritual for getting dressed on Sunday. Her wardrobe and that of her sister had consisted of dresses, shoes and even hats, meant solely for Sunday school and second service. As an adult the pews of the church she'd attended back then had been filled with parishioners of all ages who came dressed in monochromatic outfits, with extravagant, imaginative hats, one more outrageous than the next. Even her parents had observed that it was like a competition and spectator sport, drawing attention and comments away from the purpose at hand…to come together in fellowship to praise the Lord, and work on redemption.

But she also knew it would have been unseemly to confess to Jefferson's daughters that she didn't attend church on any kind of regular basis. Michaela knew in her heart it was not because of lack of belief, but of the huge contradictions between what she was taught and what she saw and experienced. But church was still the place where she felt assured that letting go of doubts and fears would be received with love and understanding.

Michaela wondered now, as she pivoted and frowned at her image in the mirror, if the sleeveless navy-blue Ralph Lauren dress with its bold print of pink tea roses made a fashion statement that was a little too garden party rather than church service. She deemed it appropriate, and made final adjustments. And it wasn't like she'd never been to service before in the South. Visiting

Alice and Ben and their own son and daughter, there had been Sunday services. It was often followed by an hour of saying hello to everyone they knew. She had silently endured being all dressed up in the brutal Memphis heat as the grown-ups socialized and commiserated on local events.

Behind her reflection in the mirror, Michaela could see Lady sitting sphinxlike on the living room sofa, watching her. She turned around and posed for the cat.

"Well, what do you think, Lady? Will I pass muster? Is my dress too short? Should I cover my arms?"

Lady stared at her from her queenly position as if she couldn't care less.

"A lot of help you are," Michaela murmured.

Her summer sandals had two-inch heels and were all straps and ties. Would her exposed toes be okay? She'd swept her hair back into a ponytail and then twisted it into a knot. Should she wear a hat? She gnawed her lip. She didn't have one, but recalled that Aunt Alice had several straw hats hanging on pegs inside the hall closet. She was still looking over the selection when the doorbell rang. She snatched a hat, picked up her purse and rushed to the door.

"Good morning," Michaela said as she opened it, expecting to greet the two girls. But it was Jefferson who stood outside on a day that was already hot, and promising to become humid as the hours passed.

She hadn't seen him since the night they'd discovered Eugene Terrance in the Underwoods's garage, almost a week earlier. For Michaela, it was like seeing him for the first time. Jefferson was dressed for church, of course, in a medium-brown suit. He looked proper, serious and quite handsome. She was pleasantly surprised, remembering that she was none too pleased with the way he'd conducted himself that night.

"'Morning. You look very summery today."

"Thank you," she said, closing the door, and accompanying Jefferson to his SUV, which was idling at the curb.

She waved to his daughters, who had taken the backseat, and who were again dressed exactly alike.

"Are you going to be comfortable in those shoes? They don't look like they offer enough support," Jefferson said, holding the passenger door for her.

"Maybe I should put on a different pair." Michaela hesitated getting into the car.

"No, wear them. They're so cute," Kimika said.

"I think your dress is pretty," Kyla added.

"Thank you. You both look lovely, too."

They all settled into the car, which was comfortably air-conditioned, but Michaela thought belatedly that she should also have brought along a shawl.

When questioned about what they'd been up to recently, Kimika excitedly explained that she and her sister were leaving the next day to visit family.

"We get our own vacation," Kyla said.

"So do I," Jefferson reminded them. "You know, I'm not going to sit around feeling sad because you're gone."

That comment led to a round of teasing between Jefferson and the girls that Michaela silently listened to, admiring the obvious affection. But their cheerful conversation reminded her of ET, and she wondered, as she had been since seeing him at St. Jude, how he was doing.

She still could not get over his parting statement to
her and still didn't know how to react. Was he being
flippant and melodramatic, announcing that he was
going to die? Was he overstating his diagnosis or prog-
nosis? Was it true? And even if she wanted to entertain
that it was, she still had no idea what was wrong. But
she would bet anything that Cooper knew everything.

Michaela's focus shifted and settled on consideration
of Cooper Townsend. Getting to know him was almost
as frustrating as trying to deal with Eugene Terrance.
There was so much about him she didn't understand,
and she wanted to. She was curious about a man who
could command so much respect from both children and
adults. Whose opinion was sought and heeded, but who
made no attempt to control anyone or anything...except
himself.

And she found herself thinking about him at the
oddest moments. Like now, as she was accompanying
another man and his family to church...and wondering
when she might see him again. Was he possibly at Miss
Faye's this morning having breakfast? Would he be
alone? Had he ever shared his buttery grits with anyone
else? Probably. It was certainly a unique pickup move.

"...after service today?"

Suddenly conversation stopped, and Michaela realized
that she'd been asked a question. She jerked to attention.

"I'm sorry, I didn't hear that," she apologized.

"I said, if you don't have any plans for later, maybe
you'd like to come with me and the girls to the children's museum—"

Before he could finish, there was a simultaneous
groan from Kimika and Kyla.

"Daddy, we always go there," Kyla said.

"We're too old for the children's museum," Kimika added.

"How about the botanic gardens?" Michaela asked. "I haven't been there in years. It will be nice to spend some time outdoors. Does that sound okay with you girls?"

"Sure." Kimika shrugged.

It was clear to Michaela, as she listened to the conversation that followed between Jefferson and the girls, that they were used to activity, and being exposed to the culture that Memphis offered. She was again reminded of ET, and the sharp contrast between his life and that of the McNeill girls. Having met ET's foster mother, Michaela was not inclined to suggest any neglect on the woman's part. Perhaps inattention was a better word. At the very least, maybe indifference. She wondered how ET would react to having as many choices and opportunities as Kimika and Kyla.

A quick glance out the window showed that they were heading out of the city.

Michaela had never considered that Jefferson's place of worship would not be within Memphis proper, and was surprised when he got onto one of the expressways for a drive that took them beyond the city limits. The church, which looked like a tiny cathedral, was a beautiful building but seemed architecturally out of place with the surrounding country setting and local farms.

The parking lot was already pretty filled when they arrived. Everyone knew Jefferson, Kimika and Kyla, and there was a lot of stop and greet before they all finally entered the building. Michaela gave up trying to remember everyone's name she'd been introduced to.

And more than once she was asked, "Where are your people from?" There were accepting nods of approval when she mentioned that her father was from Virginia.

The men were courtly, welcoming and polite. The women, although polite and friendly, sized her up, asking meant-to-be-amusing but less-than-subtle questions about Jefferson's relationship to her.

Of course, Michaela thought.

Jefferson was not only known and respected in the community, he was a widower…and available. Michaela developed a standard, brief, smiling disclaimer.

"I'm only visiting in Memphis for the summer."

Although Jefferson did some things to still leave their relationship in question, much to Michaela's confusion. He stayed close to her side, and used a gentle touch of his hand to guide or lead her, or placed it on her back as he introduced her around. Adding to any misconception were Kimika and Kyla, who behaved and spoke as if she did have a special connection to their family.

The service began when a stout, fiftyish man came to the front podium with a hand mike. In the background began the first quiet chords of an organ.

"Let's praise the Lord, this Sunday morning. Say, hallelujah," his voice intoned.

"Hallelujah," came back a chorus from most of those already seated in the congregation.

People continued to arrive from that point on. Michaela hazarded a look around. The church was almost full.

The leader continued his invocation of praise and beseeching Jesus for forgiveness and mercy. The worshippers added their own shout-outs, as his voice gained in volume until it was booming with intensity that went on for nearly twenty minutes. Michaela looked at Jefferson's profile for his response to this excitable recitation. His hands were clasped loosely, and extended between his parted knees. Jefferson's gaze was lowered, but there was a barely perceptible nodding of his head in agreement with the praise, now and then murmuring, "Thank You, Jesus...Hallelujah."

Michaela knew that Kimika and Kyla had asked to attend this service because of her presence, rather than go to church school. They both sat still and quiet, mesmerized by the oratory of the man at the front of the church, whose voice had now reached a frenzy of conviction, generating clapping and standing and outreached arms of supplication from those in the pews.

"God have mercy on us..."

Michaela found herself riveted by the energy of this prelude, quietly and thoughtfully taking it in.

When the congregation had reached a peak of emotional exultation, the leader said a prayer and amen. Then the choir, consisting of six women, stood up to sing a hymn that, with solo verses and refrains, lasted another half hour.

The service ended some time later with a hymn and instruction to greet one another before departing with the command that all remember to love one another as they go out and do God's commandments.

Michaela was momentarily startled when Jefferson turned to hold her by the shoulders and touched his cheek to hers.

"Peace be with you," he recited in a quiet voice.

"And also with you." Michaela quickly recovered.

Kimika and Kyla awkwardly embraced her with the same command, as did those in pews nearest to her.

Everyone began leaving, again stopping in the aisles, in front of the church and in the parking lot to chat. It was twenty minutes more before Michaela, Jefferson and the girls actually drove away.

The girls complained of being hungry and, in truth, Michaela hoped that no one had heard the unseemly grumbling of her stomach throughout the service. Jefferson suggested they eat at one of their favorite places before heading over to the Memphis Botanic Garden. The restaurant was lovely and airy and filled with after-church patrons. The food was standard fare, but Michaela couldn't help comparing the modern and stylish restaurant to Miss Faye's. It was nothing to write home about, but the food there had very much reminded Michaela of real home cooking.

And she resolutely stayed away from any comparison of Jefferson and Cooper.

Later, strolling through the extensive acreage of the botanic garden, Michaela was once again struck by the warm and close relationship between Jefferson and his daughters. He was a good father. He was firm with them, but also patient and hands-on, actively taking part in broadening their worldview in a way that could only serve them well as they grew to adults. Michaela found herself wondering if a boy like ET, with his fragmented past and uncertain future, would ever have the same opportunities.

Kimika was proud of the fact that her father knew a candidate running for mayor of Memphis, and that her class had been invited to visit city hall on a field trip to learn how local government worked. Kyla could identify a number of plants and foliage in the gardens because she had helped her paternal grandmother work in her own.

Michaela smiled as she listened to the twins' understandable boasting. Did they have any awareness of how blessed they were? Had Jefferson taught them that there were kids their own age who weren't as fortunate? Had they learned yet about giving back, in actuality as well as in prayer?

Despite her enjoyment of the charming afternoon, Michaela was glad when the decision was made to head home. The girls, with their attention span finally worn-out, were ready to leave and trotted ahead toward the parking lot. Michaela walked more leisurely beside Jefferson, as she listened to his discourse on an issue in his business, and a problem with the opening of his second franchise. Michaela listened and commented empathetically, but the issues didn't seem difficult or insurmountable. In her head, the phrase from a Rolling Stone song kept repeating: "You can't always get what you want," because it was true in all areas of life.

Once more, ET came to mind. She could easily guess what he might want.

And then, for no apparent reason, Michaela suddenly had an image of Spencer Childress, her former fiancé, when she'd announced, distressed and guilty and tearful, that she couldn't marry him after all…*you can't always get what you want*… Instead of even asking why,

Spencer had ranted and raged about how much time he'd put into the relationship and how it was now all wasted.

What was it she wanted then, if not him?

Michaela became aware of a vibrating rumble on the main road, coming from her right. It grew louder and was quite near before she realized it was an approaching motorcycle. Unexpectedly her stomach lurched, and her attention was immediately drawn to the street beyond the grounds of the botanic garden. Her eyes scanned the traffic, recognizing the unique engine noise, and waiting for the appearance of a cobalt-blue bike.

But when it finally rolled into view, it was not Cooper's, but a massive Harley Hog. The front rider was a big man in jeans and graying ponytail, white T-shirt worn under a sleeveless leather vest. His back passenger was a woman with improbable platinum-blond hair, a mini denim skirt and cowboy boots.

There was another bike right behind the first. But again, she was disappointed to find that it was not a blue bike like Cooper's.

And then, Michaela twisted her ankle and lost her balance.

Jefferson was alert and quickly reached out to grab her arm, his other hand gripping her hip to pull her back upright.

"Are you okay?" he asked, concerned.

Michaela, embarrassed and annoyed with herself, regained her footing. Her ankle was a little sore, but she didn't say so, and she could walk.

She nodded in response to Jefferson's question. "Sorry. That was pretty clumsy of me."

"No need to apologize. Be careful and watch your step."

Yes. She was trying to.

Cooper drained the rest of his coffee and carefully placed the delicate porcelain cup on its saucer. He wiped his mouth with his napkin and, folding it in half, placed it next to his plate.

"That was good apple cake," he said, nodding to the woman sitting on the other side of the dining table from him. "Did you make it?"

The lovely woman gave him a mock look of affront. "I should be insulted, Smith. You know I do all my own cooking."

"No harm intended. I know women these days have busy lives."

"Well, I'm never too busy to cook a decent meal for people who are important to me. Sure you don't want another slice? There's plenty left."

Cooper made a gesture with his hands to indicate he'd had enough.

He secretly watched his attractive hostess as she sipped her own coffee. She'd only eaten half her dinner and only picked at a sliver of the cake. He accepted that, like many women, Judith worked at maintaining her looks, understanding that it was an important asset. But to be fair, she'd also experienced a tragic loss recently and it was understandable that her decisions of late might be emotionally driven, rather than self-serving.

For instance, he'd accepted Judith's invitation to dinner believing that there would be other guests: her lawyer, who was also a close friend of the family, and his wife. Despite Judith's apologies that the other couple had backed out at the last moment, everything so far that evening had pointed to her planning to entertain only one person. Himself.

"I wish you hadn't gone to all this trouble just for me. You could have postponed tonight, and I would have made myself available to get together with you and your lawyer another time."

She demurred with a wave of her hand. "It was no trouble at all. You've been so kind all these months. I don't know what I would have done if you hadn't been near when Winston was brought home. I appreciate everything the military tried to do after he was killed, but it's always your own people you can depend on. You know what I mean."

Cooper nodded. "Yes, I do."

As he watched the feminine tilt of Judith Macklin's head, the twisting and clasping of her small hands, the sad eyes and sadder tones of her voice, he also couldn't help but notice how her emotions seemed to jar against the carefully coiffed hair, makeup and matching manicure, the Sunday dress that was very pretty and flattering to her curvaceous body. It was not what she had worn to church that morning. She was small of stature, giving her the aura, at least in that moment, of needing to be protected and cherished.

"How are you and your family doing?" he asked.

"We're managing, thank God, and the church fellowship has been there for me. But it's hard. My boys miss their father and were looking forward to him coming home for good this fall."

"They must be very proud of him. Their father will always be a hero to them."

"That's true, I suppose. But it's hard on me, too."

Cooper rested his chin on this clasped hands. "Of course you miss him."

Judith nodded, gnawing on her bottom lip. "I have to do everything by myself. There's no man I can depend on."

Cooper spoke carefully. "You can depend on yourself. I know you have a strong faith in God, and that will see you through. This will pass and things will get better."

She gave him a weak, pained smiled. "Smith, is this where you tell me that when God closes one door, he opens another?"

He raised his brows. Maybe he had come off a little too pious. "You already know that. You're in pain now, but things change. Winston's been gone, what? Five months?"

She looked at him, holding his gaze. Her eyes seemed to convey much more than her words. "Yes. It is time to move on, isn't it? I've been very lonely." Her words ended on a mere whisper.

They stared each other down, the sudden silence in the room engulfing them in a tension that was really only shared by one.

Cooper pursed his mouth and sighed deeply within himself. "I know."

"What am I supposed to do? And if you tell me to pray on it, I'm going to be very upset with you."

"It can't hurt. But I think what you really need, Judith, is activity. I'm sure there's still a lot to settle because of Winston's death. Before long you'll have to think about getting your sons ready for school in the fall. You have a job with a lot of responsibility. There's your church committee…"

"There's you."

She'd said it.

After weeks of coy hinting and maneuvering, Judith had finally gotten to the point, put her cards on the table…called his hand. Cooper had been waiting for it to come, and now that she'd said it out loud, he found he didn't have a ready response. Because the truth was, in another life, a different incarnation of where he was now, he wouldn't have hesitated a second to accept her offer. But that was a long time ago. By his count, seven years and five months…and two other lives.

A sudden intense veil of darkness washed briefly over him, but Cooper forced the memory away.

There was nothing wrong with Judith Macklin. The package was near perfect and, under normal circumstances, even desirable. She was pretty, gracious, charming, well liked even among her female peers. She was talented and smart, operating her own well-established day-care center. And she wanted a man in her life. A new husband.

He shook his head. "I'm sorry, Judith. I don't mean to say or do anything to add to your pain. It can't be me. I'm not what you need."

"Why? I know you're attracted to me, Smith."

"I find you attractive, yes."

"In your position, you should know a wife is an advantage, an asset to your career. It's not like you've never been married. Someplace up north, I heard."

He tried not to show his surprise, or the unsettling sense of the invasion of his privacy.

She shrugged.

"Memphis is a small town. People talk. I heard there was an accident."

Cooper nodded, his gaze deep and fixed as the memory returned. "Yes. There was an accident." That's all he'd admit to.

Judith tried to hold his gaze longer, but when he refused to blink, firm in his position and truthful in his decision, Judith succumbed and closed her eyes and wisely did not pursue the matter. There was no shame or remorse in her body language. Only defeat. She was used to getting what she wanted.

Cooper realized that she had enjoyed the respect and attention that had come with being the wife of a soldier serving overseas. But once her husband had been killed, returned home and buried with the full regalia of military pomp-and-circumstance services, Judith had begun a search to fill the place left vacant by Winston's passing. But if she'd misinterpreted his compassion toward her, maybe he was partially to blame.

Had he, too, been reaching out for something he hadn't realized he needed?

Cooper wasn't about to fault her for wanting someone to share her life with. It served, however, to remind him of what he'd been denying himself, because of a single act of mindless anger that ended with horrific consequences.

Judith opened her eyes and stared at him, a hint of both despair and frustration in her dark eyes.

"Are you seeing someone else?"

The question caught Cooper off guard. Not that he owed her a direct answer, but suddenly he had to stop and think. Because as soon as the question was asked he immediately conjured up an image of Michaela Landry.

Unexpectedly, he could see her as they'd first met, in her no-thought, pulled-together outfit, her hair unkempt…but her beautiful eyes filled with genuine empathy and concern. He could still see her from the encounter at St. Jude days later, when she'd appeared in the hopes of visiting a young patient who, under different circumstances, might have meant her harm.

He'd been thinking about her ever since.

Is there someone else?

"This shouldn't be about me," Cooper responded.

When she continued to look hopefully at him, he used her silence to quickly change the subject. And he stood up.

"I'll help you clear the table."

"No," she said, standing herself. "I don't need your help in the kitchen."

The innuendo was clear but Cooper ignored it, knowing that her ego and her pride had just been offended, even if it wasn't meant to be malicious. And he was sure she knew that.

As Judith stacked the dishes and gathered the silverware, Cooper brought into the kitchen what remained of the leftover food. There wasn't much, again suggesting that she'd only intended him to be the dinner guest that night.

He already knew that her two boys had been spending much of their time, since the news of their father's death, with grandparents, aunts and uncles and cousins or local friends. And he believed that Judith's loneliness was for real…but for the wrong reasons.

He helped her load the dishwasher, which they did

mostly in silence. He gathered her garbage and deposited it in the bin outside the kitchen door, making sure to lock it securely behind him when he reentered the house. She offered him a glass of sherry, which he declined.

"I should get moving. I have two home calls to make in the morning before I start work."

Judith shook her head as she walked him to the door. "You work more than any person I know. You're a good man, Smith. But what do you do for fun?"

He arched a brow, his eyes sparkling. "What you mean is, who do I date, where do I hang out?"

Judith seemed pleased that he knew what she was talking about.

"The Lord isn't going to think any less of you if you do. You need someone else in your life. A good woman," she emphasized.

He laughed lightly at her astute insight. "I'll take it under advisement."

"But I know you won't. You're always into something, or someone's life."

"There are a lot of people who need help. I try to do what I can," he said honestly.

"Can't you see that I need help, too? What about me?" she asked softly, plaintively.

Cooper turned to her, sincerely moved by what she thought she was going through and had to face.

"You're not alone. There is help and comfort whenever you need it. Just ask—"

"'And ye shall receive,'" she said quietly. "'Pray, and He will hear your words.'"

"Make sure you're asking for what's really important." He opened the door and turned to look at her. "Are you going to be okay?"

"Do I have a choice?" she asked.

"Always, and I hope you pick only the ones that are good for you." Cooper smiled.

Judith nodded. "That's what I did. I'm the right woman for you, Smith. No one would disapprove. I think Reverend Wallace would be happy for us. You don't know what you're passing up."

"Oh, but I do, and I'm honored," Cooper responded, taking hold of her hand. "That's why you need to give yourself time. I don't think you've finished mourning yet. When you're really ready, in your heart and your soul, you'll find the person who's right for you."

"Don't be so righteous. You want what every man wants."

"I never said I didn't."

"Then don't be so modest, Smith. You would do just fine for me." She squeezed his hand. "Can I get a kiss, a hug? You're making it hard for me to get anything else."

He wasn't offended or put off by Judith's boldness. And in a way that only made him smile privately at the irony of the situation. He was also ready, but he wanted more for himself than instant gratification, or what looked right, or was the right thing to do.

His sacrifices shouldn't have to go that far.

Cooper lifted Judith's hand. He pressed a warm kiss on the back in an affectionate and courtly manner. He then stood back, releasing it.

"I'll see you next week?"

"You know you will."

Cooper got into his car and began the long drive

home. But he felt dispirited and uneasy now, recounting the evening with Judith, and wondering if he'd behaved like a chump. Had he been too noble, too pious, too self-righteous? Or just scared?

He racked his brain trying to figure out if he, at any time, had led her to believe he held an interest in her. No, he had not. It had nothing to do with Judith Macklin. This time, it was all about him.

He was suddenly very tired. Bone weary. He kept the car at a consistent fifty-five miles an hour. He'd learned how to do that until it was now second nature, not willing to risk losing control again. But in his mind he was propelled back into time, to being in a different car late at night, in a different city, and accelerating to a dangerous speed in reckless pursuit of another car. He'd been more than angry then; he'd been enraged, blinded by a fury that had been fueled by his ego and poor judgment.

Cooper gripped the steering wheel as the scene played out in his head....

He'd repeatedly hit his horn, the tires of his car screeching as he swerved back and forth across lanes to try to overtake the car ahead of him, screaming commands. Cursing, he tried to get to the side of the other car in an attempt to force it onto the shoulder. But he knew the driver was equally emotional and not as confident a driver, motivated, as she was, by hurt and humiliation. There was a third person in the front car that night whom they'd both ignored, and who ultimately paid the price for both of their actions.

A car horn broke into Cooper's reflections and he slammed on his brakes. He'd almost run a stop sign.

Cooper sat there another few seconds, regaining control. His thinking about the past was not Judith's fault. But her blatant interest in him brought up, once again, how much he'd changed from the man he used to be. And thank God for it.

He was living the second chance he'd prayed for and been given. He was working hard to justify it. For all he knew, he'd been saved that night for a reason. He would first do unto others with the hope of that being thanks enough. And then, if he had been truly saved, perhaps he would find his heart's desire.

If Judith's proposition that evening had done anything, it had reminded Cooper, and awakened in him, the need for more than just absolution and peace of mind. It would be nice, he thought, if love and respect came with it. Had God forgiven him enough his trespasses to grant that?

Cooper felt himself start to slowly unwind. He stopped beating himself up about old history and mistakes. He hoped he'd learned from both. He chanted under his breath, something he'd learned after pulling himself back from the abyss years ago, and that never failed to calm him or remind him of God's infinite love.

Then he glanced around in time to realize that he was just driving past the entrance to Chickasaw Gardens, where Michaela was staying.

This was not the route he'd meant to take home.

Chapter 6

Frustrated, disappointed and a bit distracted, Michaela put on her turn signal as the approach to Chickasaw Gardens came up on her left. She was still reacting to her failed attempt to see ET again at St. Jude, and desperate to know how he was doing, and wondering exactly how much truth there was in his confession that he was dying. But after arriving at the hospital she'd been informed that ET had been released back to his foster family. Of course, the receptionist would tell her nothing more.

Did the release mean that he'd lied to her? Or that things were so hopeless there was nothing to do but send him home?

Marilyn Caldwell could not be reached, and the only other person who she was sure probably knew the full story was Cooper. Unable to get any satisfactory answers, Michaela had gone shopping instead.

Not for clothes, but for ingredients to try out three more of the recipes for her proposed family collection cookbook. With a wry twist of her mouth, Michaela wondered what Aunt Alice was going to say when she returned from her long holiday and discovered enough frozen cooked meals in her basement freezer to feed her and Ben through much of the fall…courtesy of her project.

But Michaela's thoughts kept returning to ET, her stomach tensing at the thought that his announcement might be true.

Driving slowly as she approached the house, she noticed that there was a large commercial van parked in the driveway, and a SUV behind it. The side doors of the van were open to show the interior loaded with construction equipment and supplies. Michaela frowned. now concerned that perhaps something had happened on the property in her absence and a neighbor had called for needed service of some sort.

She quickly parked in front of the house and, leaving her groceries and even her purse on the front seat of the car, got out to walk the driveway path to the back of the house. She could hear what sounded like drilling, and then hammering, and two male voices.

"Hello," she called out as she got near the yard and the garage, whose door was raised open.

No one was immediately visible, but there was stuff strewn over part of the yard as proof that someone was around. There were sacks of cement, a small wheelbar-row to use as a mixing trough, a stack of stone bricks, various tools and several commercial nursery planters containing shrubbery ready to be placed in the ground.

The original shrubs, which had covered the hole through which she believed ET had gained access to the property, had been uprooted and removed, leaving an ugly, gaping empty corner.

Then, from the other side of this opening, a young man suddenly appeared. He was probably in his early twenties, dressed in work jeans, construction boots and a red T-shirt wet with perspiration and streaked with dirt and dust. A red do-rag covered his head.

"Hi, ma'am. It's okay. We're here to fix this up for you."

Before Michaela could ask who he was and what he meant by we, another man appeared. It was Cooper. He was similarly dressed, but wearing a tan baseball cap, and in the now familiar black T-shirt. In the late-June heat, Michaela could only wonder if he wasn't uncomfortably hot. But while the younger man was visibly sweating, Cooper was not.

His cap added an interesting dimension to his appearance, the bill shadowing part of his face, but also creating a distinct masculine sharpness to him. Michaela realized she was reacting in a very physical way to his presence.

Cooper put up his gloved hand in a brief greeting and stepped over some debris into the yard to face her.

"Hope we didn't scare you. That's Rodney…" he said, introducing the helper. He approached with his usual calm and stealthlike stride.

"Not scared but curious. What's going on?"

He stopped next to her, pulling off the gloves and pushing up the bill of his hat. He began to outline what he intended to do. Cooper spoke easily with knowledge and confidence about the repair work he had planned and the outcome he expected.

"Cooper, you don't have to do this. I was going to find someone to fix that fence before my godparents returned."

"Well, now you won't have to. Frankly, I was hoping to surprise you," he said. "I tried calling you this morning but didn't get an answer, so I thought you were out for the day. I thought we'd be done and gone before you got back. I pulled Rodney off another job to get this done. It'll only take a few hours, if the weather holds out."

"You know, sooner or later you're going to have to tell me what it is, exactly, that you do for a living. You're like this giant elf who keeps showing up here, there and everywhere. If I'm around you long enough, I'll probably find out you also speak two other languages, can knit and make a mean pot of chili."

Cooper laughed outright at her remark, his voice booming across the yard. It was a wonderful sound that made Michaela smile if only because she had never heard him laugh like that before, and because it transformed his face and expression. She was rather pleased with herself for being the cause of such a reaction from him. For the first time he didn't appear so austere, so serious, so…careful. She suspected that this was a side of Cooper he rarely showed to anyone.

She wondered why.

"The rig is mine," he admitted, his amusement passing. "I own and operate Building Blocks. It's a contracting outfit I started several years ago for building homes and small businesses. It's a one-person operation and I sometimes subcontract work."

She was impressed, but silently waited for him to continue.

"As to why I'm doing this…consider the work a thank-you for all you've done for ET."

She shook her heard, demurring. "I haven't done anything special."

"More than you realize, even though it might not seem like it. But I'm also a little concerned about the easy access to the property from the back beyond that fence. I thought about you being here alone. This is a pretty safe community, but you never know. Things happen."

Michaela slowly smiled at him, surprised and pleased by his admission. He silently returned her regard and she wondered what he was thinking…and if his thoughts were anything like her own.

"That's very thoughtful of you," she murmured.

Cooper tore his gaze away. "I promise we'll clean up all the mess."

"At least let me repay you for the shrubs, Cooper. The old ones were dead anyway."

He started backing away, putting his cap and work gloves back on. "The shrubs are part of my package deal. Shout out if we make too much noise."

"It won't bother me. I have some cooking to do."

He frowned at her. "You can cook?"

It was a second before she recovered from the fact that he had actually teased her.

"I'm going to make you eat those words," Michaela said, beginning to retrace her steps to the car to retrieve her bags.

During the course of the next few hours, Michaela

could occasionally hear the two men in the yard yelling out questions or instructions to each other. Other than that, she couldn't actually hear any activity from the backyard. But as she spent time typing up anecdotes, recipes and comments for her book, or selecting others of what remained of the list to be tested, Michaela was aware of how strangely peaceful the day had become from the disappointment she'd felt that morning.

She began and finished one dish, something her great-grandmother used to bake called Potato 'Poon Bread. It turned out to be easy to construct and sampling the finished bread drew a surprised "mmm" from her. When it cooled, she covered it with freezer wrap and put it aside. Next she went to work on a dish of sautéed shrimp in brown gravy that her own mother used to make. Michaela remembered how she and her older sister used to fight over who had gotten the most shrimp in their serving. When it, too, was done, she marked it another success.

Rodney knocked on the door once to ask to use the bathroom, and she directed him to the one across the hall from the kitchen. Michaela finally realized, at some point, that she was anticipating that Cooper would also come to the house with a request…any request. She sometimes looked out the kitchen window and caught glimpses of him and Rodney as they worked. She saw when they began cutting up the dried and dead branches of the shrubs that had been removed, and collecting the scrap in large black garbage bags. And they neatly put the replacements in the ground, stamping around the base of the new planting to set it.

Michaela couldn't see the sweat staining Cooper's

shirt, but the fabric was plastered to his skin, his chest and across his back and shoulder blades, outlining a toned body that was more athletically built than slender, but with his own grace and agility. She recognized and admitted to a strong attraction to Cooper, but it disturbed her a little that such feelings were coming on the heels of a recent breakup from a man she'd almost married. Was it rebound emotions, loneliness, or simply something about Cooper?

Whatever was happening, Michaela decided to roll with it. She could use a little flirtation about now, she mused. And it no longer looked like an endless summer to her.

The sky grew dark, not from a setting sun but a gathering storm. It was as the two men were cleaning up and reloading the equipment back into the van that it began to rain lightly, water falling in fat drops to splatter on the windowpane and flagstone patio outside. She couldn't see either Rodney or Cooper as it started to rain in earnest and water pelted the house and the grounds. A car door slammed and the engine turned over.

They're leaving, she thought, disappointed.

She couldn't blame them. The weather had turned wicked. Rodney and Cooper had been working most of the afternoon in muggy, oppressive heat. They wanted to get home, shower and change clothes. Very likely they had plans for the evening. Dates.

So much for flirtation.

Michaela sighed, the emptiness of the big house closing in on her.

She started when there was a firm knock on the back kitchen door. On the other side she found Cooper, hunched a little under the force of the downpour, with rainwater running off the beak of his cap. He'd pulled on a windbreaker, but it didn't offer much protection.

"I thought you'd gone," she said. "Come on in, you're getting soaked. Where's Rodney?"

"I told him to go on. He has a rehearsal tonight. He plays bass guitar in a local band. I wanted to let you know that I covered the repaired wall with a plastic tarp. It's going to take a while to dry because of the damp air and rain, but it's done."

"Thank you. Now come in…"

"I'm going to head on out…" He took a step back.

"Cooper…stay and have dinner. Unless you have something else to do, I'd really like you to."

"Are you sure?"

"It won't be anything fancy but it's edible."

He grinned and she smiled slightly to soften her fear that she might sound as if she was pleading. But her spontaneous invitation did feel like a defining moment to Michaela, although she could not explain to herself how…or why.

Cooper seemed to hesitate for another moment, but finally took off his cap and vigorously shook the water from it. She took it from him, and held out her other hand for his jacket.

"The bathroom's over there, if you want to clean up and dry off a little," Michaela indicated.

Unprompted, Cooper bent over, unlacing his muddy work boots, pulling them off. He left them on the doormat and went off in his stocking feet to the bathroom.

Michaela hung the jacket and cap on the door handle, watching his retreat before she went to the laundry room to get a towel for him.

On her return, she found Lady sitting outside the bathroom door, still and alert, waiting for Cooper to come out.

"Would you like me to find you a dry shirt? I'm sure my godfather won't mind."

"No, thanks. I'm good," he shouted.

Michaela realized that the door was slightly ajar. Unintentionally, through the crack of the door, she witnessed Cooper peeling the damp black shirt over his head. What she saw made her react with a silent gasp. There was evidence of burns across his back and, reflected in the mirror, across his chest. Less so, along his arms. She stared at the sight, reacting instinctively as a spasm of empathy twisted her insides. All she could think of was how much pain he must have endured. Whatever had happened to him, he might also have died.

Cooper bent over the sink to wet his face, and then used soap to wash his forearms and hands.

She recovered, stepping directly behind the door, out of sight, and took a deep breath. She knocked.

"Here," she said, holding out the towel so that he could reach it through the narrow space.

"I'll be right out."

"Take your time. I'll start dinner."

But all Michaela could think of was the sight of Cooper's horribly damaged skin. What had he gone through to sustain such an injury? At sometime, someplace, somewhere, Cooper had been in a fire or explosion that had left a cruel reminder on his body. She'd had her first awareness of it on that motorcycle ride, holding on to him around his waist and chest. She'd known then that beneath his shirt the skin was stiff and oddly textured.

She wanted to touch him, nonetheless. She'd wanted to even then.

Her thoughts swirling with speculation, Michaela absentmindedly surveyed what was in the refrigerator. She had chicken cutlets and decided to sauté them in butter, and make a lemon sauce to go with it. She added potatoes and string beans to her menu.

Michaela had just finished dredging the chicken in flour and placing the pieces in a hot skillet when Cooper came back into the kitchen.

Lady let out a plaintive cry for his attention and Cooper scooped her into the crook of his arm, scratching her behind her ears.

"That's Lady." Michaela introduced them, keeping her attention on her cooking. "She came with the house."

"She's friendly," Cooper said as the cat purred loudly, sounding like a vibrating motor.

"No, she's not." Michaela chuckled, remembering how the cat had backed away from Jefferson. "She seems to like you, though. Are you a cat person?"

Holding the cat, who was in ecstasy under the gentle stroking of his hands, Cooper sat in a chair balancing Lady as he watched Michaela at the stove.

"I don't know. Never had one. I grew up with dogs."

Michaela didn't hesitate. "Where are you from?"

"Here," he said quietly.

"No, you're not. You don't have that regional rounding of your words, that little drawl. You're polite and gentlemanly, but not terminally cheerful."

"Is that your idea of a compliment?" he asked with a straight face.

Michaela could detect his amusement, nonetheless.

"And you've never once called me ma'am." Slowly pouring lemon juice into her mixture of flour dissolved in water, Michaela spared him a glance. "Is it a state secret?"

His brows furrowed and he chortled to himself. "No, of course not. I'm from the Chicago area. I chose to make my life here in Memphis."

"Alone?"

He nodded solemnly. "Alone."

"But why here?"

"It was the right place at the right time. It had what I was looking for. I've been here almost five years."

"Are you happy here?" she asked, tilting her head.

He pursed his lips. "Happy? I don't think that's what I was looking for at the time. But I've been at peace here."

Michaela silently nodded to herself. She understood the need for that. It was part of why she was in Memphis. She also admitted to herself that, to some extent, she was in hiding, living incognito from her normal existence. But it was only for a short period of time, until she was ready to go back and face the real world.

"Any plans to move back to Chicago? You probably still have family there."

He took longer to answer this time.

"I don't know that, either. Every now and then I feel like I need to move on. I'm not sure where."

Michaela asked no more questions. The answers

she'd already gotten were intriguing enough, but had only created more questions. She sensed that to push any further would be stepping on the boundaries Cooper had erected around himself. He had something to protect. Maybe even something to hide. The image of his scarred back flashed in her mind. There had to be a story behind that.

Michaela admitted to herself that whatever else there was about Cooper's background, for the moment, didn't matter. Memphis was her only frame of reference for him and the kind of man he might be. Their knowledge of one another was here. So far, she liked what she'd seen and heard. She liked him.

She began preparing the two side dishes.

"You said you're in Memphis just for this summer."

"That's right. I guess it's my turn," she said lightly at his prompting.

"Only if you want to."

Michaela put the chicken in the oven to stay warm, and began to set the small table for the two of them.

"If everything had gone as planned, I'd just be returning from a two-week honeymoon on the Amalfi Coast with my new husband. I called the engagement off in February."

She glanced at him over her shoulder. Cooper was regarding her with a steady, almost penetrating gaze. She couldn't read his expression, and he didn't interrupt with questions. She continued.

"After I ended it with Spencer, that's my ex-fiancé, my mother wouldn't talk to me for a week. She adored him. He was every mother's dream son-in-law. My girlfriends thought I should be committed. Spencer was furious.

"I'd been so afraid of hurting him by breaking it off, but he was more concerned with his image and his pride and two years wasted, and what to tell his friends, how to split up all those wedding gifts from our registry. I felt so guilty I let him have everything.

"He cleaned up good, he came from a lovely family, has a solid career, no tattoos, and he sure knew how to…" Michaela suddenly stopped, realizing what she was about to confess. "Too much information," she murmured with a nervous laugh.

After sitting and listening without comment or movement, Cooper put Lady on the floor, got up and approached her. He leaned against the counter, studying her face.

"Any regrets?" he asked.

She was very aware of his closeness. He had stepped into her space and it was having a definite effect. "Only that I didn't do it sooner. I mean, what was I thinking for the past two years we were engaged? What was I feeling for him?"

"Not enough of what you wanted to feel. So you found out you're not perfect, and sometimes you make a bad call and mess up. Sometimes you fall in love and…it goes wrong. You find out, maybe it wasn't love at all."

Cooper looked at her with understanding, and a wry smile. He abruptly leaned toward her and, for a startled moment, Michaela thought he was going to take her in his arms to comfort her. She stayed her ground. But Cooper was reaching for a dish towel on the counter next to the stove. With his left hand he cupped her face, holding her chin and jaw. With his right hand he used the towel to carefully wipe at her cheek and nose.

"Flour," he said simply.

Michaela held still under his ministrations, feeling nurtured in a way that was tender and thoughtful. Her innate reaction to him, however, also made her feel as if she was being completely unfaithful to her relationship to Spencer. Or, at least, her once idealized memories of their relationship.

"Thank you," Michaela murmured.

Cooper released her face and slid his hand down her arm, caressing it for a moment. "You've probably heard this before, 'what doesn't kill you makes you stronger.'"

She nodded. "Do you believe that?" she asked him, feeling she could trust anything he said.

"I think we learn from everything we do. Breaking off was a brave thing to do. Fear and embarrassment might have forced you into a marriage you didn't want." A pensive faraway look came into his eyes and his voice got lower, deeper. "You learn and you learn, and let go, and say goodbye. You start over again. You find a way to open your heart again as if it had never been broken." His hand slid away from her arm.

"Is that what you've done?"

"I'm working on it."

She took another chance. "Is that why you're in Memphis?"

"Yes."

His gaze became suddenly dark and reflective, a little bittersweet. But there was also a light that she couldn't mistake, a way he had begun to look at her that she was drawn to, as if his glance and the deep prophetic tone of his voice could touch her, and heal.

Michaela turned away abruptly from the thought. She fumbled for a pot holder.

"Everything's ready."

The conversation became superficial while Michaela served food. She instructed Cooper to get the carafe of iced tea from the refrigerator, and he poured them each a tall glass.

In the background was the quieter repetitive sound of continuing rainfall, which only added to Michaela's sense of safety and peace in Cooper's company. Lady had taken up a place to sleep next to his chair. She couldn't help the thought that the setting seemed so cozy. Very domestic. Very much like home.

Everything was ready and they took their places at the table. She was instantly reminded of breakfast at Miss Faye's, and looked up sharply to find Cooper waiting.

"I'll say grace," she offered awkwardly.

Cooper nodded once and gave her a small smile.

Michaela put her palms flat together, but quickly changed her mind. That's how she did it as a child. Then she rested them in her lap instead. She closed her eyes.

"'God is good, God is great, and we thank Him for our food. Amen.'"

She opened her eyes to see his reaction to the one grace she remembered that she learned from her grandmother at the age of six.

"Amen," Cooper said in his deep voice.

Feeling a little shy about her simplistic offering, she launched into another thank-you for the work he'd done behind her godparents' house.

That led to him wanting to know about her godparents and her being in their house for the summer. She

told him about her book project of family recipes, and
that led to telling him about her position as a dean for
professional development at Howard University in D.C.
He wanted to know if she'd really taught high school,
or had she said that for the benefit of Betty Wilson.

"No, that was real. It was a challenge," Michaela
admitted. "I was just out of graduate school. The kids
all had things to deal with that are so much more complicated than when I was growing up. Or maybe it just
seemed that way.

"Sometimes they were so much smarter than I was
at that age. I mean, street smart. But then they'd act out
and do dumb things like little kids. They wanted to be
treated like adults, but then behaved like they wanted
to curl up in your lap."

"It used to be called growing up," Cooper said. "And
it is harder than it used to be. That's not an illusion, but
I don't believe you failed as a teacher. ET thinks you're
a teacher."

That completely surprised her.

"Really?"

"He says you ask a lot of questions."

She grimaced. "Doesn't sound like he thinks much
of me."

Cooper shook his head. "Not true. He says you're
fresh. I think that's the same as saying you're hot."

Michaela laughed merrily.

"ET also said you have spooky eyes. He said, if he
tried to lie to you, you'd know it."

"Wow," she murmured, ET's observations surprising
her.

"He talks tough, but you won him over a little when

you came to visit him at St. Jude. He's confused about why you bothered."

"Have you seen him?"

"Day before yesterday. He was about to be released from St. Jude."

"I didn't know. I went to visit him this morning and found out he was already gone. No one would tell me anything else, of course." She looked at her half-finished food and put her fork down. "Cooper, ET told me he was dying. He said it like he was absolutely sure. Is it true?"

She could sense his holding back, see tension in the flexing muscles of his jaw. "I don't know, Michaela. ET and Betty Wilson have met with doctors and social workers. He's been told what his condition is."

She leaned forward eagerly, but Cooper shook his head, regret reflected in his eyes.

"I can't talk about his case. I know you care, Michaela. I don't doubt that for an instant. But any information has to come from ET."

"I understand," she said quietly. "I'm so scared for him, Cooper. In a way I can't explain, I feel responsible for him."

"So do I. He has a lot of strikes against him right now, but he's not a lost cause. He needs all the support he can get."

"If there's anything I can do…"

"There's going to be a July Fourth celebration up in North Memphis where he's living. It's at a church center. I'll make sure ET will be there."

"Can I come?" she asked.

"I'm hoping you will."

Michaela miraculously regained her appetite. They were chatting about some of the sports that Cooper coached when the telephone rang. She got up to take the call, on the other side of the kitchen.

"It's Jefferson. Is everything okay over there?"

"Oh, hi. Why do you ask?"

"I drove by on my way home earlier and saw a van in the driveway. It was raining pretty hard so I didn't stop by. Did something happen at the house?"

She glanced covertly at Cooper, but tried to keep her voice low and words neutral. He didn't appear to be listening, and was starting to clear the table. "Nothing wrong, just the repair work on the fence behind the house."

"I would have taken care of that for you. I was trying to find someone who could be trusted to do a good job."

"Don't worry about it. It's done. Listen, I don't mean to be rude…"

"Caught you at a bad time?"

"I'm in the middle of dinner…"

"I wondered if you had any plans for this Friday. I'm going to a benefit dinner at the Peabody. If you're free, I thought you'd like to join me."

She looked toward Cooper who was now at the sink, rinsing off plates. She was so glad that he'd figured out a way for her to see ET. But she was also so glad she'd get to spend time with Cooper. It was an admission she had not expected, but she now couldn't deny.

"That sounds nice, but I may already have plans," she said cautiously. She crossed her fingers.

"Why don't I call you tomorrow. We can discuss it then."

"That's fine. Thanks for calling."

When she got off the phone, Cooper was no longer in the kitchen, but the table had been cleared. Michaela walked into the living room and found him seated on the sofa. Seeing how comfortable he was padding about in his socks again gave her a sense of playing house.

Lady was perched on his thigh. The cat raised her rump and furry tail in the air as Cooper slowly stroked her back. Michaela's imagination suddenly began to run wild at the thought of herself being the object of such attention.

"Would you like some coffee? Maybe something stronger? Uncle Ben keeps a small bar."

"No, thanks. I enjoyed dinner. I like your lemon chicken."

She shrugged. "My sister still thinks I'm a disgrace as a Black woman because I can't cook greens. I can't even think what she'd say to me if I admit I don't like greens."

"Do you have a greens recipe in your family collection?"

"Absolutely. I don't want to be excommunicated, or whatever."

Cooper laughed. Lady didn't seem bothered by the sound of his deep voice, but protested when he began to stand up, forcing her to the floor again.

"Other attributes would be more important to me than your cooking skills. But I was satisfied."

There was a sudden lurching in her chest. Other attributes? Was he speaking generally or specifically? She grinned at the implied compliment.

"Sounds like the rain has stopped, so I'm going to say good-night."

"Where do you live?"

"Right now, downtown. I'm fixing up a little property I own out east of Germantown."

"So you are planning on staying in Memphis?"

He sighed with clear ambivalence. "I haven't decided. I got a good deal on this house I found. I saw potential in it, and wanted to fix it up. I put on an addition, raised the dormers. Put a solarium in the back."

"Sounds nice."

"But I don't know if it's going to be home for me."

Together they walked back into the kitchen. Cooper put on his boots, and Michaela stood by ready to hand him his hat and coat. She could feel an anxiety, anticipation, begin to gnarl at her. It was affecting her breathing…her equilibrium. It was a little frightening.

He didn't bother putting on the hat and jacket when she opened the door to the yard. They were assailed with muggy, thick air and the sweet smell of the freshly planted and watered shrubs.

"I guess I'll be seeing you," she said.

"You will. I'll let you know about the Fourth," Cooper said.

There was just a second when he stood considering her as if he didn't know what to do next. She'd experienced the same thing the first time they'd met, when he'd brought her home on his motorcycle. They'd taken two huge steps forward since that morning, but Michaela didn't want to be the one to take the next. She gave him a wave and he did the same.

Cooper headed to his van and she stood watching him walk away. From the vague shadows, she heard the driver's door open and Cooper tossing his things on the passenger seat. The door closed and the engine turned over and idled. Then, he just sat there, in Park, not moving.

It was nearly a full minute before the door opened again and Michaela realized that Cooper was walking very slowly back to her, emerging out of the dark. The Man in Black. Her heart began to pound.

She waited, watching. He looked at her, and his gaze was so direct, so clear and purposeful. With the dark covering on his face, she wondered if Cooper realized how compelling he appeared to her. Dangerous…but not. He said nothing, standing about two feet away. Despite her resolve, she took a step forward.

He was taking too long. He could change his mind.

"Yes," Michaela said simply.

His brow lifted, as did the corner of his mouth. She had correctly read his mind. With that one word Cooper once again held her face, bent his head and kissed her. She was shaken by the instant charge of their lips meeting and melding, by the gentle movement of his mouth against hers. It was subtle, not demanding or passionate, but deeply stirring. He tilted his head in the other direction, and kissed her again. Firm. Sure. Right.

The kiss made a connection that Michaela imagined could be felt in her very soul. She was surprised at the relief that swept through her, as if something between them had been resolved.

Yes was a positive statement from her.

Yes, because she'd been waiting.

Yes, because she really wanted him to.

Chapter 7

With relish and a giddy excitement, Michaela pulled the helmet on and fastened the chin strap. The engine of Cooper's bike *put-putted* as he sat balancing it until she'd climbed on behind him. He'd reminded her to bring the hoodie she'd had since their first meeting, and it was tied by the sleeves around her waist.

"Where are we going?" she asked above the noise.

"Miss Faye's," he answered, as the bike began to roll away from the front of the house.

Her reaction was one of silent, giddy joy.

It was a beautiful day to celebrate the nation's birthday. It was going to be hot but dry. The air blowing on her face made Michaela catch her breath, and cooled her skin. In that moment she felt life couldn't get much better than this wonderful sense of freedom.

As they rode to that part of town where Miss Faye's

café was located, Michaela could see signs of the high summer celebration everywhere in Memphis. There were flags flying at full mast on public buildings, and hanging from the front of nearly every home. The unexpected sight of homemade floats proceeding to the start line of a planned parade. July Fourth team sports being played in parks and playgrounds as family members and onlookers made it an occasion for picnics and barbecues.

Michaela realized that the circuitous route Cooper was taking across town to the restaurant was for her benefit. This was part of what he referred to as his dollar tour of Memphis, after she'd admitted to not knowing the city very well, and never having been to many of its attractions.

When he'd called the day before to confirm that she really could attend the July Fourth celebration at the church center in North Memphis, Michaela had been pleased when he'd also asked if they could spend the whole day together.

Do birds fly?

They pulled into the alley next to Miss Faye's and secured the bike, and then entered the café. Michaela immediately felt like a regular. She walked in carrying the helmet the same way she'd first seen Cooper tote his. Miss Faye herself, bustling around the tables and her customers, looked up to greet her.

"Welcome back, darlin'. It's good to see you again. You know where to sit."

Michaela was astonished to see that Cooper's table was empty and waiting for them.

"I can't believe she won't let anyone else sit here,"

she said across the table to Cooper as they settled into their chairs.

"I've told Miss Faye she doesn't have to give up a table just for me," Cooper said.

Michaela smiled at him. "She thinks very highly of you."

"I don't think I deserve it."

Before Michaela could tell Miss Faye what she wanted for breakfast, the older woman appeared and shook her head.

"Don't have no English muffins today, darlin'. I got plenty of oranges but my bananas are gone."

Michaela stared at Miss Faye, surprised by her total recall. She chuckled. "Bring me whatever you feel like, then. I know it's going to be wonderful."

Miss Faye beamed. "Aren't you sweet. Yes, ma'am."

Michaela swiveled her head, looking around. Through the open serving window she spotted the cook, Jake. He lifted a spatula in greeting to her. She smiled and waved back. Turning in the other direction, she looked for Pete, the older man she recalled who'd commandeered the back table with his spread of newspapers and his toothless grin. He was there.

"Smith. Pretty lady," he croaked out across the room, causing heads to turn in their direction.

Michaela turned her smiling countenance to Cooper, and found him watching her with a warm but amused expression.

"What? Is it my hair? I know it's a wreck. Sorry, but your helmet doesn't help. 'What you see is what you get.'" She mimicked him.

He spread his hands in surrender. "I have no complaints."

"Well, I'm on vacation. I didn't expect to…"

"There's no scorecard. Just be yourself and you won't have anything to worry about."

His declaration made her feel shy and tongue-tied. But she believed him. Cooper had eyes that didn't lie, as far as she could tell. And it was pretty nice to feel that, after the fiasco with Spencer, she hadn't scared off the rest of the male species.

While waiting for breakfast he told her a little bit of what went on around Memphis on a patriotic holiday like July Fourth.

"The church party is this afternoon. I thought we'd just ride around and see what we stumble on, unless there's something you had in mind."

She shook her head vigorously. "I'm up for anything. Surprise me."

They'd done no more than say hello to Miss Faye when they arrived, but she was already coming to their table with their food. Cooper was served with his standard order. Michaela looked at the plate set in front of her.

"I'll get your coffee," Miss Faye said, hurrying away and yelling out commands to Jake in the kitchen as the tiny café began to fill with her local regulars.

Michaela realized that she had the same order as she'd had her first visit to Miss Faye's. She turned a mischievous grin to Cooper. She could tell that he understood her reaction.

But first, they followed the routine and ritual they'd established together from the very beginning. She accepted that it was important to Cooper to say a blessing before his meals, and she had grown comfortable with that. He'd never indicated any judgment because she didn't. But she had to admit that she certainly felt grateful now, and fortunate.

Miss Faye returned with mugs of coffee and then bustled off to see after another customer. Michaela waited expectantly while Cooper stirred melting butter into his grits. Without a word he pushed the plate toward her. Michaela glanced at the plate, and then at him. She shook her head. She could see the momentary confusion in his eyes, but then it cleared. Michaela watched as Cooper filled his fork with grits, and then carefully held it out to her. She leaned forward so that he could feed her.

As Michaela ate and relished the texture and taste of Cooper's breakfast, she felt that this was possibly one of the happiest moments of her life.

There were people everywhere, and the sound of children's voices, and music playing over the entire area from a public PA system. Michaela walked leisurely with Cooper as they visited stalls and tables of home-made baked goods, handcrafts and collectibles that were part of the fair set up on Mudd Island.

It was crowded and hot, but there was an air of congeniality, goodwill and national pride that seemed widespread throughout the diverse population enjoying the activities.

Walking past the offerings of local vendors, Michaela stopped momentarily to check that Cooper was behind her, and that they hadn't been separated by the crowd. He was wearing very dark sunglasses against the bright sunlight, but gave her a silent reassuring nod, communicating that he was fine and he was keeping his eyes on her.

She couldn't help drawing a comparison between Cooper and Spencer, who would have been bored out of his mind by the slow, aimless strolling. She would have known not to suggest that they attend such an event together. So Michaela was pleased when it was Cooper who asked if she would like to see what was going on.

Michaela had turned her bike helmet into a tote. She'd already bought several items, including a small bag of shelled pecan nuts that had been dry-roasted and rolled in sugar, and a small old pocket mirror where the outside lid was done in fine petit point stitching.

By noon Michaela felt like she was being baked by the sun. And while neither she nor Cooper were inclined to eat another meal for lunch, they drank lemonade or iced tea and shared a cup of cut chunks of cold watermelon.

On a stretch of park on the bank of the Mississippi, they came across a trio of amateur musicians playing lively tunes to an audience of picnickers. Michaela and Cooper sat in the grass under a tree for a while to listen, and to enjoy the slow, sweeping breeze coming off the river. She removed her sandals and stretched her legs out, content to watch everything going on around them. Very content to be with him.

She thought, momentarily, of all the years with Spencer. He was not a person to be still, stay silent, enjoy the quiet. One of the things that had drawn her to him was his unflagging energy. And it was one of the things that contributed to her withdrawal, among others. She couldn't keep up with him. She'd loved his curiosity and penchant for adventure, but he bored easily. Only now did Michaela consider that perhaps she was convinced that it would just be a matter of time before Spencer became tired of her. She didn't need to be constantly entertained. She just wanted to know that being who she was was enough.

Beside her, Cooper eventually lay down and used his helmet as a pillow. Her hand was playing idly in the cool grass and his fingers brushed against hers resting close by. Cooper's reaction was instantaneous. He reached out blindly to take hold and thread their fingers together.

It was such a simple gesture, but Michaela realized at once the significance of it, the implied intimacy. She caught her breath. Cooper's hand was large and strong, yet he held hers loosely. If she wanted to pull away, she could. But she didn't, and neither did he.

For the first time since their brief acquaintance, she was suddenly acutely aware of time. For her, July Fourth marked just about the halfway point in her summer stay in Memphis. In a very short period, she would have to give thoughts to returning home to D.C., to preparing for the fall semester and her responsibilities at the university. She'd have to deal with the fact that it was her decision that she and Spencer had not married, but they still had mutual friends, common interests and activities that might cause their paths to cross. Resuming her routine would mean an automatic closure to her unstructured life, and its surprises, here in Memphis. It would mean having to eventually say goodbye to Cooper.

Inadvertently Michaela's hand jerked, and Cooper tightened his hold on her. His doing so did little to calm her, because she was suddenly faced with the truth of their lives. His was here in Memphis and hers was somewhere else. Their relationship was tenuous, fashioned by circumstance. It had nowhere to go.

A flirtation.

But the very thought of leaving made Michaela feel panicky and apprehensive. It was a stunning revelation to recognize she wasn't ready. And she was unable to tell how much of what she was feeling was real, and how much was caused by being away from home and her normal life.

Was it really possible for her to have fallen hard, in just three weeks, for a man she knew next to nothing about, based on his sensitivity, the tone of his voice, his calm demeanor…the steady probing gaze of his eyes? The safe haven she experienced now by his touch?

Michaela closed her eyes, feeling the prickly rise of heat and sweat on her brow as she tried to predict the coming weeks.

The impromptu concert ended and people began to move on to other activities, or to leave the island. Michaela felt Cooper hanging back a bit until they were more or less alone. She wasn't sure when it happened, but a tension now seemed to develop between them. She knew what it was all about.

But she tried to stay away from what was surely inevitable by asking Cooper about the odd, and out of place, pyramid structure at the opposite end of the area where they stood. It was a distraction. She wasn't fully listening as he explained the failed project, and then launched into a general commentary about other changes and development going on nearby in the downtown area. Then he suddenly stopped talking and turned silently to her.

Michaela's anticipation skyrocketed, but this time she didn't have to offer any encouragement to him. As it turned out, Cooper didn't seem to need any.

"Do you believe in fate?" he asked, frowning.

"I…don't know. Isn't that like asking if I believe in magic, or miracles?"

Cooper sighed. "I think miracles happen all the time, if you pay attention."

He came very close to her but she was unable to see his eyes behind the dark glasses. She didn't like the distance it created even if, for whatever reason, it made Cooper feel safe. She reached up and removed them from his face. He didn't even blink at her action.

"Why do you want to know if I do or not?"

Cooper reached out a hand and braced it on the tree trunk next to her head. He leaned in toward her so that she could smell him, a heady freshness that spoke of vitality, maleness, warm sunshine on his skin.

"Because everything seems perfect right now. In this moment. For all we know, maybe this is where you and I are supposed to be. Things happen for a reason."

"That sounds so…mystical. But…I think maybe you're right. At least, right now."

She held her breath, but reached up to lightly trail her fingers down his hair-covered cheek. He turned his head to brush his lips against her palm.

"Cooper…" Michaela whispered, deeply moved by… She wasn't even sure by what. Except that she was so glad to be with him.

"I don't know what it means, but something's different. I feel different," he struggled to explain. "Ever since we met, I've felt strange."

She smiled gently. "Strange as in strange? Or strange as in something new but nice?"

"Yes."

"Me, too."

The energy between them, the obvious attraction and desire, maxed out. In one syncopated, fluid movement, she lifted her face and raised her arms as Cooper tilted his head to meet her and he gathered her close to his body. It wasn't a desperate decision or movement, but seemed to have a natural grace and rightness.

Their kiss, deep and intense, released a wellspring of yearning in her. His instant response in the way he held her and moved his lips over hers, the restless caressing of his hands on her back, the languid warmth of their bodies at every place they touched, said everything about how far they'd come together. But it also left no doubt in Michaela's mind that they were both right where they wanted, and needed, to be.

Michaela knew she'd seen communities before like the one in North Memphis she and Cooper rode into. They existed in parts of the nation's capital and surrounding areas. Neighborhoods where the buildings were run-down and sad, some of them even boarded up.

Here, the pavement was cracked and split in many places with weeds growing through. There were vacant lots and haphazardly dumped garbage. Side streets off the main boulevard were lined with small, detached houses that showed deferred maintenance and little landscaping.

But families lived here. Children played, and men and women went about the business of living and doing the best they could with what they had. Riding behind Cooper as he headed toward the church where the afternoon celebration was to take place, Michaela appreciated even more his dedication to the community.

Where had that come from?

The church, at first sighting, didn't look like a church. It was redbrick, and laid out in a low rectangle, its white roof adorned with a simple cross. The windows, five narrow panels on each side, appeared to be frosted glass. There was one main and centered entrance, but Michaela could see that most people probably entered through a side door because it came directly from the parking lot.

There were people and activities going on all over the property. Behind the church was a flat field upon where a soccer game was in progress. There was an open cement court with basketball hoops positioned at two ends, and five rows of bleacher seats on the two long sides. It, too, was occupied with two teams of adolescents in the middle of a game.

Hearing the motorcycle approach and seeing Cooper, nearly a dozen kids ran to meet him. Michaela smiled at the enthusiastic greeting they yelled out to him.

Cooper cut his speed and carefully let the bike roll into the parking lot where he found a space and parked. Michaela climbed off, listening to the questions being hurled at him in a confusion of voices.

"Who's that?" they asked, pointing at her.

"Her name is Michaela Landry." Cooper introduced her.

She pulled off her helmet. "Hi."

"She your girlfriend?" a young boy boldly asked.

"That's privileged information," Cooper responded smoothly. He took their helmets and attached them to the handles of the motorcycle.

"What does that mean?" a young girl asked.

"It means I've already told you what you need to know." He grinned at her.

"Smith, gimme a ride on your motorcycle. Please?"

"I can ride it by myself…"

"Stop pushing! I want to hold his hand…"

The kids groused good-naturedly, but all of them, Michaela noticed, were vying for Cooper's attention. Even while trying to direct everyone out of the lot and back to the gathering, he took his time listening to and answering endless questions, deftly deflecting personal questions about her. Michaela trailed behind, amused and touched.

It was like following the Pied Piper.

He eventually encouraged the kids to go back to what they'd been doing, promising that he'd see them all again. Beckoning to her to stay with him, Cooper headed for a table set up outside the church that seemed to function as information central. There were several men and women seated behind it, handing out flyers and giving directions. Each was wearing a black cloth baseball cap with the name of the church embroidered in yellow above the bill. There was a poster taped to the side of the church wall with a schedule of events listed for the afternoon.

An older man wearing glasses stood up and stretched out his hand across the table to Cooper.

"You made it." He smiled broadly. "Thought maybe you had other plans." He gave Michaela a quick but open smile.

Cooper gripped the hand. "How's it going?"

"We got quite a turnout. Everybody seems to be having a good time. The good Lord blessed us with beautiful weather. Can't complain." The man turned to

Michaela as she stood back watching the two men greet one another.

"I'm Reverend Wallace. Welcome to the celebration."

"Michaela Landry," she said.

He raised his brows and studied her closely. "Michaela. Yes, yes. Smith here told me about you." He reached out to pat her shoulder in a fatherly manner. "You've got a good heart. I can see it in your eyes. They don't hide much with that golden light behind them."

She smiled shyly. "You make them sound so pretty. My sister used to tell me I had the eyes of the devil."

The reverend laughed uproariously. "I bet it was because she thought you could see right through her. You know, they say the eyes are the windows to the soul."

Michaela frowned. "That's not in the Bible, is it?"

"No, but I think it's still true. God will bless you for taking an interest in Eugene."

She was embarrassed by the praise. "I just hope he's going to be okay."

"He will be," Reverend Wallace said with a serene, knowing grin. "No matter what happens, he'll always be in God's good grace."

She nodded, feeling relieved by Reverend Wallace's certainty.

"He's around here somewhere," the reverend said, squinting out over the crowd. "You'll see him." He bent and began to rummage in a large open carton behind his chair. He straightened and presented her with one of the black hats. "A little gift so you won't forget us."

With that, he turned to greet another arriving acquaintance.

Michaela turned away, pulling the cap on her head, and found that Cooper had moved along to a group of men and they stood chatting. Deciding not to distract him, she began to explore on her own, hoping that she might run into ET, and yet fearful that he might again reject her overtures of concern and friendship.

He was not among the boys on or near the soccer field, although she hung around the game in progress long enough to peruse everyone in the crowd sitting or standing along the sidelines. She eventually moved on to the basketball court with the same results. It was hot, and she was thirsty. She stood in the shade cast by the bleacher seats and watched the game. But she had no idea what the score was or even who was winning. Her gaze kept wandering off in hopes of spotting Eugene Terrance.

And then suddenly she did.

He was seated at a picnic table behind the church with a number of other kids his age. The bright yellow T-shirts that all the adolescents and teens were wearing identified them as being members of the church's varsity teams. ET appeared to be listening more than taking part in the conversation. But for all the people and noise and things going on around him, he still somehow looked like he was alone. Michaela made her way in his direction.

She was within a few feet when he noticed her. Michaela half expected that he would abruptly get up and leave, but he sat still although he was staring at her balefully.

"Reverend Wallace told me you were here," she said, sliding into the seat opposite ET.

He was also wearing one of the event hats, but it was a little too big for him. And he was sniffling; he had another cold.

"Yeah, I know. He said you was looking for me. How come?"

"You sound so suspicious," she said. "It's not like I don't know you or we haven't talked before."

He stared off rather than look directly at her.

"I went back to St. Jude earlier this week to see you."

That seemed to surprise ET, and he shot a curious glance at her before resuming his pout. "They let me go. I went back to Mrs. Wilson."

"I know. Smith told me."

"What else he tell you?"

Michaela could hear anger beneath the question. She shrugged casually. "Nothing. I would like to know what the doctor said about your condition. He said only you could tell me."

He scowled. He remained silent, bouncing that nervous knee.

Michaela clasped her hands and leaned across the table. "ET, I only want to be your friend," she said in a quiet, coaxing voice. "Like Smith is your friend. I know you trust him. I do, too."

He shook his head stubbornly. "I can't."

She rested her hand on his forearm. "Then, it's okay. Don't tell me if you don't want to. It won't make a difference to me anyway. I'm always going to think of you as kind of cool and special." She chuckled silently.

"No, I'm not. Mrs. Wilson said that God is punishing me and that's why I'm sick."

Michaela was stunned. She swallowed, trying to recover. "She can't think that. I don't believe that God punishes little children because they get sick and need a lot of care."

"She says I'm going to die."

Now, his voice quavered despite his valiant attempt to stay strong.

"Eugene…look at me." She held his arm tighter. He turned a deeply troubled gaze on her. All she saw was a boy, perhaps a bit small for his age, with a slightly runny nose, and a sadness that no child should ever have to face or endure alone. "Did the doctors tell you that? Did Smith say it?"

"No," he croaked.

"Then it's not true. Period."

For a moment Michaela thought she'd finally gotten through to him. But, without warning, ET snatched his arm from her and struggled out of his seat on the bench.

"I got HIV," he spit at her. "I'm gonna die of AIDS."

With that, he hurried off around the side of the building, off into a line of trees, and disappeared into the overgrown weeds and shrubs. Michaela stared after him, his last words reverberating in her head.

HIV…AIDS…dying.

He just said again he was dying.

"No," Michaela murmured under her breath, her brows furrowing in confusion. "No, that's not what it means, ET!" she yelled after him, but he ignored her and kept going. "ET…" Now she'd lost sight of him.

People turned to stare at her as her voice carried. Her mind, however, was racing with all the ramifications, the implications of what the boy had blurted out. If the diagnosis was true, then she knew that he already had a lot to process and deal with. But what twisted at

Michaela's heart and made her feel both empathy and outrage, was knowing how people might respond to ET when they learned what he had. Was this why he wouldn't talk to her? Was this why he'd walked away? Make the rejection his own before it was done to him?

Michaela got up from her seat wondering if she should go after him, or leave him alone for a while. Ambivalent, she considered going in search of Cooper, knowing that ET would certainly listen to him. But the longer it took to find him the more anxious she became about leaving the boy on his own. Resolved to do something, she followed the path he'd taken away from the church.

Michaela stepped carefully into the overgrown underbrush, her imagination conjuring up poisonous snakes and other unseen dangers that might grab her leg and drag her down and out of sight. Her heart raced, worried about the wisdom of walking into the unknown woods. Only the knowledge that Eugene Terrance was somewhere out there by himself kept her going.

"ET?" she called out in as calm a voice as she could. Nothing.

"Please answer me."

Dried branches and twigs cracked and snapped under her feet.

"I'm not leaving so you might as well come on out."

Something ran across her path and scurried away. Her heart lurched. Michaela swallowed.

She tried another angle. "I… I'm not afraid of creepy crawly things…"

Out of the corner of her eye, she spotted a snatch of yellow fabric through the bushes. She recalled that ET was wearing a yellow T-shirt. She slowly made her way in that direction. As she got closer, she recognized, with relief, that it was ET. He was sitting on a fallen tree trunk in a small opening surrounded by garbage and enclosed by overgrown trees and bushes. All of it was set back from a local side road. He was sitting perfectly still, bent forward with his elbows on his knees and his hands supporting his face.

Michaela inched her way forward and sat gingerly next to him. He did not move or do anything to acknowledge her presence. They remained like that for several minutes. She knew it was a standoff she had to respect. ET had to make the first move. But they were still for so long that her mind began to wander back to Cooper's whereabouts. He must be wondering what had happened to them both.

"You can go if you want. I won't be mad."

Even though she had to wait ET out, Michaela still started when he spoke.

"I'm not going anywhere unless you tell me to go away."

He didn't respond.

"Then we'll just sit quietly together."

"Smith is gonna be lookin' for you."

"You think so?"

"Yeah. He likes you. I can tell."

"Then I don't think he'll mind waiting. He knows how concerned I am about you. We can just sit. We don't have to talk if you don't want to."

The silence stretched. He began to fidget.

"At St. Jude, the doctor said I was lucky." He was still bent over, talking to the ground.

Michaela sent up a silent, fervent prayer. "Did the doctor say why?"

"He said I have the…the germ. He said maybe I won't get…you know."

"AIDS. Do you understand the difference?"

"Not really. But I know when people get AIDS they die."

"Some die, but not everyone. Anyway, you just told me you might only have the virus. That's what you're calling the germ. Listen to me. It's really important for you to know what the doctors are talking about and to understand. Because if what you're telling me is correct, you don't have AIDS and you might never get it."

"How do you know?" he asked caustically.

"I'm a teacher and I read a lot about what's happening to kids. What else did they tell you at St. Jude?"

"I have to take some medicine, like, every day," he moaned. "Why do I have to take it every day?"

"Because otherwise you will get very sick."

ET turned his head and looked at her over his arm. "I could die."

"Exactly."

He hid his face again. "I don't know."

"What don't you know?"

"I don't know what to do."

"Have you talked to Smith?"

"Yeah."

"And?"

"He said, nobody can tell me what to do. But he said I can trust the doctors at St. Jude. He said, don't be another stet…stitis…"

"Statistic. Know what that means?" He shook his

head. "It means you're no longer a person. You're a number. Another Black kid who's dead."

"I don't want to die."

Michaela felt her throat quickly closing up. She swallowed hard. "I know, ET. But it doesn't have to be like that, now or next year. You could grow up and live to be an old man like Smith."

"He ain't that old. He still cool."

"He is." She nodded her agreement. "So, what next? Are you going to believe the doctors? Listen to Smith and me, or give up?"

ET sat up. "I'm supposed to go back for treatment. Mrs. Wilson's mad 'cause she got to take me. Maybe I can go by myself."

"If you tell me when, maybe I can take you."

"I don't know," he muttered, ambivalent.

"Well, think about it, okay?" Michaela considered that they'd been away from the activities long enough. She thought it important that ET now try to enjoy himself. She wanted to find Cooper.

She had a lot to think about.

"I think we should get back to the celebration. But I want to give you this first."

Michaela opened her tote and pulled out a gift bag. It was the same one she'd tried to give ET a week ago. She held it out to him.

"Now that you and I understand you're not dying, I still think you could use these. Please take it, because I'm getting tired of carrying it around with me."

Reluctantly, ET took the bag, opening the top enough to see that the DVD player, the disks and batteries, the book, were still inside.

"Thanks," he mumbled.

"You're welcome. Now, is there anything else you'd like to tell me before we head back?"

He thought. "Yeah. I'm sorry I broke into your garage that time. But I'm glad it wasn't somebody else's house."

Cooper was only mildly concerned that Michaela seemed unusually quiet. They'd watched fireworks together, choreographed to patriotic music exploding in one of the city parks that had marked the end of July Fourth. She was probably tired, he reasoned as he navigated the motorcycle through traffic and back into central Memphis. Too much sun, too many sweet teas during the day to keep cool, too much stimulus. It had been a long day. But beyond what he'd planned for the two of them, not the least of which had been her private talk with ET that she had not shared with him, had been the surprising comments and observations of two people whose opinion he respected. The first was Reverend Wallace. The second was Miss Faye.

Rupert Wallace had been more than just a local contact when he'd first come to Memphis, Cooper knew. Reverend Wallace and his family had welcomed him and embraced him, asking no questions about his past, but showing infinite interest and concern about his future. Cooper would forever be grateful for the reverend's guidance, patience, but most of all his wisdom and blessings. It had been Reverend Wallace, and he alone, who had been able to perfectly read his motivations and fears about starting over here, and to temper and redirect his need to prove himself. Cooper could never forget how desperate he'd been for forgiveness back then.

With great humor and understanding, the good reverend had also reminded him not to neglect his own heart. That his physical and emotional needs were every bit as important as his devotion and love of God, and the caring of his soul. The two were not mutually exclusive.

So it was humbling when Reverend Wallace said to him, shaking his hand as he and Michaela were about to leave the church festivities, that he approved.

Cooper knew exactly what the reverend was talking about.

Earlier that morning, about to leave Miss Faye's café, he'd stood at the counter chatting with the proprietress while Michaela was drawn into conversation with Pete, the local vagrant who she found to be sweet and interesting.

"She ain't from Memphis." Miss Faye had shaken her head.

"Something wrong with that?"

"No, sir. I ain't gonna hold that against her. I like her. She's friendly and don't have an attitude, if you know what I'm talking about."

"I do." Cooper nodded.

"She look real good beside you, Smith."

He'd stared at her with a frown. "It's not like I bring women here all the time."

She cackled. "Lord, chile', don't I know it. That's what I'm sayin'. She look like she belong…"

His consideration made him pensive, as he and Michaela headed back into Memphis.

At the next red light, Cooper took the moment to

cover Michaela's arm with his hand, where she had hers wrapped around him. The touch was not only to reassure her, but himself as well. It was a spontaneous demonstration of affection. His comfort level with her was growing exponentially as was his sense of urgency, of hurry. Everything in his life recently had been thrown into fast forward with accelerated actions and stampeding emotions. He'd worked hard to not let that happen again. Now he was all about taking his time and being sure.

Michaela's interest in ET had developed on its own, and now melded with his. They had both arrived at the same place of wanting to do whatever was needed to keep the boy healthy so that he'd have a better shot, a fair shot, at life. But that was not the only thing between them.

The light changed and they were in motion again, the night air cooler than usual for July, but Cooper was reluctant to take Michaela home. What he really wanted he knew he could not allow. He'd have to satisfy himself with whatever closeness they could create. Like now, with Michaela's slender body leaning against his back.

"Cooper, please stop."

He turned his head briefly, wondering if he'd heard right. "You want me to stop?"

"Yes. Please."

"Where?"

"Anywhere. I have to get off. I have to get off."

Hearing what sounded to him like rising hysteria, Cooper immediately responded to the palpable emotions in her voice. He turned off the boulevard onto the nearest side street and slowly coasted down the quiet residential block. They weren't far from Kennedy Park, but he decided against riding any farther, and slowed the bike on the edge of a lake just off Covington. Here, they were more or less alone.

Cooper barely had time to shut off the motor before Michaela was struggling to get off behind him. He could hear her breathing, feel her agitation. He reached out for her arm.

"Michaela?"

She pulled away.

"What's wrong? Talk to me."

Cooper got off the bike and kicked up the stand. He pulled off his helmet and turned around in time to see her remove hers, and then bend over as if she was going to be sick. She gasped as if trying to get air.

Scared now, Cooper dropped his helmet and rushed to her. He was about to touch her when Michaela straightened awkwardly, turned and fell into his arms. His awareness changed instantly.

She wasn't sick. She was crying.

"Michaela…" He whispered her name and it came out a ragged sound of emotion. He held her tightly, his body absorbing her racking sobs.

"We can't let him give up. We can't let him die. We can't."

He shushed. He stroked her back, cupped her head and held Michaela's face pressed into his shoulder. He murmured comforting sounds. He let her cry.

Cooper was caught off guard by the depth of her feelings and deeply moved by Michaela's concern for Eugene Terrance. He knew what the boy faced, and it was more than just the prospects of death, if he didn't get consistent proper care.

He made a promise to himself that he would not let Michaela or ET down.

It was late when they rode back into Chickasaw Gardens. Whatever celebrating that may have taken place in the neighborhood had already played itself out, and everything was very quiet. Cooper kept his bike engine quiet as he pulled into the driveway. Michaela was subdued as she let them into the house where they were greeted by Lady whose meow might best be interpreted as, "And where have you been?"

Seeing that the cat expected his attention, Cooper lifted her into his arms while Michaela went to put out fresh water and cat food. He sat with her on the sofa as she purred in contentment. After a few minutes, he put her down and she trotted off to eat.

He looked up and found Michaela standing in the entrance to the living room. He recognized the bewilderment in her weary gaze, most especially since what had happened on the ride back.

Michaela slowly came to sit next to him, and Cooper raised his arm so that she could rest against his side, her head on his shoulder. She curled her long legs up onto the sofa next to her. Cooper stroked her arm.

"I'm so glad you included me in your plans for today," she murmured.

"Me, too."

"I'm sorry I fell apart on you." Her voice was barely a whisper.

"Don't be. You showed how much you care."

She laid a hand on his chest, and Cooper felt an instant reaction to her touch. He hoped Michaela was not aware of the hesitation that would then only allow him to kiss her lightly on her forehead.

"Cooper," Michaela murmured.

Cooper knew that she wanted much more from him.

Deep inside a sudden fear gripped him, twisting his insides with the weight of his resolve to hold back. He knew that his decision had nothing to do with whether or not he liked or desired Michaela. The simple answer was yes to both. But he felt his own history creep up between them, reminding Cooper that he was a different man now than he used to be. And that difference now shaped his life and was important enough to make him risk his unfolding relationship with her.

"You're tired," he responded, his tone low and throaty and vibrating with regret.

"Aren't you?"

"Yes. Yes, I am," Cooper said, his voice filled with more meaning than he knew she would understand.

"So stay."

Cooper closed his eyes. There it was. An open invitation.

You know you want to.

But any chance he had for a future now rested completely on this moment.

"I think Lady might get jealous," he started out teasing. Michaela made a slight *humph* of humor. "I think you could use a good night of sleep. You've had enough emotional upheaval for one day. I know I have. And I want to be respectful of your godparents' home, Michaela. I hope you understand."

There was no response and Cooper held his breath,

waiting for her to withdraw and pull away from him. But if anything she relaxed against his chest.

"Michaela?" He said her name quietly.

No answer.

She was asleep.

Cooper let a rush of relief wash over him. He continued to sit and hold Michaela, occasionally stroking or caressing her arm, but he did no more than that. Instead he allowed himself to sit there, reflecting on the entire day, the entire summer for that matter, since meeting her.

But the most important thing he'd learned was that his emotions and ability to feel, his desire to love, had not been lost in the accident, nor in his vow to serve others. If anything Cooper felt even more sensitive and receptive. He wanted exactly what Michaela Landry was offering.

She, of course, knew nothing of promises he'd made that he meant to keep. He wondered if it would make any difference if she did.

She felt so sweet, so light and trusting in his arms. He stayed to enjoy the experience for as long as he could.

Then, extracting himself carefully, Cooper lowered Michaela to the sofa. He remained crouched down beside her, and gently laid the back of his hand against her cheek. Her lashes fluttered but she didn't awaken. He gazed down on her almost as if he believed he might never have another chance to do so.

Cooper finally stood. He took a throw that was over the back of a side chair and spread it over Michaela.

He turned off the lights and let himself out the front door.

Chapter 8

"'Morning, Miss Landry."

"Hi," Michaela responded, walking past the reception desk and navigating to the elevators through the now familiar corridors of St. Jude's main building.

With a sense of purpose, she mentally reviewed her agenda for the day. Originally it had included a morning to test the last of the recipes that were to be included in the side-dishes section of her cookbook. She also needed to update the document files she'd created on her computer of the basic manuscript of recipes and anecdotes for the collection. She'd fallen a little behind on the weeding she'd promised to do for her godmother in the backyard.

However, Michaela was finding that her days were becoming consumed by the needs of Eugene Terrance, St. Jude, Cooper and, to a lesser extent but still to her surprise, Jefferson.

She was aware that, in an unusual and unsettling way, Memphis was taking over not just the summer days but also her thinking and plans, and expectations. Michaela felt herself sinking deeper and deeper into the needs of others which, while interesting and fulfilling in its own way, was only masking and distorting her own.

She'd come to Memphis to escape, to heal, to catch her breath and to get focused once more on her life. Instead she'd become involved in the lives of a number of people whom she liked and cared about. But the cold, hard, unavoidable fact was that in four weeks she was going back home.

Michaela took a deep breath as she got off the elevator and headed to the office of Marilyn Caldwell. She quickly tried to organize her thinking, putting into compartments the issues surrounding ET, Jefferson and Cooper. The relationships with all, she was confident, would work out to a positive and natural conclusion as the summer wound down. The only one that was confusing and keeping her up at night was the roller-coaster ride between her and Cooper.

In the most essential and significant part of their attraction for one another, he was holding himself back. Was it her? Or was there someone else?

Michaela was about to knock on the closed door when it suddenly opened and Marilyn swept out into the hall.

"Oh! Glad you're here," she said, stepping away from the door.

"You seem in a hurry. Should we cancel our appointment?"

"No, of course not. I need to run across the hall to get some paperwork from another office. Go on in and have a seat. As a matter of fact, Cooper is on hold. Why don't you talk with him until I get back."

Before Michaela could react, Marilyn was jogging away, her lab coat flapping open around her.

Michaela entered the office and put her things down on a vacant chair. She stared at the blinking red light on Marilyn's phone. Cooper wouldn't be expecting her to pick up. What would she say to him? What could he say to her?

She abruptly picked up the phone and punched the hold button.

"Hello, Cooper."

"Marilyn?" he asked, sounding puzzled.

"No, it's Michaela."

"Michaela," he murmured.

She strained to hear not just his voice but the tone, the emotional inflections.

"I'm here to see Marilyn about ET. Now that he's told me about—"

"I'm sorry. I know I confused you the other night," he interrupted.

"It's probably not your fault, Cooper. I shouldn't have assumed... I mean, you never said..."

"I owe you an explanation, and it's not at all what you're thinking."

She frowned. "You don't know what I'm thinking."

"I don't want you to doubt anything I've said, or any of our time together. It's all sincere, and real."

She closed her eyes. Being with him, listening to his mesmerizing voice, the way he kissed and held her, certainly had seemed real to her.

"I..."

Marilyn returned.

Michaela straightened and pulled herself together.

"I have to go. Here's Marilyn. Bye."

Michaela handed the phone to Marilyn. She tuned out the rest of Marilyn's conversation with Cooper, thinking only that she wanted to believe him. She couldn't make sense of why he hadn't made love to her when the perfect opportunity had presented itself. Even more embarrassing, in the light of day, she'd done the asking. More or less.

She could still feel the crushing emotions she'd felt after ET had revealed his diagnosis. It had been difficult to maintain a calm and cheerful demeanor during the rest of the July Fourth festivities with that revelation running on a loop in her head. Michaela thought she'd make it home before it all caught up to her and she could allow herself a private reaction. But just thinking about all that lay ahead for ET had finally gotten to her on the ride with Cooper as he was taking her home.

He'd been so good and strong and understanding when she'd broken down and started to cry. He held her up, his arms cocooning her with warmth and empathy. And when she'd calmed down enough so that they could continue the journey back to Chickasaw Gardens, she'd anticipated spending the night with him. Michaela knew she couldn't have been wrong about Cooper's feelings, either.

Except that during the prelude of cuddling while sitting in the living room, she'd fallen asleep. And when she'd awakened near dawn the next morning, she was still on the sofa, alone, and Cooper was gone.

That had been three days ago.

"Sorry I kept you waiting. Cooper said he'd like to

speak with you later. Something about correcting mis-information you have. Does that make sense?"

"Yes, thank you," she said, keeping her voice calm.

But she couldn't think of anything that he could say that would be strong enough to counter the impression he'd left that he was just not that into her.

Michaela sat her tray down and waited until ET joined her at the table. The cafeteria on the main floor was mostly empty since the lunch period was long over. He'd just finished a consultation session, and she'd wound up her conversation with Marilyn.

Marilyn had filled her in on the extent of ET's condition, the good, the bad and the promising. There was, apparently in his case, a lot to be hopeful about. While Eugene had the AIDS virus, he did not have AIDS. His T cell count was excellent and, other than chronic colds and ear infections, his other symptoms were considered manageable. With the right cocktail of medications taken regularly, ET could expect to survive.

Michaela, in turn, had reassured Marilyn that ET's foster mother, Betty Wilson, had given her permission to bring ET to the St. Jude campus in her place. Michaela had no way of knowing if Mrs. Wilson might have willfully neglected to bring ET in for treatments, but she was concerned that his foster mother might not have made it a high priority.

She'd brought him once, since she'd made arrangements to meet with Marilyn and other willing staff to learn more about HIV. And now it was routine. Michaela didn't want to risk that he'd miss a single important treatment, and he had to come until the doctors had found the right dosage and amount of medication to give him.

ET sat down and immediately began to wolf down his French fries and slurp his drink through the straw.

"Slow down. You're eating like this is your last meal."

He shrugged and laughed lightly. It was a relief to her that he got the humor.

"Everybody telling me I'm doin' good. This ain't my last meal."

"So how did it go today?" Michaela asked, pouring a prepackaged balsamic vinaigrette over her salad.

"They keep changing my pills, man. It's messed up."

"They're trying to get how much you need to take right. It takes time."

"I don't know why I gotta take pills every day."

"How many?"

"Five," he said, sounding very put-upon.

"Do you understand what could happen if you don't take the medicine?"

"I know. I'll get sicker and sicker, maybe."

"No maybe, ET. It will happen. This has all been explained to you. I don't want to keep harping on it, but if you want to stay well you have to do what the doctors say. You have to trust them. Otherwise you'll have me and Cooper to answer to."

He made a face. "Cooper?"

"I mean, Smith."

"Mrs. Wilson say, what if the doctors are wrong? She say the medicine makes me sick."

"Marilyn Caldwell is going to have a talk with her again. There are some videos she can watch that will explain it all."

"I seen them."

"You saw them."

"Yeah. I watched one with Smith. There was this one dude in the film, he was Black and, like, almost twenty. He got HIV when he was four years old. Now he's in college!" He chomped on his hamburger thoughtfully.

Michaela tried not to react to the mention of Cooper, but was unsuccessful. She stirred around in her salad but didn't feel like eating anymore. She pushed her tray aside.

"Have you thought about going to college?"

"Man, that's a lot of work. Smith said I'm smart and I can do it."

"What do you want to be when you grow up?"

He shrugged. "I never thought I'd grow up," ET said with nonchalance. "I got to think about it. Maybe I can be a pilot. Fly planes."

"Maybe by the time you go back to school in the fall you'll have some ideas."

He groaned when she mentioned school.

"I guess I shouldn't complain, right? At least I'll be able to go, and I can hang with my friends."

"Exactly. Good attitude, ET. I'm proud of you."

"Yeah," he crooned, pleased with himself. Then he frowned. "You won't be here, right?"

She was pulled up short by ET's comment. Her stomach somersaulted as she again felt time pressing in on her, along with the realization again that her summer in Memphis had been temporary. She nodded her head.

"That's right. I'll be back home, and back to work at my own college."

"You ever coming back here?"

"I don't know."

"Maybe Smith can make you stay."

Michaela's eyes popped open, wide. "Why do you say that?"

"'Cause I know he like you. He talk about you a lot."

"Does he?"

He leaned across the table, closer to her.

"Can I ax you something?"

"Ask. Of course. Well, maybe nothing too personal," Michaela said, still trying to get her head around ET's last observation.

"Miss Caldwell told me my real mother died of AIDS. Then how come I don't have it? How come I have HIV?"

Michaela knew that Marilyn had explained this fact, this connection to ET and his foster mother. She knew that sometimes it had to be explained over and over, and that counseling was also necessary. She'd been warned that it took some kids a long time to accept what was happening to them, or even to accept how they'd gotten sick to begin with.

Michaela felt an enormous responsibility to help ET understand, and she counted herself lucky that he now trusted her enough to listen to what she might tell him.

"Why don't you start by telling me what you know or remember about your birth mother."

"She was a drug addict," ET said immediately.

There was no emotion to this pronouncement. He was simply stating fact.

"That's right. It's believed that she got AIDS from using needles she probably shared with other drug addicts. You got the virus from your mother when you were born. You were taken away from her when you were two, Marilyn said."

"Yeah. By one of her friends. Then when she couldn't keep me and my mother's family wouldn't take me, she turned me over to the state. That's how I got into foster care."

"So, it sounds like you were never tested for the virus when you were a baby. But you now know that you have only the virus in your body. That's what makes you HIV positive. You don't have AIDS. That's when the virus multiplies in your body and you get the full disease.

"If you take your medicine and take care of yourself, ET, and do whatever the doctors say, you could grow up to be a pilot like you said."

He was silent for a moment and she knew that he was putting all the pieces together.

"I bet if my mother had come to St. Jude they could have saved her."

"Maybe. Maybe not. The good news is, they're able to save her son. You."

Michaela sat back from the dining table, giving her attention to the conversation between the five other adults but not contributing very much herself. So far her input hadn't been required or sought during the evening. Jefferson was more gregarious than she'd ever seen him, but then these were his friends and he was comfortable around them.

"Would you like some more coffee? It's no trouble to brew another pot."

"No, thanks. I'm fine." Michaela smiled, briefly lifting her cup to show Brenda, the hostess.

"I'd like some more. I'll go start another pot," Edward said, pushing away from the table.

There was a surprised *"ooooohh"* as Brenda's husband got up and left the table.

"What's that for? Y'all act like I don't know my way around the kitchen," he said with mock indignation.

"You don't," Brenda cracked, drawing laughter.

"He's being put to shame by Jefferson, who can cook with the best of us," Lorraine piped up, pushing her glasses back up the bridge of her nose with a beautifully manicured fingernail.

"Yeah. Unfortunately he had to learn the hard way," Paul, Lorraine's husband, added. "I'm sure he's told you about his late wife. He's not afraid to talk about it. Good man."

"No need to feel sorry for me," Jefferson said staunchly. "I can take care of myself and my girls now."

"We know, darling," Brenda cooed. "But it's not the same thing, you know that. You need to have a woman in that house for the girls. They need a woman role model. They're at that age when they're so impressionable."

Lorraine turned her attention to Michaela.

"Well, don't you think Jefferson should be thinking of that? He should be trying to find himself a good woman."

"I don't think we need to go there," Jefferson said.

Michaela was stunned that particular question was being asked of her. She shifted in her chair and sat up straight. "Well, I don't think it's fair for me to say. I mean, Jefferson and I only met a little over a month ago and we don't know that much about each other. But I think he's a wonderful father. His daughters adore him."

There was nothing but silence after her little speech, and Michaela was puzzled to see that three pairs of eyes were staring at her in curiosity. Edward was still in the kitchen. At first Michaela thought that he probably couldn't hear what was going on, until his voice rang out.

"Oh, leave the poor woman alone. She's here for the summer to relax and enjoy herself. Don't make this an inquisition."

"I don't think we're being rude, honey," Brenda said sweetly. "I'm sure Jefferson has been showing her a Memphis good time."

"Yes, but I want to know, doing what?" Lorraine asked eagerly. "I mean, besides going to the botanic garden with Kimika and Kyla. That's hardly a date. What have you two been doing together?"

Michaela shifted again. She covertly looked at Jefferson, but he didn't seem inclined to help her out. If anything, he seemed to also be waiting to hear how she would answer.

"We really haven't seen each other that much, I'm afraid," she added with a smile. "And it's not Jefferson's fault. I've actually been very busy almost from the minute I arrived."

"Oh, yeah? Doing what?" Paul asked.

He was a local attorney and Michaela found that his conversation did tend to sound like a voir dire.

Again, Michaela felt like she was under a microscope. "I'm writing a book, and..."

"A book! Did you hear that, Edward? Michaela's a writer."

"It's not really a book. I'm compiling some old family recipes into a collection. I'm going to self-publish just for my extended family."

"Oh."

It was a collective comment and she couldn't help feeling that either they were unimpressed, or uninterested.

"I've also become involved with a young teenager here who's in foster care, and…"

Jefferson turned his head to regard her sharply, his brows furrowed. "You can't be talking about that kid who tried to break into the Underwood house and almost terrorized you."

"What?" Lorraine gasped. "Jefferson, what are you talking about?"

"What do you mean, you're involved with him?" Paul asked.

Edward returned with the fresh pot of coffee, at which point Michaela was the first one to indicate she'd like a refill. She avoided Jefferson's gaze. Very briefly, and not giving the version of the story that Jefferson chose to believe, Michaela told about the incident the night she encountered ET, and explained everything that had happened since. Almost. She didn't think they needed to know about ET being at St. Jude and what the doctors discovered.

"I told her she should have called the police," Jefferson groused.

"That's what I would have done." Brenda nodded. "You have to be careful."

"I told her that," Jefferson said.

"Well, I admire that Michaela realized the boy needed help," Edward said seriously. "We see too many of our young Black boys in detention or jail."

"That's not our fault." Brenda shrugged. "We can't save every kid who has a sad story."

"Why not?" Michaela heard her own voice.

They once again all stared at her.

"I know you're right. We can't save all of them. But shouldn't we try to do something about the ones we can help? This boy is not a criminal. But no one wants him, and he's defensive and angry and, if left on his own, he could be just another boy in jail. That doesn't have to happen."

"Well, it sounds like you're serious about this boy. Who is he?" Lorraine asked.

Michaela became cautious. "He's just a boy. He's in foster care right now. He's also dealing with a serious illness."

"AIDS," Lorraine said succinctly.

Surprised, Michaela stared silently at her.

"Lorraine works in the neonatal department at another children's hospital," Paul said. "She sometimes gets cases like that. I believe the hospital sends those kids over to St. Jude."

Michaela carefully poured cream into her coffee, but suddenly she didn't want it anymore. "He doesn't have AIDS," she admitted. "But…he has HIV. The doctors at St. Jude are pretty sure it was transmitted at birth."

There was an even longer silence this time.

Jefferson was staring at her as if he was seeing her for the first time. Michaela resented feeling so uncomfortable under his scrutiny.

"He's going to be okay." She felt compelled to defend ET. "He might not ever get AIDS. He'll be living with a chronic illness, like diabetes. He's got a good attitude, and there's someone here in Memphis who's mentoring him."

"Who's that?" Edward asked.

"Cooper Townsend. Everyone seems to just call him

Smith." She looked at Jefferson. "We met him that first night at the hospital."

Jefferson nodded. "Yeah, I remember."

"I know that name," Brenda said.

"Me, too." Edward frowned and then turned to Paul. "Isn't that the guy who has the construction company? Does a lot of pro bono work?"

"That's the one. Cooper Townsend. Now there's an interesting man. How well do you know him?" Paul asked Michaela.

She was appalled to feel the lurching in the center of her chest, the pull of tension in her stomach as the question hit a nerve.

"Not very well at all," she said quietly, realizing that was the truth. At least, in some ways. "He volunteers at St. Jude, and he coaches a lot of sports. Kids seem to adore him."

"If he's the one I'm thinking about, the women are hot after him. He's single. Widowed, I think the story goes. Good-looking and gainfully employed," Lorraine said.

Her husband turned to her. "How do you know so much about him?"

"Don't you remember? Pastor Nichols talked about him at this very table about two years ago. I think he also has something to do up at a church in North Memphis."

Widowed.

Widowed went through Michaela's mind, and for that moment it was the only thing she could retain. She felt oddly demoralized. She really knew nothing about Cooper.

"I think there was a write-up about Townsend in the paper a while back, too," Jefferson murmured thoughtfully. "He helped some woman who was about to lose her café because it wasn't up to health code, or something like that. He put in all the work, got her the right certificates and didn't charge her."

Miss Faye's, Michaela guessed immediately.

"I remember that story." Brenda nodded. She turned to Michaela. "It also hinted at a mysterious or tragic past. Is it true?"

Michaela shrugged. "Like I said, I don't really know him."

"Well, that's so interesting." Brenda sighed. "So when do you leave Memphis?"

Michaela couldn't help but smile.

All evening she'd had the feeling she was also on display. She knew it was a big deal that Jefferson wanted her to meet some of his friends, and that he'd been asked to bring her for dinner to the home of one couple. But she pretty much knew it could go either way. His friends could be suspicious of her, or they could embarrass both her and Jefferson by trying to force them together. They had done neither.

Instead, Michaela had found, they had been gracious and friendly, taking a familiar attitude with her that had, at first, put her immediately at ease. What she hadn't expected were the guilt-free observations made about her to her face. She couldn't tell if they were teasing, or what Jefferson's friends actually believed.

Upon being introduced, Brenda had pulled back and stared at Michaela.

"Oh, look at her eyes. They're like cat's eyes, right, Lorraine?"

"Down here some folks would call those devil eyes," Lorraine helpfully supplied.

"I always thought they were real beautiful," Jefferson said.

Michaela had smiled at him for his honesty, and for defusing his friend's comment.

Edward had asked about her name. What was the origin and the meaning?

"Unusual, but it has a nice sound. Kind of like Mahalia."

Michaela had lifted her shoulders, helplessly.

"I have no idea. My mother said she read it somewhere and liked the sound. And she didn't want me to have a name like everyone else. She said she thought I was going to be special."

They all went "aaawwww."

And then it was Paul who'd said, in the middle of cocktails, crab dip and pita chips, "She doesn't sound like she's from up north."

"I'm not that far up north," Michaela had responded. "Funny, I was going to say none of y'all sound very Southern."

That had evoked a genuine stream of laughter that had finally broken the ice...until now, as dinner was concluding.

She thought she'd done well, held her own, not put Jefferson on the spot, and not thought too much about Cooper. But with all the conversation inadvertently turned to ET and the saga surrounding him, Michaela was, once again, reflective.

Where was Cooper? Was his silence his way of ending it between them?

Ending *what* between them?

Michaela was glad when Lorraine said she thought it was time for her and Paul to leave. They had a baby-sitter to get home. It was the women who cleared the table, left the coffee and extra dessert, while the men sat in the family room watching what remained of *Sunday Night Football.*

In the kitchen, Michaela was no longer the topic of discussion and only another pair of hands. She worked efficiently with Brenda and Lorraine while the two women discussed their schedules and mutual social events for the coming weeks. Michaela politely asked about their children and preparations for school in the fall. Neither woman asked her about returning to Howard.

On the drive home Jefferson was chatty, not about the evening but about his thoughts on possibly running for the local city council. It was a safe topic and Michaela gratefully held up her end until they reached her godparents' house. Jefferson walked her to the door and made sure she was safely inside.

"Thanks for a really nice evening. I enjoyed meeting your friends," she said dutifully.

"They're good people. At least it's four votes I can count on if I go into public office."

Michaela smiled but made no comment.

Jefferson took a step closer. She'd known this was a possibility.

"Look, I think it's admirable that you want to help this kid, but I still feel you should be careful. You might be in way over your head. Be careful he doesn't try to rip you off."

She stared at him. "I appreciate your advice."

"I'm only trying to watch out for you."

"I go home soon. I think I'll be okay. Are you and the girls coming over on Saturday afternoon?"

Jefferson pursed his mouth. "If nothing comes up. This is a busy time for me. I'll give you a call, okay?"

With that he squeezed her arm and kissed her briefly on the cheek and then left.

Michaela stood there, thinking about the irony of the situation. Jefferson was a good man, she knew. But he wasn't like Cooper.

On the other hand, she now felt in limbo with both men.

I'm definitely losing my touch, Michaela thought dryly.

Cooper got out of his truck and immediately identified the sedan parked in front of the offices for Building Blocks as belonging to Betty Wilson. He thought he'd have about a half hour before meeting with her, but was surprised to see she'd already arrived. This is not promising, Cooper considered. When someone was this anxious to see you, it generally was not with good news. At least, that had always been his experience.

He suspected that Mrs. Wilson was going to complain either about the time that was needed to devote to Eugene Terrance's medical issues, or about ET himself. So far, he'd been unsuccessful in getting ET's foster mother to understand that, instead of trying to control the boy by dictating to him, it would be more helpful if she listened and gave him a chance to present his own point of view.

As he closed his cab door, Cooper's cell phone rang. He hoped it might be Michaela, but he knew it would be unfair to expect her to read his mind when, in his own mind, there was so little he was sure about.

He answered as he headed for the door to his business.

"Cooper," he answered, pulling open the door and entering. "...I know about the delivery. Do me a favor and check it against the order sheet. Don't sign off on it unless all the equipment is there... I expect to be back this afternoon. I'm heading into a meeting at the moment... Sure. If I'm not back by five go ahead and leave. Make sure you lock up everything, and let the client know I'll be back later. We need to discuss some changes on his blueprint. Talk with you later."

He closed the BlackBerry and slipped it back into the cradle attached to his waist.

"Mrs. Wilson, good to see you," Cooper said, smiling at Betty as he stopped before the chair where she was seated. Already he was discouraged. She looked firm and resolute. "Can I get you anything? I have some coffee, or soda, if you like."

"No. I can't stay long. I have to get back to the house so my husband can leave for work."

"Okay." Cooper nodded. Instead of sitting at the desk, he sat one hip on the front edge facing her. "What can I do for you? You said it was very important that you see me."

"You know I try to do the right thing. My husband and me, we've taken in a dozen kids that nobody else wanted."

Cooper nodded again. "Yes, I'm aware of that. I admire all you've done."

"The thing is, I can't keep Eugene Terrance anymore."

"Excuse me?" Cooper said, although he'd heard perfectly clear the first time.

"He has to go. I can't deal with him anymore. Lord knows I tried, but I'm afraid of what he has. I don't want to get sick. And I have other kids I'm responsible for."

Cooper felt a chill of defeat pass over him. It happened when he'd reached pretty much the last option in a situation and no other was available to him. Eugene had been a tough sell from the beginning, and he was sincere when he told Betty Wilson he admired that she sometimes took on the hard cases. But this was different. She was saying she was rejecting ET because he was sick. Because he had an illness that was still cloaked in misconception and fear, and which could be easily dispelled with available information.

"Have you heard from Marilyn Caldwell? I asked her to call you and explain the situation with ET. There's no reason for you to be afraid, Betty…"

She was shaking her head. "What she had to say makes no difference. I can't have that boy in my house. I have to watch out for myself and my family. I'm sorry."

Cooper realized it was useless to argue with Mrs. Wilson, no point in using reason. She'd already made up her mind. Against all the known facts, she believed what she believed.

"What do you want to do?" he asked.

"I called Children's Services downtown. I told them I can't be Eugene's foster mother anymore. They have to take him out of my house. They have to find another family for him. That's it." She finished with an emphatic slice of her hand through the air.

"Betty, I appreciate your honesty. I know this must have been difficult for you," Cooper said, trying not to sound tired and helpless.

He was raging inside at the ignorance that precipitated Betty Wilson's decision. He was even more annoyed with himself for not being able to think of a way to make her change her mind.

Slowly Cooper got a grip on himself. Betty Wilson's decision notwithstanding, something still had to be done about ET.

Betty Wilson stood up. "I'm sorry, but…"

"Don't be sorry. You've done more than a lot of people might have. I'll call the city, but I'm going to get right on trying to find Eugene another home."

"Well, I wish you luck," she said. "But I think the minute folks hear what he got, they're not going to want to take him in."

"I hope you're wrong," Cooper said, walking her to the door and holding it open for her. "As a matter of fact, I know you are. I don't blame you for being more worried about yourself, but I believe there are other folks who will step forward to help him."

Cooper closed the door and stood watching her leave through the glass window. But he was deep in thought, and deeply concerned. Betty Wilson could be right.

Seated at his desk again, Cooper could only think of one option, and it was an obvious one. He planned on calling Reverend Wallace to discuss his plan. But he also knew he wanted to call Michaela. It bothered him that he was using the latest development with Eugene as an excuse to reach out to her, but he'd come to another decision and it had nothing to do with ET.

He was now willing to trust his feelings enough to know he had to risk being totally honest with her. He'd not felt so lonely in a long time, as he had in just the past three or four days of not being with her. As a matter of fact, the thought of possibly not being able to see Michaela and to tell her what she needed to know had also given Cooper an equal number of sleepless nights.

Still, it took him another fifteen minutes to work up the courage to call. She answered on the second ring, her voice distracted. But just hearing her sent Cooper into a tumble of emotions that caught him off guard and made him anxious. She meant far more to him than he'd realized.

"What are you cooking today?"

"Cooper," she said in surprise.

"Hello, Michaela. How've you been?"

"I've been keeping busy," she said smoothly, non-committally.

"I consider myself fortunate that you haven't hung up on me yet."

"I'm too curious about why you're calling to do that."

"I think I deserved that," he murmured ruefully.

"Sorry. I… I'm just not sure what to say, Cooper. I really don't know what to think right now."

"I know. My fault. Something came up that I didn't know how to handle. So, I think I handled it badly. I want you to forgive me, if you can."

"I don't think there's anything to forgive. But I would like to understand what's going on. You know…between you and me."

"Understood. And that's fair. First, I have two things I have to tell you."

"Okay."

"I've just learned that Betty Wilson is withdrawing as a foster parent to Eugene Terrance."

"Oh, no…"

"The reason isn't important."

"I know the reason," Michaela said sadly.

"The thing is, I don't want this to be a setback for him. I don't want him to believe that everyone will turn against him for any reason."

"What are you going to do?"

Cooper took a deep breath. "I plan on calling Reverend Wallace and see if he can talk about this…at church on Sunday. Once the congregation knows about Eugene Terrance I know someone will come forward and take him in. I see it as temporary, until the city agency can work out something else, find him another home."

"Cooper, that's a wonderful idea. Someone is bound to volunteer from your church, don't you think?"

"Let's pray on it," he said carefully.

"Cooper, I want to be there. I'd like to come to the service. If you need me to, I'll even speak on ET's behalf."

Cooper's eyes closed briefly with the granting of his own private prayer. He smiled to himself. He'd been right all along. She most definitely had been worth taking the risk for.

"I'm really happy to hear that. Yes, please come. It'll be important to ET…and to me," he added.

"Really?"

"Yes, I mean it."

"Then I will. You said there's something else you wanted to tell me?"

"I've missed you."

Chapter 9

Pulling open the bathroom door, Michaela, wet from her shower and trying to wrap a towel around herself, paused, sure she'd heard the phone. The distinct ring tone on her cell phone confirmed it, and she hurried across the hallway to her room. Lady, ensconced not only in the center of the bed but on top of the outfit Michaela had selected to wear, fled when Michaela shooed her with a wave of her hand.

"Hello?" she answered breathlessly, sitting on the side of the bed.

"I thought you were going to call me. You said after three weeks you'd probably be bored out of your mind. Good thing I wasn't holding my breath."

"Jill! Hey, girl. It's good to hear you."

"I don't believe you. Go on and admit it. You forgot all about me and everyone else in D.C."

Michaela chuckled and settled more comfortably on her bed. "The truth is I haven't had the time to think about anything since I got here, let alone get bored."

"Are we still talking about Memphis?" Jill asked with amused skepticism.

"Don't sell Memphis short. It's got a little bit of a lot of big cities, plus it has that Southern thing going on."

"I'm not sure what that means, but are you enjoying your stay? Are you glad you decided to go or are you dying to come home?"

"There's no yes or no answer. Yes, I'm enjoying my stay, but it's not anything like what I thought it would be. My cookbook project is coming along. I'm glad I decided to come but…it's gotten complicated. And I'm trying not to think about coming home. There's just so much…"

"You sound serious. Are you okay?"

"I'm not trying to scare you, Jill. It's not like that at all. I'm not going to be a drama queen about what's been going on, but let's just say the summer has taken on a life of its own."

"Hmmm," Jill murmured. "Does this have anything to do with a man?"

"What? Why would you ask that? Did I say anything about a man?"

"I thought so. There is a man involved."

"Well, it's not exactly what you think. Anyway, I don't have time to go into it. Jill, I'd love to spend the next hour catching up but I can't right now. I have to get dressed," Michaela said with sudden urgency, glancing at the nightstand clock.

"For what? It's eight-thirty on Sunday morning."

Michaela began to feel absurdly like a kid caught with her hand in the cookie jar. "Well, how come you're up so early?"

Jill sucked her teeth. "Bad date. I woke early remembering all the things I wish I'd told him last night."

"Anybody I know?"

"You've heard me mention his name. I had him short-listed." Jill sighed. "Now I know why. I really need to broaden my horizons. The men in D.C. are seriously getting on my nerves. They're so adept at playing games. They tell you they're not married, and you know they're lying."

Michaela smiled. "That never used to bother you."

"Yeah, well…maybe I'm finally growing up. I'm really tired of being disposable."

"Or short-listed?" Michaela suggested.

"All right. I get your point."

"I'm so sorry," Michaela murmured, not sure what else she could say. Jill wanted to talk. She wanted to listen. But she looked anxiously at the time again. "I really have to…"

"Okay, I won't keep you. Make me feel better," she whined. "Tell me the men in Memphis are no different. Have you met anyone interesting?"

Michaela plucked at the old-fashioned chenille bedspread. "Actually I've met two men."

"Excuse me? Did you just say you met two men? Michaela, you've only been there six weeks."

"Well, it's been a busy six weeks."

"I hate you."

Michaela laughed. "I'm sorry. Jill, look…I am serious. I'd love to talk but I can't."

"If you think I'm getting off the phone after you dropped that on me, you're out of your mind. You can't leave me hanging like this. Tell me these men are married. Tell me at least one of them is gay. Tell me they're homely and wear overalls."

"I can't. None of that is true."

Jill whimpered.

"One is a neighbor of my godparents. They kind of bullied him into looking out for me. He's not really my type but..."

"I didn't know you had a type. And I don't count Spencer."

"...he's a good man. Nice-looking. He's a widower with two teenage girls. They're twins, about thirteen."

"You're breaking my heart. What does he do for a living?"

"He owns and operates a couple of businesses. And he's thinking of running for political office."

"Well, if you're not interested, I hope you told him about me, your very best friend."

"Jill, I don't think Jefferson..."

"Jefferson. Nice name. Manly."

"I was going to say I don't think Jefferson will have to go far to find someone eligible if he's interested in an affair or a new wife. Memphis is rich with gracious, smart and attractive Black women."

"Okay, but has he hit on you?"

"No, he hasn't. He's been a real gentleman."

"An endangered species," Jill said sarcastically. "On the other hand, maybe you should be insulted."

"I'm not," Michaela responded honestly.

"Oh. So, you're not interested."

After a quick moment's thought, Michaela realized there was nothing to dispute. Nothing to second-guess herself on, or to beat herself up about. There may have been a nanosecond when Jefferson might have engaged her interest. But it didn't take.

"I think that's a fair statement."

"Okay, scratch him. What about the other one?"

The other one.

What an interesting way to put it, Michaela thought, but she was also biding her time. The truth was she really wanted to talk. She wanted to tell Jill about Cooper, but she had no idea how to begin. Her very ambivalence would be a dead giveaway to her feelings. She was very much afraid that not only would she be totally transparent, but that Jill would hone in on it like a smart bomb, and blow all of her excuses, her doubts, her yearnings, to smithereens. She couldn't handle that just yet.

The real truth of the matter, Michaela considered, was that she was terrified of the directions her feelings for Cooper were leading. Basically, down the garden path, around the bend and over the rainbow.

"Hello? You still there?"

"Yes, but I've got to go. I'm not kidding."

"Okay, okay. I just have one quick thing to tell you and then I'll let you go, but only if you swear you'll call me tonight so we can talk."

"Promise. What?"

"Spencer is seeing someone."

Michaela felt a somersault in her stomach. Not because her former fiancé was dating, but because it put a definite end to their relationship. She didn't feel as though she'd taken a personal hit with the news, but there was this sense of moving on. Cooper had once said something about it. All things in their time.

"You mean, seeing someone as in…"

"Yeah, you got it. I haven't met her but folks are saying she's all that."

"And a bag of chips," Michaela murmured wistfully.

"I know what you're thinking, girlfriend, but don't forget you're the one who wanted out. Can't blame the man for rebounding."

"But how do you know if you're rebounding, or if it could be the real thing?"

"Oh, oh. Are we still talking about Spencer?"

"Who else is there?"

"I changed my mind. I want to know about the other man right now. I don't care if you're going to be late for whatever. I want to know what's going on. Am I going to have to come down there and hurt someone for messing around with your feelings? You're very vulnerable right now, Michaela. You don't know what you're doing."

"Thanks for the support, Jill. I might need it later…but not yet."

Michaela allowed her body to relax against the pillows. Lady sprang up silently on the bed again and padded over to lay down next to her. Absently, Michaela began to stroke the cat's back. She suddenly recalled watching Cooper do the same thing much to the delight of Lady. She wondered how she would react if Cooper were to…

"I really don't know that much about him. As a matter of fact, I can't quite figure him out."

"Him who?"

"Oh. His name is Cooper."

"Jefferson. Cooper. Girl, you have to tell me how you do it."

Michaela smiled, tickling Lady's ears as the cat rotated her head and gave her a look that, roughly translated, probably meant don't stop.

"I don't have time to go into how we met, but I like him. Actually, I'm very attracted to him. I think he feels the same, but he's been real polite about it. He's very good-looking. He has this incredible voice, and the way he walks…"

Jill groaned. "This is so unfair."

"He's really one of the most gentle, caring and strong men I've ever met, but I think there's an interesting backstory."

"I knew it. Too good to be true."

"I don't know anything about his background or family. He's complicated."

"Did you hear what I just said?"

"Yeah, but I don't agree. He's very much for real. This is a man who says grace before eating, and is compassionate, and…"

"I get it. Jefferson never stood a chance."

"I can't help if I found one more appealing than the other."

"But you did find two. Do I still have time to come down for a quick visit?"

Michaela laughed. "If you really want to. It would be fun to see you."

"I'll think about it. So where is it you're off to in such a hurry this morning? Does it have anything to do with Cooper?"

"Well, I'm meeting him for Sunday service. But in all fairness, I've also attended church with Jefferson. It's a very important part of life here."

"So I guess I shouldn't remind you that you've been very critical of the folks who faithfully attend church every Sunday but then forget to practice what they're taught on the other days."

"I have questions, but it's not like I don't believe the Word or the message."

"You think this Cooper is any different?"

"I know he is, Jill. I've seen him in action."

"Well, I must say Memphis sounds very surprising. So, you'll call me later?"

"I will. You haven't said much about how your summer is going."

"I'll warn you in advance—you'll need a glass of wine while you listen. To be continued. Enjoy the service. Bye."

Michaela smiled at Reverend Wallace, who stood at the entrance of the church, personally greeting everyone arriving.

"Well, it's good to see you again, Michaela," he said, his eyes bright and warm behind his glasses.

"You remember my name," she commented.

"I'm not senile yet." Reverend Wallace cackled. "Cooper said he thought you'd come this morning." He took her hand and held it cocooned with his own. "He'll be glad to see you. I am."

Michaela murmured a thank-you, sensing significance in the reverend's words that she couldn't quite figure out. It did make her wonder exactly what Cooper may have said to the reverend about her.

She had only a moment to look around before approaching the door leading into the church. She'd hoped that maybe Cooper would be there to meet her, but there were only two elderly women standing on the other side of the great oak doors, handing out programs and directing people to seats. Once into the apse Michaela again paused to look around. Inside there were two side aisles that divided the seating sections and were wide enough for processions.

Michaela took a seat in a pew somewhat toward the back. And she sat near the aisle so that Cooper could easily see her when he arrived. She looked around at the already seated worshippers but did not see him. She did see, much to her surprise, Miss Faye walking purposefully down the right aisle to sit with several other people with whom she was obviously acquainted. Michaela watched the exchange taking place, but was beginning to experience a sense of familiarity because already there were people here she knew. And while she'd only met Reverend Wallace once before, from the very beginning he'd put her at ease.

The church pews were filling up, and still she did not see Cooper. Suddenly an organ began to quietly play the chords of a hymn. People settled down. Through a door at the front and to the left of a podium, came a dozen men and women, clothed in royal-blue robes with white collars. The choir members positioned themselves in two rows of seats. A woman separated herself from the others, and it became clear that she was the musical director as she used her hands to motion the others to stand ready.

The organ music became more complex and rich as the organist began to play the full arrangement. Everyone stood up and Michaela followed suit as the processional began. The choir started to sing in strong melodic voices.

Down the two aisles came the deacons, also in robes. Among them was Reverend Wallace. Toward the back were two men. Michaela audibly gasped, drawing quick glances from one or two people near her. But her eyes were wide, riveted to the sight of Cooper walking into the church as a member of the procession. Totally bewildered, and trying to make sense of what she was seeing, Michaela simply couldn't.

What was he doing?

Michaela felt like her brain was shutting down. She could not take her eyes from him. The man she witnessed taking a position far off to the side of all the others who'd entered with him, was a completely different man than the Cooper Townsend she'd known all summer.

Or was he?

She could not follow the rituals of the service, the greetings and prayers and hymns. She stood when everyone else stood, and sat as they did. She never bothered opening her hymnal because there was no question that her voice would have cracked if she'd tried to sing. She simply stared at Cooper, willing him to look around and see her there. More than anything, she wondered what she would see now if she looked into his eyes.

Reverend Wallace gave the sermon, and it was only as he began to speak that Michaela allowed her atten-

tion to be drawn away from Cooper and her tumultu-
ous reactions to him. Her first thought was that he was
a stranger. The second, that he was not. His stride and
walk was known to her, as was the calm, chiseled
features of his face, subtly masked behind the shadowy
beard. The third and most disturbing of all, Michaela
confessed to herself, was how devastatingly handsome
he looked, even in his officiating robes.

Finally she pulled her gaze away. Inside she was a
jumble of nerves and conflicting emotions. Her heart
was pounding.

What was he doing? What was he doing?

Michaela closed her eyes and hung her head. Her
hands were twisting around something. She remembered that she held the program given to her at the beginning of the service. She opened her eyes and began
to read it. There, listed among the names, and several
lines below Reverend Wallace, was Cooper Townsend,
Youth Pastor. She squeezed her eyes closed again.

Pastor.

Officer of the church.

Man of God.

Inside, Michaela felt her emotions intensify. She
fought against tears. She struggled against anger. She
tried to perform a one-hundred-and-eighty-degree shift
in what she'd come to feel for Cooper. Too late. It had
already happened. She didn't even know when, but she
knew it now.

She lifted her head and took in a deep breath. The wish
to leave was sudden and strong. And then Michaela
opened her eyes again. Her gaze met, with unerring
directness, the probing scrutiny of Cooper's. For the

longest ten seconds of her life, they stared at one another, and Michaela could neither hear nor see anything else. She had the sense that he'd known all along where she was sitting. Yet choosing that moment to make eye contact also said to Michaela that Cooper was well aware of what she was going through right now.

She changed her mind about leaving.

Finally Reverend Wallace's voice penetrated her fog. His words took hold and rooted. She relaxed and began to listen. Cooper lowered his gaze to his clasped hands. She silently responded, as if he might actually hear her.

Okay. I'll wait.

The sermon was thoughtful and provocative. It surprised Michaela because of Reverend Wallace's modern take on spirituality and faith. When it was over, and prayers and amens had been said, the reverend announced a special message from Pastor Townsend.

Michaela's stomach roiled with tension as Cooper stood and slowly made his way to the podium. In prayer, he welcomed everyone. His voice resonated through the gathering with such quiet power that it gave her a chill. When he reached out in particular to all visitors and first-timers, Michaela wondered if it was meant just for her. When asked to stand, she was the only one to do so, and she received nods and smiles of approval. He waited until she was once more seated and spoke again.

"When I was in high school, I remember reading something that went like this—the true sign of any good society is in how it treats its most helpless and vulnerable citizens. These citizens might be the sick and poor, children and the elderly. I want to make an appeal today for a child. I call him one of our own. He lives in the community, goes to school with our kids and is a pretty good soccer player. He's bright and, in my opinion, will someday grow up to be a strong and intelligent man. But, in order to ensure that he might reach his full potential in the future, for now what he really needs is a home."

Michaela's heart began to beat faster. She covertly let her gaze travel over the congregation. Most of those in attendance were women. Most were middle-aged or older. All were attentive, but it was impossible for her to tell who would be most likely to come forward, on the basis of Cooper's pleas, to champion a boy that they didn't know.

"You can probably already tell that I like this young man, and I believe in him. Right now he's a ward of the state. A more permanent foster home is being sought. But he could use a hand right now for a few weeks. I don't want to influence anyone's consideration, and rather than listening to me go on and on, I want to give him a chance to speak for himself."

Cooper used his hand to beckon someone sitting in the first pew. There was no hesitation as ET stood and went to stand before him.

There was a slight rustling of sound as people craned their necks or shifted to get a good look at the slight boy at the front of the church. Cooper rested an arm around ET's shoulder, and Michaela felt an odd constriction in her chest. She knew them both under different circumstances than where they were at that moment. It suddenly occurred to her how fortunate she was. Cooper said something very quietly to ET who, with his eyes downcast, nodded. With one final pat on ET's shoulder, Cooper returned to his seat.

ET stood alone in front of the congregation of some two hundred or more people. He seemed even smaller standing at the front of the large, open room with its vaulted ceiling and solemn air. He was wearing a suit that was too big for him, the sleeves falling past his wrist, the shoulders sloping from lack of support. It looked like a zoot suit from decades ago. Michaela couldn't help smiling because he looked so adorable. She also couldn't help admiring him because he was so fearless.

"'Morning."

"'Morning," came back the murmured reply.

"Peace be with you."

"And also with you," the congregation answered.

"My name is Eugene Terrance Dunne, and I'm fifteen years old. Everybody calls me ET but I ain't like that thing in the movie…"

There was a low rumble of laughter from various parts of the congregation.

"My mama is dead, and I never knew who my daddy was. I been in foster care since I was two years old. I met Smith when I was in detention after school one day. He taught me how to play chess. One time I almost beat him.

"Like he said, I don't have a place to live right now. So I would appreciate if somebody could help me out for a little while."

ET stopped suddenly and glanced back at Cooper, and Cooper sat watching the boy intently. Michaela held her breath because she knew what was coming next.

"Smith told me to be sincere." He said the word awkwardly. "There's something else you have to know about me. I got HIV. I mean, I'm HIV positive…"

Immediately there was a reaction through the church in gasps and exclamation. But she couldn't tell if they were sounds of sympathy or shock. Again ET turned to Cooper, but then faced the gathering with renewed self-confidence. When he began to talk again, everyone quieted down.

"At first I was scared, but then I found out HIV means I got the virus inside me. I'm gonna have it the rest of my life 'cause I was born with it in my blood.

"Also, I'm a Sagittarius. When I grow up I want to be an astronaut. Thank you."

He bowed stiffly from the waist.

ET went back to his seat at the front of the congregation. Cooper smiled at the boy, approaching him to shake his hand and affectionately clapping him on the shoulder. The murmurs and undercurrent continued until Cooper stood once again behind the podium for attention.

"I hope that everyone here today will give some thought to Eugene Terrance's needs, and will reach out to contact either myself or Reverend Wallace. Or if anyone wishes to, you can talk with me on my after-service number listed in the program.

"For now I will close today's program with this. It's in keeping with what Christ teaches us when He commands us to care for one another. There are three things in life that, once gone, can never come back—time, words and opportunity. There are three things in life that could destroy you—anger, pride and not forgiving. And, last, the three things in life that are most valuable are love, family and friends, and kindness."

Cooper raised his hands to the congregation.

"'The will of God will never take you where the grace of God won't protect you.' Let us pray…"

By the time the service ended, Michaela felt emotionally drained and confused. She stood through the last hymn, one that she knew and loved. The words and music moved her, as it always had, but it was a temporary lull in the turbulence she'd already experienced from the rest of the service. She sat as parishioners, known to one another, stood in the aisle to greet and chat, slowly filing out. Michaela could see Cooper up front, suddenly surrounded by a swarm of worshippers. To a person they were all women and, as far as she could tell, all under the age of forty.

Cooper was patient, gracious, but did not single out any one person over another. She did notice, however, that the women clustered around him were vying for his attention. One in particular—stylish, petite—kept touching Cooper's arm. She also seemed to have a lot to say, holding up the line. Despite everything that she was feeling just then, Michaela realized she had to add a twinge of jealously to the list.

She suddenly realized that someone was heading toward her, and recognized Miss Faye. She stood to say hello to the older woman.

"I knew it was you." Miss Faye gestured with her hand. "I saw you when you stood up."

"And I saw you when you came in. I didn't know this was your church."

"Smith didn't say," Miss Faye confirmed, not surprised. "He don't talk 'bout other folks' business. You like the service?"

"I did," Michaela said sincerely. "I... I came because of the boy, Eugene Terrance. I know his situation."

Miss Faye looked very skeptical. "Is that all?"

"What do you mean?"

"I like Reverend Wallace, but I always come to hear Smith if he's on the program. Lord, he sure got a way about him when he talks. And he's always tryin' to fix folks' troubles. I sure hope somebody gonna take that boy in. Nobody should hold it against him for what he has. Everybody got something God give them to deal with. I'm already raising my two grandbabies or I'd sure try to help.

"And I liked what Smith had to say about the grace of God protecting us all. Ain't he something?"

Michaela nodded at Miss Faye's beaming countenance. Her words fought against a sudden obstruction in her throat. "Yes, he is."

"Now can we go? I'm hungry," ET complained.

Cooper turned away from Judith, the last of the stragglers who invariably kept him long after the service had ended, complimenting his sermon, or offering suggestions for making it shorter, or asking for advice.

"Me, too. I'm almost done here," Cooper answered.

In Judith's case, it was to explain why it was impossible for her to take in and care for a child right now. Her own two boys were already a handful. She was looking for a pardon and he gave it to her.

Cooper unzipped his robe and took it off, folding it and placing it across his arm.

"Eugene, you did good," Cooper congratulated the boy. "I'm proud of how you handled yourself in front of so many strangers."

ET shrugged. "I wasn't scared," he said.

With his hand on Eugene's shoulder, Cooper steered

him in the direction of the church offices. He had to put away his robe and check for any messages that might require his immediate attention. But his real destination was Reverend Wallace's office. He was positive that was where the reverend would have taken Michaela after talking with her briefly following the service.

"Nothing to be afraid of," Cooper said. "Remember what I said about everyone deserving respect. That includes you."

"What if nobody wants me? What if I don't find someplace to live?"

Cooper could hear the youthful anxiety behind the question. For someone like Eugene, he understood how hard it was to have to depend on the kindness of strangers who might reject him for things that were beyond his control.

"Stop worrying. Someone is going to offer you a place to stay. You wait and see. Now, give me ten minutes. I have to stop by the office before we go."

"Is Miss Landry coming with us? I saw her."

"I don't know," Cooper said, his answer weighing heavily on him.

He realized that it was possible Michaela might not ever speak to him again. She might have, at that very moment, complained to Reverend Wallace about his duplicity and dishonesty. She might accuse him of leading her on. He would not have been able to deny any of it, even though it wasn't exactly true.

Cooper stopped in the corridor. "If I see her, I'll ask. Is it okay with you if she says yes?"

"Yeah, I don't mind. She's all right."

"Then wait for me in the parking lot. I won't be long."

He stood watching Eugene walk away before heading toward Reverend Wallace's office. But just as he was about to knock, the door opened on the reverend.

"I was just coming to look for you," Reverend Wallace said. "Are you finished?"

"Yes, I am. The boy is waiting for me. I told him I'd take him for something to eat before dropping him off at Mrs. Wilson's."

"I'm afraid nobody came to me and offered to take him in. You have any better luck?"

Cooper arched a brow. "None. And you know how I feel about luck."

"I do." The reverend nodded solemnly. "But for all we know, Cooper, luck, fate and timing are all rolled into one. You should know that better than anyone. Don't discount how goodness comes to you. Accept it and feel blessed. Remember what I always told you."

"Nobody knows what God intends," Cooper responded pensively.

"But there are signs all around us. Remember what you said this morning about opportunity. Now, I suppose you're looking for Michaela."

"I need to talk with her."

"I met her when she first arrived. Just a moment ago she looked a little shell-shocked, I would say. She's inside. Stay as long as you want." The reverend hesitated for another moment. "Is there anything I can do to help?"

Cooper's brows furrowed and he tensed his jaw. "Not yet. I think I have to work this one out all on my own."

"Just remember you're not alone."

The reverend patted his shoulder in a comforting manner before walking away, but it did little to relieve

Cooper of his sense of impending disaster, the very thing he'd hoped to avoid in the first place.

When he entered the office, Michaela was not sitting in either of the two chairs in front of the heavy wooden desk. He found her standing in front of the one window, peering through the venetian blinds out to the people milling around as they left the church. Michaela's back was toward him, but he noticed at once how lovely she looked in a simple summer dress and low-heeled sandals. He'd watched her walk from the parking lot and had tried to intercept her as she came into the building, but was stopped by another pastor with a question about the order of the day's service. By the time he was free again, Michaela had already entered the church and seated herself. The wide-brim straw hat she also wore marked her position, making it easy for his gaze to find her during the service. Now, she'd taken the hat off to show her hair was combed back and secured in a twist.

"Good morning," Cooper said in a quiet voice. But, even to his own ears, the simple greeting sounded stilted and formal.

"Hi," she answered.

Her voice was quiet and light, but the tone and monosyllable response created a distance between them. He wondered how he was going to bridge it.

"ET was really cute. He looked handsome in his suit. I can't believe how brave he was," she said. Her voice sounded strained to her own ears.

"I'm glad you could make it, Michaela."

Finally she turned around. Her unusual eyes seemed especially wide, the gaze direct...and wounded.

"How could you think I wouldn't? Of course I came,

Cooper. Because of ET. And because of you." Her voice wobbled. "You were—" she struggled for the word "—inspiring." She swallowed and rushed on. "Why couldn't you tell me sooner that you're a pastor? I feel like a fool for not knowing, just so you can look wonderful."

Her honesty tore at him. But so did the warning from the reverend weeks ago when he'd first mentioned Michaela, and he'd revealed his quickly developing feelings for her.

"I wanted you to get to know me before you found out what I do here. I didn't want my involvement with the church to influence how you might think or feel."

She took a step forward, shaking her head helplessly. "Of course it would influence me. I don't understand how you could think it was better not to say something. Right now I'm so confused. I don't know who you are. You ride a motorcycle! You wear construction boots and pour cement. I feel like I've been coming on to you and throwing myself at you all summer, and now I feel embarrassed. I practically asked you to sleep with me, for God's sake!"

Michaela covered her mouth, shocked at what she'd just said. Slowly she put her hand down. Her eyes began to sparkle with moisture.

Cooper flinched at her accusations.

"You didn't do anything wrong. Your feelings were natural and real. That's exactly what I wanted from you. I thought we were getting to know each other like any other normal man and woman."

"That's not how I feel at this moment. I'm ashamed by some of my behavior. And I'm really angry, Cooper, that I feel ashamed. What you did wasn't fair. There wasn't an even playing field. What were you thinking?"

"That I liked you. I knew it right away, and I wasn't prepared. Then I saw firsthand how caring you are, especially with ET. Fierce and protective. I was very attracted to you, and it started with that first motorcycle ride. But I wanted it to mean something."

"You knew from the beginning I'm only here for the summer. I'm not staying."

Cooper also took a step forward to be closer to her. He could feel her agitation, as if at any moment she would take flight, out of reach. He was glad that they were in Reverend Wallace's office, selfishly hoping that the sanctity of it would help to control their emotions. On the other hand, it was a definite obstacle to his desire to take Michaela into his arms and disprove some of her myths and her fears.

"I never saw that as a reason to hold back how I felt. For the first time in my life, I wanted to do this the right way, for the right reasons. You're the first woman in a very long time who makes me believe it's possible. Do you understand what I'm trying to say? I wasn't looking to score. I didn't want to play you. I don't want instant gratification. I want something solid, Michaela."

Her eyes shimmered a yellow light, but now the spark of confusion and anger was fading. In their place, Cooper could see an aching helplessness.

"Why don't you just say it?"

Cooper instantly felt the tingling sensation of sweat on his brow, between his shoulder blades. His painfully earned and hard-won ability to think and reason and make sense completely escaped him just then. And that's the one thing he'd forgotten to take into consideration. The reverend had warned him about that, too.

The heart has its reasons that reason cannot know.

It cannot be controlled.

He swallowed and inhaled deeply. "I think I'm falling in love with you."

She stared back at him, but Cooper couldn't read her expression, or the unblinking probing of her gaze. What he could see was the rapid pulse at the side of her neck, and the flaring of her nostrils. Her mouth showed just a hint of dusty-rose gloss but the rest had been gnawed off as, even now, her lips and chin trembled with emotions held in check. Almost imperceptibly, she shook her head.

"Relationships are two-way streets, Cooper. You can't test the waters to see if it's safe to go in, and then wade only to your ankles. Where's the risk you talked about? To love as if your heart had never been broken."

"I said I was working on it. I'm taking that risk right now."

Michaela briefly closed her eyes, and her shoulders slumped. "I know. But you got it wrong. I should have been in on the plan, especially because of this." She lifted her arms and glanced quickly around. "I took the bigger risk, because I went totally on blind faith."

"You're right," Cooper admitted, standing tall in the face of her pain and her truth. "I'm pretty new to playing by the rules. It's a long story, but it's what brought me here to Memphis and to this church. Both saved my life."

A slight smile played at the corner of her mouth. "I'm glad for you, Cooper. I'm serious. But you haven't left any room for me. I think that you…"

The door opened slowly and Cooper turned to see who was about to enter. ET cautiously stuck his head around the door.

"Hey, man. Reverend Wallace told me where to find you. Hi," he said, lifting his hand in greeting when he spotted Michaela.

"I didn't forget about you," Cooper assured the boy.

"It's my fault, I'm afraid," Michaela said. She walked past Cooper and placed her hand on ET's shoulder. "You probably won't like this, but I can't help myself."

She placed a light kiss on his forehead.

"Wow," he said, looking a little embarrassed but also pleased. "How come you do that?"

"You mean, how come I did that? Because you were really great this morning."

Cooper could see that Michaela was not going to give him a chance to say anything more, and with ET's sudden appearance, their time together was over.

"ET and I are going out for some breakfast. I'd love for you to join us," he said pointedly. But already she was shaking her head and inching toward the door.

"Thank you, but I don't think so. You guys go and have fun."

"Then I'll see you another time," Cooper said, trying desperately to get her attention.

"We'll see," she responded with a vague smile.

"We going on Smith's bike."

Michaela looked at him once more and Cooper could only hope that his eyes held what he was feeling in his heart.

"See? Doesn't sound like there's any room for me."

* * *

Michaela hurried down the carpeted corridor toward the exit. She had no idea where it would lead her but she had to get out of the church as quickly as possible. But tears were already beginning to spill as she pushed through the door with the crash bar and out into the overcast Sunday morning. There was no one else around and only three cars still parked...and Cooper's bike, which had been hidden from sight earlier in the crowded lot.

The flow of tears really began in earnest when she considered that, if it rained, Cooper and ET would get wet riding on the open bike.

She felt something grab her arm. She gasped and pulled away, only to find herself face-to-face with the anxious and concerned countenance of Reverend Wallace.

"Is everything all right?"

His voice was all solicitous and gentle. She couldn't talk, but swallowed. Michaela silently nodded. And then she shook her head. He took her arm.

"Now, you come with me..."

Michaela allowed herself to be led, since she couldn't even see clearly where she was walking. She was annoyed and embarrassed by her total lack of control. And she couldn't even take comfort in blaming Cooper.

How wicked would it be to blame a servant of God for leaving her in a state of misery and longing?

The reverend opened a door and hurried her inside. It was a classroom, its child-size chairs in a semicircle from a recent Sunday-school session.

"Sit down," the reverend instructed her.

Michaela did as she was told, digging in her purse

for tissues. Reverend Wallace silently waited her out until she'd calmed down.

"I'm sorry," Michaela whispered.

"I don't think you're the one who should be apologizing," he said sadly with a shake of his head. "I promised myself I wouldn't be drawn into this, but I think my nephew is still learning his way around trusting what he feels in his heart."

Michaela stared at him. "Your nephew? Cooper is your nephew?"

The reverend silently nodded, while paternally patting her arm as if suspecting she was about to bolt, again, at this latest news.

"How could he do this? Why me? I thought Cooper…"

"Yes, yes, my dear. He is everything you believe him to be in your own heart, and much more I'm proud to say. But what you've been seeing and experiencing is the new Cooper. Believe me, he's come a long way from the old one. He's been through a lot, and it's changed him quite a bit. And, like all of us, he still makes mistakes."

Michaela stared at him, puzzled. "Reverend Wallace, I'm afraid to admit it but I'm…"

"Dazed and confused."

Michaela couldn't help but laugh at his use of the popular sound bite. She felt relief at being able to. It was like opening a valve that released bottled-up tension inside herself.

"Yes, that's it exactly. I don't know anything about 'the old Cooper,' as you say. What kind of man was he?"

He sighed. "Unfortunately, I don't think it's my place to explain Cooper to you. I will only say that he's very talented and very smart. He's capable of good things. I was hoping that by now he would have opened up to you. I can tell by the state you're in that you're still in the dark."

"I am. But he did admit how he's feeling about me."

"Good. Take him at his word, Michaela. If it's any consolation to you, you've given him a couple of sleepless nights as well. Trust your own sense of what kind of man Cooper is. I promise you, you won't be disappointed.

"Now, that's really all I can say. I pulled you in here to give you some time to calm down."

Michaela stopped him from getting up, reaching out to take the reverend's hand.

"Please. I have to know something. He's not married...is he?"

"Oh, no, child. But he once was."

Michaela swallowed. "Does he have any children of his own?"

Reverend Wallace pursed his lips and shook his head, and then answered in a profoundly sad voice.

"But...he once did."

Chapter 10

"Are you sure it's okay?" Michaela asked anxiously into the phone.

"Honey, I trust you, you know that. But are you sure you can handle this boy? I know you want to help him, but there's not much you can do in the time you have left in Memphis."

"I know, Aunt Alice. But I think a permanent home may have been found for him before I go. It's just that, with paperwork and the city and state child welfare agencies involved, there's a gap of about ten days when he'll have no place to live."

"Well, okay then. Now, how did you say you met him again?"

"Er...well, actually Jefferson and I found him together. Eugene was sick and we, er, got him medical attention. I've been sort of following his case ever since."

"And you're sure he's not dangerous or anything like that? I don't want to see you hurt. And Jefferson knows what your uncle Ben will do if that happens!"

Michaela grimaced. At this point she knew the chances were slim and none that she had to be concerned about ET's behavior. She was, however, ever mindful of the issues that remained open-ended with Cooper. Jefferson had become a nonissue.

"I'm sure. I wouldn't ask to bring him into your home if I didn't believe he was not a threat. And there are other people to vouch for him. His mentor is a pastor at a church here."

"Is that right? Who is he? I wonder if I know him."

"Cooper Townsend," she said with as much nonchalance as she could manage.

She then waited for the wellspring of emotion that seemed invariably waiting just below the surface. She only had to think of Cooper, let alone mention his name, and she was overcome with longing, and a lingering sense of vulnerability by his deception. It did no good for her to recognize that Cooper's behavior was not the least bit malicious. She still felt wounded and bewildered. A little fantasy that she'd concocted had withered away.

"No, I don't think I know who that is. Anyway, go ahead and do what you think is best. I'll tell Ben all about it. But don't you hesitate to call me back if anything happens, you hear?"

"Yes, ma'am," Michaela uttered dutifully. She didn't realize how she'd responded until her godmother suddenly started laughing.

"I'm going to make you a proper Southern lady, yet."

When Michaela got off the phone, she was instantly overcome with a malaise that she'd been experiencing since attending church service a few days earlier. She was relieved that Cooper had not tried to reach her, because she had no idea how she would react if he had. Slamming down the phone in his ear had been a possibility Sunday evening. But somehow that didn't seem appropriate anymore, or Christian. Therein lay her dilemma.

How could she dare to be angry at a man who was all about spreading the word of love and forgiveness? Who consistently thought of others before himself?

How could she not, if he'd forgotten to include her in that consideration?

Michaela sighed, silently assuring herself that it was going to be all right. Everything was to a purpose…that's what Reverend Wallace had told her, and it was what she was raised to believe. It was what had allowed her to find the strength to break off a relationship that wasn't working for her, and that didn't have the kind of love she wanted to receive or wanted to express. No matter the outcome with Cooper, he'd said something she never thought she'd hear again. He was falling in love with her. She wasn't beyond hope after all.

But was it real? Was the span of hot summer days and nights enough time to know? How long did falling in love take, anyway?

Michaela began dialing another number into the phone. After a minute, she heard Marilyn Caldwell answer.

"Hi, Marilyn. This is Michaela. Things seem to be moving ahead with no problems. I have permission from my godparents to let Eugene Terrance Dunne stay here

with me for the next week or so, until things get straightened out with his new foster family…no need to thank
me. I'm glad I thought of it…I think someone from the
Children's Aid Society is coming tomorrow morning to
check me out, and the house. I understand they want to
make sure Eugene is going into a safe situation…yes, I
believe Cooper knows all about the arrangement. As a
matter of fact, if everything goes well in the morning, I
was told that he'll bring Eugene here later in the afternoon…yes, it is very good of him, and I'm not surprised,
either. I know he has great belief in the boy's potential.
Me, too…anyway, I wanted to find out about Eugene's
medication schedule. What he's supposed to take and
when. Is he still seeing a counselor at St. Jude…? I'll
make sure he keeps his appointments… It's no trouble.
I can drive in today, if you have time to see me, and I can
pick up all the information I'll need… No, I haven't
spoken to Cooper recently, but if everything is arranged
I guess I'll see them tomorrow. Thanks, Marilyn."

By the next afternoon, all the details were finalized
to the satisfaction of the city and Marilyn Caldwell, rep-
resenting St. Jude. Now, Michaela stood near the door,
occasionally peering through the side window to see
when the black van would arrive bringing ET and his
belongings. And, of course, Cooper.

She was only mildly concerned with how she and ET
would manage together for almost two weeks. Michaela
was far more nervous about how she and Cooper would
react to one another.

She'd played out a dozen scenarios in her head, prac-
ticing her dialogue and her attitude. She'd be calm and
aloof. She'd be polite but noncommittal. She'd be

gracious and thank Cooper for helping with the arrangements, and for trusting that she and ET would be fine together. That's it.

But Michaela knew she was kidding herself. She was dying to hear the full story behind Cooper "Smith" Townsend and his redemption in the city of Memphis. She wanted to know if Reverend Wallace was the person he'd run to, or if Southern hospitality, waddling ducks or Elvis had anything to do with it.

Blaspheme!

Michaela seriously doubted if Elvis had anything to do with saving Cooper's soul. But something had brought him here...she wanted to know what, and why.

Her stomach knotted and curled when she finally spotted the black Building Blocks van still some distance away, as it slowly drove along the entrance road and turned onto the street in front of the house. She hurried back into the kitchen so she wouldn't appear to have been standing right behind the front door, waiting. Five minutes later, the bell rang. She took her time walking to the door while every nerve in her body seemed to be on overload.

When Michaela opened the door, she deliberately let her gaze target ET and gave him a big, warm smile.

"You made it. I'm glad you're here."

"Hi," ET mumbled.

She realized that he was nervous as well. Perhaps he understood as she did, Michaela guessed, that this new arrangement changed all the rules. Like herself, he probably also had no idea what to expect. And she would have to take the lead. She was the grown-up. More or less.

"Well, come on in. I want to show you around and let you get settled in."

ET, practically dragging his feet, walked past her into the house. Michaela bravely turned a more aloof smile on Cooper. But the intense look in his eyes promptly caused her entire system to crash. Her smile wavered and she blinked rapidly, feeling disoriented.

In his dark, measured gaze, she imagined she saw his own uncertainty. Maybe even contrition. And yet, Cooper managed, without effort, to look so incredibly manly and in charge. He certainly didn't seem to be a man who had a doubt in the world. But there it was, nakedly displayed in his eyes. Maybe, for her eyes only.

He wanted her forgiveness.

"Hi, Cooper," she murmured, proud that her voice at least sounded firm.

"It's good to see you," he said with a brief nod, his gaze holding hers.

The betrayal of her twitching nerves again alerted Michaela to his sincerity. But she held out.

"Is it?"

"It is." He cleared his throat and pulled it together. "Seems like all I've done since we met is thank you. For all you've done, and continued to do for ET. For being kind and generous…and trusting me…"

"Stop." She laughed and fidgeted self-consciously. "I have a long and sordid past. Getting into heaven is not yet guaranteed."

He chortled silently. "If it was up to me… Well, anyway. I hope you realize the significance of what you're doing."

"I've gotten permission from my godparents. They don't mind. They understand this is temporary."

"I'll remember to have ET personally thank them."

"They'll appreciate that. Eh…are you staying for a while?"

Cooper shook his head. He pushed his hands into the front pockets of his black jeans and took a step back. "I don't think so. You and ET need some time to get comfortable together. You don't need me watching over your shoulders."

"Thank you."

"But I would like to see you sometime. Soon, Michaela. I owe you an explanation, and an apology. Reverend Wallace said my people skills need improving. My relationship skills, to be exact," he said, shyly rubbing his chin and looking down at his feet.

"You mean, your uncle, Reverend Wallace?"

Cooper's head shot up. "He told you?"

"Only that. He said the rest was up to you. And I disagree with him. There's nothing wrong with your people skills, Cooper. You just forgot to take your own advice."

"Which is?"

"Not to be afraid to risk everything. I think that's how you know you're alive. You feel things but, whatever the sensation, it isn't going to kill you."

He thoughtfully shook his head, for the first time the light in his eyes showing a spark of awareness and humor.

"When can I see you?"

The low rumble of his voice sent a curl of tension up her spine. "Well…can you make it for dinner tomorrow? The night after?"

"There's a wedding rehearsal at the church tomorrow I'm covering for the reverend. How about the next night?"

"I'll be here."

"Seven okay?"

She nodded. "Seven is fine."

Cooper suddenly stretched out his arm to her, his hand waiting to take hers. Michaela held it out to him and he engulfed hers in a grip that was firm and solid, but not crushing. He held her fast, and it felt like he didn't want to let go. Michaela again silently exchanged a look with him. She wondered if her eyes told as much as his seemed to. He gently squeezed her fingers and then released her.

"'Night." He turned and headed back to his van.

"'Night," she said quietly to his retreating back.

Michaela stepped back inside and closed the door. She didn't realize until that instant how tightly she'd been controlling herself. But now she exhaled a sigh of relief.

Then she quickly whirled around. Where was ET? She started toward the kitchen, but then caught sight of him in the living room. He was sprawled in a recliner watching Lady, who was sitting sphinxlike on the coffee table only mildly interested in his presence.

"You're not afraid of cats, are you?"

He shrugged. "I never been 'round no cat before. People say they sneaky."

Michaela walked casually into the room. "They're not sneaky, just smarter than we are."

ET chuckled. He slowly held his hand out to Lady, way above her head so he could snatch it back quickly in the event of a sneaky attack. Lady lifted her head in curiosity and sniffed at his fingers.

"She not going to bite or anything, right?"

"No. Actually, she's pretty friendly. She's not afraid of strangers."

Michaela stood back watching the scene as it unfolded. She understood Lady well enough by now to anticipate just what might happen next. But she wanted ET to discover for himself that the cat meant him no harm. All she really wanted was someone to scratch her in her favorite places. Cooper had it down cold the first time they'd been introduced.

Lady meowed quietly, came to her feet and stretched in a great arching of her back.

"Whoa…" ET said, not sure what was about to happen.

"It's okay. Sit still and watch."

Lady, calculating the distance between her perch and ET, poised, set herself and, with a gentle leap, landed on the arm of the recliner. The cat began to sniff at ET's arm, his shirt and the scent of him that she could detect in the air.

"What she doing that for?"

"Making sure you're no danger to her. She's deciding if she likes your smell or not."

Lady then stepped off the arm of the chair and onto ET's lap. He shifted, again not sure what to expect.

"Sit still," Michaela suggested again quietly. Lady made a half circle and plunked herself down comfortably on the boy's lap.

ET was grinning from ear to ear. "She likes me, right?"

"Yes, I think you pass. Remember, she's a small animal. Be gentle with her. She's already met Smith and really likes him."

"Yeah? Then I'm cool."

After a few minutes of indoctrination to cats in general and Lady in particular, Michaela asked ET if he'd like to see his room and the rest of the house. She shooed Lady from ET's lap so he could get up. But it was clear to her that he was completely taken with the cat. And Michaela was deeply touched by his reaction. It was heartbreaking to see how little affection he'd received, or never been taught how to give, in his short life.

ET walked through the house like he was afraid to touch anything. He said nothing until they reached the second floor and she opened the door to a room at the end of the hall.

"This room was used by my godmother's son. He's grown now and married. The bed has fresh linens, and there are plenty of hangers in the closet. Or you can use the dresser."

While she talked, Michaela watched as ET slowly looked around the room, tested the bed, checked out the closet and turned to face her.

"You mean, I'm going to be in here by myself?"

She nodded, grinning at his expression. "Yes. You're not afraid to be alone, are you?"

He shook his head. He shrugged. "I never had a room all to myself before. Can I use the TV?"

"Of course you can. I think that's a DVD player on top. As long as you're here, this is your room. I expect you to take care of it."

"Oh, man," he said, as if he couldn't believe it.

"And there are some house rules."

He frowned, now alert. "House rules?"

"Yes. No smoking. You make your own bed in the morning. You have chores to do, like put out the garbage and make sure the doors are locked at night. The bathroom next door is for your use, but you have to keep it clean."

He looked at her with raised brows. "That all?"

"No. While you're here I expect you to do exactly what the St. Jude doctors told you to do so you don't get sick. That means taking your medicine when you're supposed to. I'll make sure you get to any appointments. I want you to start learning about what HIV is and how it might affect you. So, the next time we go to see the doctors or counselors, they're going to give you stuff to read…"

"That's too much work," he fussed.

"You're going to meet other kids who have what you have. And there'll be no sleeping late in the morning, or going to bed late at night. Lights out at eleven. And I'm giving you an extra hour because it's summer."

"Oh, man…"

"But maybe you'd rather not stay here. If you want, I can call Smith to come and get you. He can take you back to the agency. They might be able to find you another home for the night."

He looked stubborn and aggrieved. He sat on the side of the bed, shaking his head.

"It's up to you, ET."

"All them rules. That's cold."

"While you think about it, I'll go make us some dinner." She turned to leave the room. She only got as far as the door.

"Miss Landry? There's no place else for me to go. Nobody else wants me. Can I stay? I'll do everything you want."

"Are you sure?"

"I get my own room. And a TV. I guess the rest ain't so bad."

"Isn't so bad."

"Yeah."

"One more thing. There are lots of books in the family room. I want you to find one to read while you're here. The whole thing."

He groaned. She laughed.

"I'll be down in the kitchen. Go ahead and unpack your things. Where are your bags?" she asked, looking around.

"That's it right there." He pointed.

Michaela saw two shopping bags, haphazardly stuffed with clothing. A third had at least a dozen amber bottles of pills, as well as the things she'd given him on her visit at St. Jude. It was dispiriting to see that the entire fifteen years of his life could fit into three grocery bags.

"Come down when you're done," Michaela said quietly, walking out of his room.

There wasn't much for Cooper to do once he'd arrived for dinner with Michaela and ET. That was fine with him. It had given him time to organize his thoughts, and to try to conquer his fears. The reverend had once told him that, with God on his side, he had nothing to fear. But Cooper had learned that sometimes fear served a very good purpose. It forced him to be honest with himself and sort out his feelings.

His offers to help had been brushed aside while Michaela tried to prove her multitasking skills. But one incident too many…Lady getting sick and upchucking a hairball in the downstairs bathroom…had promptly ended her reign as "Queen of the Kitchen." He had been asked to clean up the mess, and ET was assigned the task of setting the table. It was a complex arrangement of glasses, plates and flatware the boy was still trying to get his mind around with his what-difference-does-it-make attitude.

It had been insightful and sometimes downright funny to bare witness to the interplay between Michaela and the boy. In just two days they'd fallen into a routine of sorts, a tango dance around each other. He was amazed at ET's attempts to manipulate and play on Michaela's goodwill, and her equally strong will and more successful outsmarting of him. But what really made Cooper sit up with renewed respect and profound admiration and affection for Michaela was that never once did she belittle ET, yell at him, or use her adult authority to gain points. If anything, Cooper could see that she sometimes struggled to be fair and even-handed, not wanting to push him too hard, but making it clear that she was in charge. ET was, after all, a teenager, adept at trying to play on her feelings. And losing.

It was a game of duke and bluff between them. Cooper grimaced to himself when he recalled he'd taught it to ET himself. It was meant to be used as a weapon against an opponent in the game of chess. Not against someone genuinely concerned about his welfare and not trying to do him in. Cooper admitted it had taken him a while to realize that Michaela and ET were somewhat evenly matched. More than that, they both seemed to enjoy challenging each other.

He was impressed...and relieved.

Whatever invisible caution signs he'd unknowingly

erected to prevent crashing and burning again as he'd grown comfortable with his feelings for Michaela, vanished almost the moment she'd opened the door to him. He'd barely had time to say hi before she'd beckoned him in, and then fled back to the kitchen. Something about her raisin sauce for the ham was over-cooked. No pretense there.

Cooper decided that any woman who could make him laugh automatically went to the top of the list. It had been too long since he'd felt so positive, so deeply about someone. But with Michaela it was already way past that.

He frowned thoughtfully, wondering when it was he knew he was in love with her. Had it been at St. Jude's when she'd come to find out about ET? Or watching her chat so openly with Pete, in the back of Miss Faye's? Or had it been at church when he'd seen the shocked and disappointed look in her eyes because he'd not been completely open with her, and that he might lose her because of it?

Dinner was over, and that had been the easy part. From his position at the dishwasher, he glanced over his shoulder to where Michaela stood preparing coffee. Lady was crunching away on the dry food in her dish, recently filled by ET. It was one of the chores that Michaela had given him that, by her own admission, ET was taking very seriously. At the moment, the subject of their attention was rattling around outside the house, putting out the garbage. Cooper realized it was the first real moment he'd had alone with Michaela, but still not the right moment for what needed to be said.

After pouring in detergent, Cooper closed and locked the dishwasher door and turned it on. He leaned back against the counter, watching Michaela measure out scoops of ground coffee, add water and turn on the coffeemaker. He sighed, feeling content and peaceful. The domesticity of the moment seemed surreal. It was just this kind of moment, this scene, that he'd been trying to achieve without a clear idea of how. Now it was clear and, of course, made sense. You first begin with someone you want to spend time with.

"How's it going?" he asked.

He could see by her expression that Michaela knew exactly what he was referring to. "Not bad. Exhausting. You know, I taught high school for several years. I forgot how much teenagers get on your nerves. But I also remember how incredibly wise and smart they can be. That's what I'm trying to keep in mind when ET starts to push my buttons. That, and the fact that he's been through a lot. For the most part, it's interesting having him here."

Cooper smiled. "Want me to have a talk with him?"

"No," she responded emphatically. "I can handle ET. He's a good kid, but he believes the only way to get what he wants is to disregard rules. I want to change his way of thinking."

"Oh. Teenager 101. How To Build A Better One In Ten Days." She laughed. "Let me know if he gets out of hand."

She shook her head. "I want you to stay out of it. You're the big-brother figure in his life and that's a different relationship." She took two mugs out of the cabinet and set them next to the coffeemaker.

"What does that make you?"

"The interested teacher, maybe. Or just that crazy lady from D.C."

Cooper laughed lightly and shook his head. "Why not a big sister? Better still, how about a stand-in mother?"

He was surprised at what seemed like a sad and pensive reflection in her eyes.

"I don't think so. I'm here just a few more weeks. It wouldn't be fair to set myself up that way and then leave. Don't you see? For ET, adults are always leaving him or letting him go. Now that he knows he's HIV positive, it might not get any better. I just want him to have this time being a kid, and feeling safe."

"If I haven't already said so, Michaela, I think you're amazing."

"Thanks. It's nice of you to say that."

They stood just a few feet apart and, for a long moment, just silently appraised one another. He had the feeling that, even unintentionally, she might have been sending a message to him as well. He hoped she had forgiven him his trespasses. While it was true that since his arrival she'd been warm and gracious, he hoped he would be given some of the leeway she'd so willingly given to the boy. Could he and Michaela pick up where they'd left off before it had all blown up in his face, or would he have to start all over? Cooper hoped not. It would take too long. She was going home in three weeks.

The kitchen door to the backyard burst open and ET came in. The spell was broken between them. Without missing a beat, Michaela turned her attention to ET.

"Did you remember to latch the top of the garbage bins?"

"Yeah. I found a block of wood and put that on top of it, too."

"Smart thinking." Cooper nodded his approval.

"I'm gonna watch some TV," ET announced, heading toward the stairs.

"How's the book going?"

He moaned. "Man, it's boring. Why can't I watch a TV show and then tell you what it's about?"

"I don't consider *Survivor* to be educational and it won't help your vocabulary. Pick another book. Or do you want me to?"

"That's okay. I'll find something. But can I do it tomorrow?"

"First thing in the morning. Before you have breakfast."

Again bemoaning his fate, ET started shuffling off in the direction of the staircase.

Cooper chuckled to himself. While ET protested and complained, what he didn't hear was a refusal to do what Michaela had asked.

"Thanks for helping tonight," she called after him.

"You're welcome," ET said.

Cooper raised his brows and gave Michaela a silent, surprised look. She merely grinned.

ET stopped and turned back. "Miss Landry, can I get some more cake?"

"Yes, but eat it down here at the table. Crumbs all over the place lead to insects."

"Yes, ma'am."

Cooper moved away from the sink to watch as Michaela took a dessert plate from a cabinet near him, handed it to ET, and they both watched as he carefully cut himself some of the lemon pound cake she'd made for dinner. He wrapped the rest and sponged away any counter crumbs. ET then sat at the table, quickly scoffing the cake down. Cooper followed Michaela's instructions to get the cream from the refrigerator, while she got spoons and the sugar for their coffee.

When ET was finished, he placed the plate in the sink. But before reaching the stairwell, he did an abrupt about-face and returned to the sink to hand-wash the plate and leave it in the drain board. Then he left again, taking the steps, rather noisily, two at a time.

Cooper and Michaela exchanged looks and quietly chuckled. The coffee now ready, she filled the two mugs.

"I'm impressed."

"When my sister and I were kids, my mother used to say our antics would drive her to drink. We thought it was funny, but now I get it."

"Does that mean you're not interested in having kids?"

She wiped at an imaginary spot on the counter. "I don't know if I've ever had a serious conversation with myself about it. I enjoyed teaching. My sister's kids are great. I like being around kids. I think I have great empathy for them…"

He slowly nodded. "Yes. I can see that."

"I don't think Spencer cared one way or the other. It was another detail about our future that never came up. Maybe that's what made me uneasy. There was no plan for a real commitment. There's still time. I won't rule it out," Michaela murmured, almost shyly. She glanced at him, her eyes bright, drawing him in. "Reverend Wallace said you were married and had a child. Are you going to tell me what happened?"

Her voice was barely a whisper.

Cooper tensed his jaw muscle and silently nodded. He picked up the two mugs. "Let's sit outside. It's a nice night."

She opened the back door again, and when they stepped out, they elected to sit side by side on the top step facing the yard. It was peaceful and quiet, and Cooper considered that they could be in another place, another time, and the chance to be alone was all about the two of them, except it wasn't. Not yet. There was the past that, somehow, still needed to be dealt with.

He handed one of the mugs to Michaela, but neither of them drank. They sat silently for a long time.

"I don't even know where to begin," Cooper said, feeling very much like he was opening Pandora's box, or at the very least, peeling back the scab of old wounds and history.

And then, unexpectedly, Michaela put her hand on his back and gently, slowly, began to rub up and down. Her hand traveled down to the waist of his jeans and began to pull the shirt free.

Cooper forced himself not to move. He held his breath. Michaela's fingers snaked their way beneath the shirt and right onto his skin, tentatively feeling her way.

"Why don't you start here? I saw the burns by accident the night you stayed for dinner after fixing the fence." Her voice was very low and encouraging.

He involuntarily stiffened, and then relaxed his shoulders and closed his eyes. She'd been aware for all these weeks and never said anything. Never asked… never pulled away or rejected him. Instantly the whole terrible episode played out from his memory. It took a while for him to vanquish the emotions that invariably went along with the memories.

Her fingers were tentative, barely touching him, but not afraid to. He did flinch then, because of a sudden phantom pain that drew him back to a horrible nightmare of fire and death.

"I was in a bad accident about eight years ago. It was a crash on a service road just outside the Chicago city limits. I was in one car. My wife…and my daughter were in the second car. She was trying to get away from me, with good cause, I should add," he admitted, his voice gravelly. "She was taking our daughter with her and I was trying to stop her. We'd had a showdown, a big fight just before. It wasn't the first time, but it was about the same thing."

Cooper couldn't bring himself to say that it was his unfaithfulness that caused the fight. That was another story for another time. It was not a part of his past life that he was particularly proud of. All the while Michaela's hand explored farther, with curiosity, but also with a tenderness that literally made him weak in the knees.

He had to stop talking. He began to feel very hot. A fine sweat was beading on his forehead but he didn't bother wiping it away. His skin was on fire…or maybe it only felt that way.

"I killed them," he said baldly.

Michaela's caressing faltered but she maintained contact.

"Oh, Cooper…no," she moaned in sympathy.

"It was an accident, but it was all my fault. They're both dead because of my arrogance and stupidity."

"And you've been beating yourself up about it ever since. You survived. You get a second chance."

It was a simple statement, but had an instant, odd effect on him. Having survived had always made him felt guilty, and wrenching remorse for the awful loss of his child. All because of his ego and selfishness.

My little girl...

There was never going to be enough he could do to live that down and make it right.

My baby...

"I didn't exactly survive." He looked at Michaela, his eyes reflecting the same puzzlement he'd experienced back then. "The way the crash happened, the fire after, I shouldn't have survived. But I was saved."

"You mean, EMS got to you and pulled you free?"

Cooper closed his eyes. He'd done this a thousand times before. Try to see clearly how he'd gotten out of the crushed, burning car.

"No, Michaela. This was before the police or fire trucks or EMS even got to the scene. The crash was really bad. Very violent. My wife lost control of her car. It fishtailed and spun, and flipped over. I plowed into a truck trying to avoid running right into her. I was dazed, trying to stay conscious. At first I heard my wife screaming. Then she stopped. I never heard my daughter cry. Nothing. I knew they had to be hurt bad, and I had to get to them. But I couldn't move, and I hurt all over."

Michaela sat stock-still and he wondered what she was thinking. Did she understand he'd behaved like a fool? Would she think less of him?

"There was a point when I knew I was going to die. I couldn't get out of my seat belt. The car was on fire. I was on fire. My clothes felt like they were melting on my body."

"Cooper," she murmured. Her tone mirrored the agony he was recalling.

She removed her hand from his back and placed her hand on his thigh, patting him. Cooper grabbed at Michaela's offering as if it was a lifeline. He threaded their fingers together, grateful and comforted.

"Then, how did you get out of the burning car?"

He shook his head, frowning. "I don't know for sure. All of a sudden I heard someone say my name, loud and clear. I think I was nearly unconscious, and now I was alert. I'd stopped trying to get my seat belt off. I figured, this is it. Game over. Then this man was leaning in the window, staring at me. I couldn't see his face through the smoke, but I remember feeling calm. And I stopped feeling any pain. There was a sense that everything was under control. He said, 'I'll get you out,' and he opened my door. He just opened it!

"I said, 'my wife, my daughter.' He sort of smiled and said, 'They're going to be fine. They're being taken away right now. They're not suffering.'"

Cooper stopped. He suddenly felt overwhelmed as he relived those moments. He'd been so relieved that they were okay.

"The next thing I knew I was lying on the ground away from the car. I don't remember how I got there. The stranger was standing over me. I still couldn't make out his face. I said something like thank you for saving my life. And he said, 'You will thank me by saving others.' Then, he walked away. I tried to call him back, to get his name. I sat up, but he was gone. Just like that. I couldn't see him anywhere. Then I heard the sirens, and other drivers and bystanders were trying to help me. I passed out."

"*'You will thank me by saving others,'*" Michaela repeated softly. She looked at his profile. "I thought you said your wife and daughter died."

"That's right, they did. I didn't know that until a little while later. When I came to, I was strapped to a gurney in the back of an ambulance with an oxygen mask on my face. I remember pulling it off and calling out for them. One of the EMS workers had to hold me down. I felt the pain again. I asked to see my wife and child and he told me it was too late. They died before help could arrive."

"I'm so sorry."

He shook his head. "I don't deserve sympathy, Michaela."

She said nothing to that, and they both fell silent. It was the second time he'd purged himself to someone and he was glad he'd told the whole story to her. The first time had been to his uncle, who'd flown to Chicago to visit him while he was recovering. It was getting easier. But he knew he would live the rest of his life with "what ifs."

"What do you think happened?"

He silently shook his head.

"Do you believe in miracles?" Michaela quietly asked.

Cooper considered the question for a moment. "I'm not sure. I want to. I think about what that man, that stranger, said to me about my wife and daughter. He said that they weren't suffering. Finding out they'd died, I asked myself, was he just trying to comfort me, or was there another message? I only know I'm alive today because of something that happened that I can't explain. It doesn't even make sense, except that I believe what I went through was for a reason. The person I am today is because of that accident and how I survived it. I've heard other people say the same thing. They're forever changed.

"Eugene Terrance is going to be a different kind of man because of what he's going through now. I think that, against all odds, he's going to have a long life."

"'You learn and you learn and you say goodbye...'" Michaela quoted back to him.

Their heads were close together. It would have been easy, and natural, for him to press his lips against her temple or her cheek. But he didn't.

"What I hope I've learned is we're all in this together. We are connected. At the end of church service the reverend always tells us to love one another as we would love the Lord. That's how you worship. That's how you praise Him. But I lost my family and my pride before I got it."

"Is that why you became a minister?"

He chuckled silently. "I'm not a minister. I didn't go to seminary and I don't have a degree in theology. I don't have that kind of calling. I'm a pastor. I volunteer to be part of the church, to teach, to help officiate where I can. I don't think I'm good enough to be like my uncle."

"I bet he would disagree."

"Maybe. I'm grateful for what I can do. But I have a long way to go."

"Are you happy?"

He chuckled again, a little puzzled, and tried to see her face in the dark. Purposely or not, she had hit on just the thing he'd been doing, even inadvertently, to make happiness possible. Holding back. Was he still afraid to take a giant leap of faith off the precipice without knowing if there was a safety net below? Michaela was right. He had been given a second chance when his life was saved. Dare he ask for anything more?

"I think so. What I'd like is another chance to love someone. Maybe have a family again."

Michaela was still for a moment, and then began to withdraw her hand. He didn't attempt to hold her, but he wasn't sure how to interpret her reaction.

"I'm confused about one thing," she said, cutting him a curious glance. "What's with the motorcycle?"

He pursed his lips, surprised that she'd picked up on the one thing in his current life that probably seemed out of place. He shrugged sheepishly.

"Maybe I'm pushing my luck, living a little on the edge. It's a way for me to remember I'm not invincible. I have to learn to be careful for myself and other people. You and Eugene Terrance are the only passengers I've had. I feel free on my bike. It's just me and…"

"I get it," she murmured.

With a sigh, she stood up, taking the mug of completely cold coffee from his hand. "Let's go in. I'll zap these in the microwave."

Cooper stood as well, took the mugs back and placed them on the steps. He looked Michaela right in the eyes.

"Are you still angry with me?"

She became flustered. "No, I… What makes you say that?"

"I should have been open about my connection to the church and to Reverend Wallace."

"I don't understand why you weren't, Cooper."

"Because I wanted you to respond to me, not to what

I do." He slowly took her hands and pulled her a step closer. She resisted, and then gave in. "Because of the way you and I met there was no pretense, no act. No time to do a pedigree or background check. You were just yourself and I liked that, Michaela. I liked that a lot."

She shook her head, not looking at him directly. "That's fine for you to say. There is a big part of who you are that I knew nothing about."

"I know." He nodded, feeling contrite and frustrated.

Michaela stared into his eyes, holding his attention. "There's something else, Cooper. I feel like I'm not good enough. I'm not going to measure up to…to what you expect, or want, or need. I'm afraid to even touch you because that's like…like coming on to you, tempting you. I could burn in hell for that."

"Michaela, you just did…" He fought the urge to laugh again.

She placed her fingertips lightly on his lips to silence him.

"Listen to me because it's important. I think your faith is so beautiful. It's very moving. But I don't think I'm there. I have a lot of questions and a lot of doubts. You're sure about everything…"

He chortled, quietly and affectionately, at her wild assumption.

"I wasn't trying to be funny, but you're a believer. I shoot from the lips and then have to deal with the fallout."

He pulled her hand away and forced her even close. "Michaela, shhhhhh. I want to ask you something." She looked at him trustingly. That was good. "Do you like me?"

"That's my problem. I like you very much. More than very much. But…what are you supposed to think of a woman who lusts after you? You're the pastor of a church."

Cooper felt some of his tension dissolve. It wasn't nearly as bad as he'd thought. He wanted to grab Michaela and demonstrate how faulty her thinking was. But he had a lot to atone for as well. He had no idea if their relationship might have been easier if he'd been up-front from the beginning. But it might have been different…and not as much fun.

"Pastors meet women, fall in love, marry…the whole nine yards. God knew what He was doing when He invented physical attraction." Cooper took her by the arms, made sure she was paying attention. "You're right, I wasn't fair. I let you know how I felt. But I let you take the lead. I made the decision, when I came to Memphis, that when and if I found someone I cared about, someone I really wanted to be part of my life, that it had to happen the old-fashioned way. Sex is easy. It's relationships that are hard. I want real intimacy. The kind that takes a lifetime to build."

"Cooper…I go home in a few weeks. Back to D.C.," she whispered poignantly.

He brushed the back of his hand against her cheek, smiled into her eyes. "I didn't hear that you're not interested. I didn't hear you say, it can't be with you."

"But I don't see how it's possible to make this work with you and me."

"I have faith that it can. All I want is for both of us to give it a chance. To keep moving forward and let's see where the path leads us. All I ask for now is that you don't use my position with the church as an excuse for not dealing with the real issue. You're as scared as I am."

"You're right," she admitted.

"I'm really glad to hear that. Now we're on the same page."

He bent his head and kissed her. Michaela was tentative but responsive. That's all he wanted for now. Just to know that the spark of their attraction was still alive. He had to coax her but the kiss became more expressive, mobile, deep. Still, he knew when to let it end, when to let his mouth release hers. Looking into her eyes, Cooper could tell she agreed.

He followed her back into the house. He knew that both of them were processing what had been said between them. Had it been a mistake to make a full disclosure? Reverend Wallace had predicted that once the past was no longer a secret, it would no longer have a hold over him. He wanted to believe that. He was ready for absolution.

In the kitchen they both stopped at the muffled but loud sounds coming from the floor above.

"It's the TV in ET's room," Michaela said, putting the mugs down and heading to the stairs.

"That's pretty loud, don't you think? He should know better," Cooper admonished.

"I don't think he can help it," Michaela said with a wry smile.

She beckoned to him and together they went up the stairs and down the hall. The noise of the TV got louder as they approached ET's room. The door was opened slightly.

Michaela knocked quietly before opening the door farther and stepping inside. Cooper was right on her heels.

ET was not watching the TV but was in the bed asleep. Despite the summer heat, he was wrapped in a spread, his eyes and nose the only parts of him exposed. Both lights in the room were turned on. Next to him, curled against his back, Lady lay asleep as well. She didn't even deign to open her eyes when he and Michaela entered. Cooper reached for the remote and lowered the volume, but was surprised when Michaela indicated he should leave the set playing.

She turned out the overhead light but left the desk lamp on. Now gesturing that they should quietly leave, Cooper stepped back out of the room. Michaela left the door open the way she found it.

"What was that all about?" he asked as they returned to the kitchen.

Michaela's eyes were a warm yellow, filled with compassion and gentle amusement.

"I think he's afraid of the dark."

Chapter 11

Michaela heard the voices as she descended the stairs from her room. She recognized ET's voice but not the other. It was a girl's voice. When she reached the kitchen, she found Lady at her food dish. That meant that ET had fed her as had become his responsibility. The voices seemed to be coming from outside the house, and when she walked through the living room into the foyer, she found the front door ajar. Approaching, she realized he was talking to Kimika and Kyla, Jefferson's daughters.

She opened the door wider. ET was standing on the top step to the entrance, and the two girls, on the ground level, were listening as he talked. He sounded boastful.

"Hi, girls," Michaela interrupted with a smile. She looked at ET with raised brows. "I didn't know you all had met. When did that happen?"

"Hi, Miss Landry," the girls said in unison.

"We saw Terry when we were walking back from the east playground the other day," Kimika volunteered.

"Terry?" Michaela asked blankly, glancing at ET. He didn't look at her.

"He was sitting right there reading a book," Kyla said, pointing to the step where she and ET were now standing. "And I said, who are you? And he said his name is Terry and he was staying with you. And I asked him if he was a relative, and he said kind of. I don't understand what that means."

Michaela was aware that ET fidgeted and was avoiding eye contact. She stood next to him.

"Yes, *Terry* is visiting for a week or so. You can say I'm like his...like an aunt."

"Yeah, that's it," ET agreed, sounding relieved.

"So how was your vacation?" Michaela directed to the twins.

"It was fun. I got to sit by the window on the plane coming home," Kimika said.

"I don't care. I watched a movie on my DVD player," Kyla countered.

"I got one of them, too," ET said casually, looking covertly at Michaela.

"Terry said you're going to the planetarium," Kimika said.

"Yes, we are," Michaela said.

"I'm gonna be an astronaut," ET said, boasting again.

Kyla giggled. "You're kind of short to be an astronaut."

"I'm gonna grow. My doctor said I would."

Kimika and Kyla exchanged puzzled looks.

"What doctor?" Kimika asked. "What's wrong with you?"

Michaela could see that ET couldn't and wouldn't

answer, caught off guard by his own comment. He did not easily volunteer his condition and she understood why. She placed her arm lightly around his shoulder. "He means he hasn't finished growing yet. Neither have you girls. As a matter of fact, you might grow taller than, er, Terry because your father is so tall."

"I don't want to be that tall." Kyla grimaced. "Daddy's like a giant."

"Can we come with you?" Kimika asked.

It was now Michaela's turn to be caught off guard by the question. She looked at ET, who looked at her, but it was hard to tell from his expression if he liked the idea or was just so surprised by it.

"Well, it's really up to Terry. He's never been to a sky show before or seen any of the exhibits about astronomy and space travel."

"I like when it gets dark and the stars come out, and then they tell stories about the constellations," Kyla offered.

"You been there?" ET asked.

"On a school trip," Kimika answered.

ET looked at her and Michaela could see that there was an element of vulnerability in his eyes. If she were to guess the cause, it would be because he was not used to being around kids like the McNeill girls who had done so much more than he had, who had been places, and talked differently. Who had a home and a father.

"I'll have to call your father, of course, and see if it's okay."

The girls enthusiastically endorsed the plan, but ET

was still somewhat hesitant. It was then that another thought occurred to Michaela. That he might not want to share her with these two girls.

"Maybe both of you can show ET...I mean Terry, around the planetarium. Afterward we can find a place to have some ice cream."

ET looked up at her with poignant uncertainty. It was the first time that Michaela could remember seeing him this way. It was interesting to note that he had supreme self-confidence when dealing with adults, but not so much with his peers. Or maybe it was just with the twins because they were girls.

"I think it will be fun," Michaela encouraged, smiling at him.

He finally nodded.

"Okay."

Michaela left the three outside together, comfortable that they were forming their own friendship, and that ET would find a way to navigate it as he had so many other things in his life.

She dialed Jefferson's number and was surprised when he answered on the first ring.

"Hi," she said. "That was quick."

"Michaela, hi. I thought that might be the girls. I've been waiting for them to get back home from the park. They're later than I thought they would be."

"Actually, they're both standing outside the front of my house right now. That's why I'm calling."

"Something happened to them?"

"No, no. Everything is fine, Jefferson. They both wanted me to call you. I'm taking a young guest who's visiting with me to the planetarium this afternoon.

Kimika and Kyla asked if they could come along, if it's okay with you."

"I didn't know you had company."

"Well, we really haven't seen or spoken to each other recently," Michaela reminded him politely. "I know you've been busy. Now that your daughters are back home…"

"Right. It's almost time to return to school."

There was a momentary silence, but Michaela waited for Jefferson to speak first. Perhaps, like her, he was thinking how fast the time had flown. Perhaps also, like her, he was considering the chances that had been missed and the distances that had never been bridged between them. It was too bad, Michaela thought, but for other reasons than just the two of them.

And, in any case, she'd made her choice.

"We'll be back before dinner. Since the girls said they've been to the planetarium before, I thought they'd like acting as our guide."

Jefferson chuckled.

"To be honest, I'm surprised they want to. You remember their response to the idea of going to the children's museum back in June. Sure, it's okay with me."

"You're welcome to join us," Michaela felt obligated to add.

"Thanks, but I've got work to do here. I've got quarterly taxes coming up and I need to get some papers filed with my accountant."

As Michaela headed back to the kids, she felt a small degree of guilt that she was relieved Jefferson couldn't join them, afraid that his sense of propriety might put a damper on the afternoon.

"Okay, we're good to go…" She stopped as the two girls cheered. She gave ET a reassuring grin. "We're going to have a good time."

And they did.

For one thing, it had been decades since Michaela herself had been to a planetarium. With genuine interest, she trailed behind the three teens as they wound their way through the chronology of the exhibits, that began with the big bang theory of how the universe began, and ended with some of the amazing astronomical discoveries of the past ten years, including new galaxies, stars and other phenomena of space that helped explain so much about the earth.

ET was also just as interested, sometimes forgetting himself and exclaiming out loud at the wonders of space. He became even more interested when they reached the hall involving space travel, with a panel showing nearly all the astronaut teams going back to the first landing on the moon. And his interest really perked up when it came to a panel devoted to African-Americans in space. There were brief bios and photographs of Guion S. Bluford, Mae Jemison, a woman, and Ronald McNair who died in the Challenger Shuttle explosion. ET stood staring at the information, reading it over and over again.

Michaela casually steered Kimika and Kyla away, allowing ET time to read the captions and stare, awestruck, at the photographs of the Black men and one woman who had flown in space for NASA. He couldn't have been shown better role models. Except for maybe Cooper.

Then they entered the circular theater, another first for ET, to watch the thirty-minute sky show. Even Michaela knew a moment of intense wonder as the

lights in the theater went down, and the simulated night-
time sky appeared, bejeweled with thousands of stars
against the background of the Milky Way. When the
disembodied voice of the lecturer reviewed the constellations, and showed Sagittarius as it arched up from
the southern sky, Michaela looked at ET's profile in the
dark theater. He turned his gaze briefly to her, and she
could see the broad grin on his face.

There was the obligatory visit to the gift shop where
the girls were more interested in the earrings and neck-
laces with pendants shaped like the sun or the moon.
But ET was flipping through books, looking for more
information about the astronaut program.

He seemed particularly quiet when they all left the
planetarium and headed to Poplar Plaza in search of
something to eat. And became animated again when
the conversation turned to movies and music. Pre-
dictably ET liked anything with Will Smith or Jamie
Fox, while the girls preferred Denzel. Michaela listened,
taking it all in, greatly enlightened and amused by the
parameters of their youth.

When they arrived back at the house, she and the girls
were surprised to find Jefferson walking toward the house.
He waved to them and stood aside as Michaela pulled her
car into the driveway and everyone piled out. While the
girls immediately accosted their father with details of
their afternoon adventure, Michaela noticed at once that
Jefferson had focused his attention on ET. Too late, she
realized that Jefferson might remember the boy from the
backyard incident at the beginning of the summer.

She tried to quickly run interference before Jefferson could say anything. But he spoke first, cutting

across his daughters' excited retelling of their visit to the planetarium.

"Okay, I'm glad you had a great time. Now I want you to go and wait for me at the house," Jefferson said with the kind of authoritative tone that would have alerted anyone that something was wrong.

"But, Daddy, you didn't listen to—" Kimika tried to speak.

Her father cut her off.

"Not now. Go on. Do like I said. I'll be there in a minute."

Michaela, realizing that he was intent on a show-down, quickly turned to ET, who was clearly alert to the cold tone of his new friends' father.

"Go on inside. I'll be there soon. I just need to talk with Mr. McNeill. Do me a favor and make sure Lady has fresh water in her dish, okay?"

"Yeah," ET said grudgingly, heading into the house and taking one final, baleful look at Jefferson.

When the door had closed behind him, Michaela turned angrily to him. "Was that necessary? Why did you have to spoil everything for them?"

"That's the kid who broke into the yard. The one we took to the medical center."

"Yes, he is. So?"

He looked first astonished and then, surprising to her, outraged.

"You had my children out with that kid? You had no right…"

"I did ask if it was okay. You have no right to assume that I would do anything to hurt your girls. Yes, that is the very same boy, and he's not anything like what you think."

"You don't know what I think. You're not a parent."

Michaela felt as if she'd been slapped.

"Thanks for making that clear."

"I don't want my daughters being around a kid like that."

"Like what? Who's poor and without family? Who doesn't meet your approval? Why are you holding him responsible for circumstances he didn't choose and has no control over? I watched you in church, Jefferson, praying along with everyone else who believe they're good people. Where's your understanding?"

"I don't think I deserve your attitude. If you don't mind, I'd prefer if Kimika and Kyla stay in their own backyard."

Without giving her a chance to say another word, Jefferson turned and walked away. Michaela glared after his retreating back, fuming at his intolerance, and disappointed at his shortsightedness. She turned and entered the house, fighting for control so that ET wouldn't notice anything was wrong.

She found him in the living room. He was slouched on the sofa at an angle that allowed for Lady to lay on his chest. He was carefully stroking her back, while the cat purred and gazed at him with something close to adoration. There was a window behind the sofa that overlooked the front of the house. Had he heard the argument between her and Jefferson?

"Well, that was a fun time. The girls are nice, aren't they? And I think they like you. I was thinking…"

"That's the man I saw with you when you found me that night. He's their daddy?"

Michaela sighed and sat on the arm of the sofa, regarding him with an understanding gaze. "Yes, that's him."

"How come he don't like me? I didn't do nothing to him."

"I know that. It's hard to explain, ET. I guess he saw you as a kid who was committing a crime that night."

He looked at her, sad and bewildered.

"But I didn't break into his house. And I wasn't doing nothing."

"I know that, too. Look, I'm so glad you and the girls like each other. But I won't let Mr. McNeill do or say anything against you. He doesn't know anything about you like I do."

He nodded silently, but Michaela understood that what she'd said wasn't enough. She had the feeling he was also thinking of the rejection he'd faced with Betty Wilson, and probably that it could happen again, and again, because of who he was and what he had. She felt the urge to comfort him, give him a hug. But she was well aware of the invisible boundaries, and that they were necessary.

"Did you enjoy the planetarium?"

Again, he merely nodded.

"See, I told you the sky was filled with millions of stars."

"That was inside," he muttered.

"Don't worry. One night you'll get to see the real thing. By the way, I have to ask you something. When did you become Terry?"

He looked confused for a second and then, if it was possible, blushed. "Oh. I changed my name. I mean, my nickname. I don't want to be ET anymore."

"Can I ask why?"

He shrugged. "'Cause it sounds dumb. I'm too old

for that kind of name. Terry sounds good, right? Better than Eugene." He grimaced with distaste.

"So, you want me to call you Terry?"

"I don't mind if you call me ET. I'm used to it."

"Okay then. Just between you and me." She stood up. "How about pizza tonight? I don't much feel like cooking." Michaela had expected him to immediately perk up at the mention of one of his favorite foods. ET only nodded, still pensive. "And I want to hear about your book. Have you finished it?"

"Yeah. Last night."

"Good. We'll talk about it over dinner."

With no other conversation forthcoming, Michaela sighed and headed toward the kitchen.

"Miss Landry?"

She immediately turned back to him.

"If they find out I have HIV will they still let me become an astronaut?"

Michaela stared at him, heartbroken that he'd even have to consider such a possibility about anything he wanted in life.

"They can't stop you from trying. That would be discrimination. How far you go is all up to you. Are you willing to work really hard? Finish school, and then go to school again? Is becoming an astronaut important enough to you to not let anything stop you, not even being HIV? I know you can do it. I bet Smith will tell you the same thing. Okay?"

"Okay," he murmured, in a quiet, little-boy voice.

Michaela, quietly working on the manuscript for her cookbook, thought to ignore the telephone when it rang.

She was on a roll and wanted to finish her thought and the sentence. She finally gave in to the persistent ringing.

"Yes?" she asked, cradling the phone between her shoulder and ear as she continued working despite the distraction.

"It's Cooper. Caught you at a bad time?"

She immediately focused on the deep, rich voice in her ear, smiling. It had been a whole six hours since she'd last spoken to him, and that had been to ask if she'd bring ET up to the church center for practice.

"Trying to figure out an index for my book. I never realized how tricky it was. What's up?"

"You mean, since we last spoke?" She laughed. "Well, I have some news for you."

Michaela was on the alert. She could tell by the nuances in Cooper's tone that whatever he had to tell her was going to be significant. He hadn't said it was good news or bad news, so she was sure it was a little of both.

"What is it?"

"I got a call today from one of the parishioners of the church. There's an offer to provide Eugene Terrance a home. Not short-term but until he's eighteen, if everything goes well."

For a moment Michaela didn't know how to respond. It was always understood that ET's staying with her was temporary, a Band-Aid on a problem that needed a more permanent solution. It was always clear that she was leaving Memphis at the end of August. But now that it was happening, Michaela found herself ambivalent about Cooper's announcement. ET would be leaving to live somewhere else. She'd always known that, always. And yet…

"Michaela?"

"Yes, I heard you. That's…great! I hope ET will be happy. Do you know the family?"

"She's a recent widow. Her husband died overseas last spring. He was in the military. She has two boys of her own. One of them plays soccer with ET."

"Oh. That's good. All in the family, so to speak."

"Michaela, are you okay with this?"

"Of course. This is what we've been hoping for, right? Anyway, it's not about me."

"In a way, it is. I know how you feel about ET."

"I want what's best for him. I want him with people who will take care of him."

"Judith Macklin is a long-standing member of the church. She's a businesswoman. This sounds cliché but she's a pillar of the community, and a good person. I'm a little surprised that she came forward, but I approve."

"Then, that's good enough for me. As long as ET is okay with it, Cooper. He doesn't need any more uncertainty in his life right now."

"I know," Cooper said quietly. "But you still haven't answered my question. Are you okay?"

She wasn't sure. Suddenly she was finding it hard to speak. In quick order she had to accept Cooper's announcement and deal with it. She had to recognize that one situation was ending, as another was about to begin. She had to be okay with it. There was no other choice.

Michaela took a deep breath. "Yes, I am. A little surprised, I guess. I didn't think you'd find someone so fast. I thought…there'd be more time."

"I'm sorry. I shouldn't have told you like this. I'm coming over…"

"No, don't. I'll be okay. Are you going to tell ET?"

"I think there's a formality. He has to report to Children's Services and meet with a social worker. But maybe you should speak to him first. As the current caretaker you can do that. I'll come with you to the interview, if you like."

"Yes, please."

"And then he gets to meet Judith and they can get acquainted. I don't expect any complications, unless…"

"What?"

"ET doesn't want to go with her."

"If you know her, and ET knows one of her sons, I can't imagine why he'd say no."

"I can think of one reason," Cooper said. "Will you talk with him?"

"Yes, I'll do that. Tonight, while we have dinner. Does Mrs. Macklin know about ET's condition?"

"I believe Children's Services discussed the matter with St. Jude. Marilyn Caldwell has been put in touch with Judith. She understands the complexities and the potential problems ahead."

"If you vouch for her then I feel better about… well…"

"About letting him go?"

"Yes," she murmured. "So, when do I have to bring him in to Children's Services?"

"Day after tomorrow."

"That soon?"

"I'm afraid so. Michaela…"

"I'm fine, Cooper. Really. I'm glad you called. Like

you said, it's good news. As a matter of fact, it calls for a celebration, don't you think? I'm going to throw a party. A backyard hot dogs and hamburger feast."

"Sounds like fun. It will be a great send-off for ET."

"For me, too. I leave Memphis in less than two weeks."

Michaela, stepping back into the yard, turned to Reverend Wallace, who was sitting in a lounge chair just outside the kitchen door. She held out her hand.

"I'll take that, Reverend Wallace. Would you like more of the salad? Another hamburger?"

"Oh, no, ma'am." He shook his head with a deep chortle. "I'm not sure I'll be able to get up and walk as it is. Ate too much, but everything was good. 'Specially your potato salad."

Michaela took his paper plate. "Old family recipe."

She emptied the plate into the garbage and looked around to see if there was anything else that needed to be cleaned up or thrown out. The yard was noisy with the excited chatter of ten young teens, including ET, who was not only the guest of honor but also acting as the host. She'd made it clear to him that the party was for him.

For the past several days, however, she kept recalling the evening when she'd told ET a new home had been found for him. She'd expected curiosity, at least. Maybe even suspicion given what he'd gone through all summer. But he'd sat at dinner, mostly unresponsive. It made her nervous. What if he didn't want to meet the new family? Worse yet, what if he suddenly took it into his head to run away again?

She tried to be positive and cheerful as she told ET about Judith Macklin and that Smith approved the choice, that Mrs. Macklin was a member of the church. And still ET had no response. So, she'd left the topic alone and she'd gone on to tell him about the party.

"How come?" he'd asked.

"Well, don't you think it would be fun to have some of your friends here? We'll have it in the backyard. There'll be plenty to eat, and we can invite anyone you want."

"I never had no party before," ET said, as if the very concept was foreign to him.

"Then this will be your first one. I know you'll have more in the future."

Still, he'd remained pensive, almost pouty most of the evening, and Michaela became anxious about what he was thinking. What was he thinking?

And then, after he'd come back into the house from taking out the garbage, he'd shuffled over to her, where she stood at the counter putting away dishes.

"Miss Landry?"

"Hmm?" she'd responded, somewhat absentmindedly, but looked up sharply at ET when he didn't speak.

Michaela looked at him and was astonished to see his young face twisted in an agony of emotion, unable to speak or adequately express himself. She gasped softly, and opened her arms.

"Oh…ET…"

He let her gather him in a gentle embrace. He said nothing, and neither did Michaela, for a long time.

"Don't tell nobody." His voice, squeaky and warbled with tears, was muffled against her chest.

Michaela had to swallow several times to keep her own tears back. "I won't," she promised in a whisper.

As she went about cleaning, she glanced briefly at the young teens, boisterous and laughing and, thankfully, seeming to enjoy themselves.

Three of the other boys were from ET's soccer team. They'd all been gathered up and brought over by Cooper in his work truck. Three other teens were outpatients, like ET, from St. Jude. There were two girls and another boy. And the last two were Kimika and Kyla. And while no one else, even ET, found their presence unusual, Michaela still couldn't get over the stunning surprise of their appearance. When she'd answered the entrance bell, sometime after the party was in full swing, to find the two girls and Jefferson at the front door…

She'd been speechless, staring at Jefferson, then taking in the hopeful gleam in both girls' eyes, and then back to Jefferson again. From his expression, he seemed not only stalwart but formal, and embarrassed, as if he was there against his better judgment, if not against his will. Suddenly Michaela felt a little sorry for him. Sorry that his inflexibility was robbing him of experiences that might make him a more understanding, tolerant, forgiving man.

"Jefferson…" She looked at the girls and smiled. "It's nice to see you."

"Hi," the girls said together in an uncertain voice.

"Can I help you? Is something wrong?" Michaela asked, confused by their sudden presence.

"We wanted to know if we can still come to the party."

Michaela stared blankly at Kimika. She had not extended an invitation to the girls, afraid that it would only incur Jefferson's wrath against her. So, how did they know about the party?

"Daddy said we could," Kyla added.

"Oh. Well…of course you can. It's already started, and everyone is in the backyard."

The two girls looked up to their father, awaiting the final go-ahead. Jefferson nodded his head once, granting permission. The girls immediately relaxed and broke into smiles.

"Go on in, then. I'll be right there, okay?"

The girls made a hasty goodbye to their father and hurried into the house, headed through the kitchen and to the yard beyond. Michaela turned a puzzled expression to Jefferson.

"I know how you feel about me, but I promise I didn't tell your daughters about the party. I would have invited them if things had been different."

"I'm finding out that if you tell your kids you don't want them to do something, chances are they're going to do it anyway. Kimika and Kyla were mad at me for not letting them be friends with…the boy. They like him. They say he's funny, and not like their other friends. Apparently they've been running into each other at the park, and the library. I'm willing to bet it wasn't all by accident. He told them about the party."

"He never said anything to me," Michaela said, in her own defense.

Jefferson took a deep breath.

Michaela stared at him, holding her breath. Waiting and wondering what else he was going to say against ET.

"He told my daughters all about what's wrong with him. I think he wanted to see if they were going to turn against him, and they didn't. I'll be honest. I don't know if I could have done the same. I know how AIDS and HIV is spread."

"You only know of one way," Michaela said firmly. "And that's *not* how children get AIDS and HIV."

"So, you're telling me I have a lot to learn."

She nodded. "It couldn't hurt, Jefferson."

"The church teaches that it's a punishment."

Michaela's mouth dropped open. "Against a child? Do you honestly believe that? That boy got up in front of a congregation at *his* church and told everyone what he had. The reverend said afterward, 'He who does not love his brother whom he has seen, how can he love God whom he has not seen?'"

His jaw muscles tensed rapidly.

"I'm sorry. I shouldn't judge you. That's not very Christian, either, is it?"

Michaela saw the momentary confusion, the stubbornness in his expression. She could guess that it was costing him to humble himself before her for the sake of his daughters. He was a strong, self-sufficient man, used to having his own way...and being right.

"Not your fault. I guess I never quite understood you. Frankly..."

"You're not used to independent women who talk back and do what they want."

He shook his head. "I'm not used to anyone who makes me feel like I'm not a good person."

Michaela lowered her gaze and didn't respond. She couldn't because the thought had certainly occurred to her, more than once.

"You know, it doesn't matter what I think. I'm leaving

in another week. It's too bad we got off on the wrong foot and never got right again."

"Maybe under different circumstances, we might have…" He hesitated, struggling for the right words.

"Maybe." Michaela shrugged. "Thanks for bringing the girls over. You're more than welcome to stay, if you like."

"I don't think so. I'll be at the house."

"I'll walk them back when the party ends."

"Thanks," Jefferson said. Then, he abruptly turned and walked away…

Michaela looked at the very natural way all the kids were getting along. The boys were more fascinated with a small telescope set up on a tripod that Cooper had brought. After hearing that ET didn't believe that there were real stars in the sky, Cooper had decided the simple way to prove otherwise was to let him see for himself. Cooper stood by to show the kids how to operate the telescope, explaining that the image was not going to stay in the same place because the earth was moving.

The girls had also managed to find a common ground and were deep in animated discussion about the latest fashions. Through the lens of the telescope, ET and his friends could see, for themselves, the stars. Michaela could tell from ET's initial silence that he was totally captivated by the sight.

Marilyn Caldwell, who'd been sitting next to Reverend Wallace, chatting, finally stood up and gathered her purse. She smiled at Michaela.

"I have to get going. I should get the kids back to the campus where their parents will pick them up. Thank you so much for inviting me and them to your party. What a great idea."

"Thanks for coming, Marilyn. And thanks for everything you've done on ET's behalf."

Marilyn laughed. "I'm told that he is the artist formerly known as ET." Michaela giggled. "I'm supposed to call him Terry from now on."

Michaela rolled her eyes and grinned. "I keep forgetting. I think I'm the only one allowed to call him ET anymore."

"And Smith. That's a privilege reserved for special people, obviously."

"Thank you," Michaela said, feeling emotional by the comment. "Nice of you to say so."

Marilyn took her hand and grew serious. "I mean it. I have to tell you I've been impressed with your steadfast support of Terry. He's got a very long haul ahead of him, and it's not going to be easy. He needs people like you in his life."

"I think his new foster family will be a great new addition."

"Yes, I think so. Mrs. Macklin seemed very sincere about her desire to provide a home for him."

"Can I ask a favor? And if you can't, I understand. I just wondered…can I call you sometime, just to find out how ET is doing? You know, with his medication and blood count, things like that?"

"I'll have to check with my supervisor and doctors to find out if your request is against patient confidentiality. But considering your involvement with Terry this summer, an exception might be allowed. I'll let you know."

Michaela signaled to the three St. Jude patients that

it was time to leave. With a minimum of protest, they began saying their goodbyes. Cooper, catching her gaze, also said he was closing down the observatory for the night so the kids wouldn't be tempted to dawdle.

That afternoon she'd gotten the idea that it might be nice to make something for the kids, a kind of end-of-party takeaway gift, and decided on sugar cookies that were shaped like stars, the sun and moon. That meant she and ET hitting the local mall in search of the right cookie cutters.

When ET said he wanted to make the cookies himself, Michaela, surprised, had put all the ingredients on the counter for him, and left him alone. In the end, the cookies were slightly cock-eyed and a little overbaked, and the kitchen an utter mess, but ET was so proud of himself. They'd put together individually wrapped portions for each of the kids to take with them.

Now, Michaela reminded ET about the cookie packages, and he went to the kitchen to return a minute later with a handful of the gaily wrapped treats and passed them out.

Marilyn waved briefly and, accompanied by her three charges, walked around the side of the house to the front, where her car was parked behind the one belonging to the reverend.

Reverend Wallace wandered over to help Cooper with the dismantling of the portable telescope. And over the top of everyone's heads, Michaela caught the watchful eye of Cooper. She was fully aware that he'd been covertly tracking not only her movements, but also her reactions to everything and everyone all evening. Only he knew the full meaning and subtext of the night's festivities and what they held for her.

Michaela looked at him, wanting to reassure Cooper that she was all right. But she wasn't. And she wasn't sure that there was anything he could do about it. Or should.

She turned away, her arms and hands carefully balancing the bowls and platters of leftover food, and went back into the kitchen. Reverend Wallace had requested a doggy bag, and she intended to send Cooper home with extras as well. When she'd finished filling plastic containers and Ziploc bags, she went back to the yard and approached Kimika and Kyla.

"Girls, I think I should walk you home now. The party's winding down."

Polite and well-mannered as ever, the twins didn't overdo their disappointment that it was time to go home, but thanked her for the party. Michaela, turning away to speak with the reverend, caught only a part of what they were saying to ET as they were about to leave.

"Are we going to see you tomorrow…?"

Michaela made a point of not listening for ET's answer. There were only a few tomorrows left.

"Reverend, I have a little package for you in the kitchen to take home."

He chuckled warmly. "Thank you, my dear. Your timing is perfect. I have to get going myself and drive these boys back home."

"Thank you for coming and bringing them with you. The kids were all great."

Reverend Wallace patted her arm. "I think the same of their hostess." His smile became faint and reflective. "You have an unusual first name."

She grimaced. "Tell me about it. No one ever knows how to say it right."

"Do you know what it means?"

"Haven't a clue. Never thought much about it."

The reverend took her hand, looking deeply into her eyes. "It's a good choice. I think you should take the time to find out. It might surprise you." He then waved a hand at the three boys he'd brought with him. "Let's go. Time to get on the road…"

"I'll be right back," Michaela said to ET and Cooper, as she prepared to escort the twins down the road and walk the reverend out to his car.

"We'll finish up here," Cooper said.

The girls were animated as the three of them walked the short distance to their home.

"Maybe we can get Daddy to let us have a party," Kimika said to her sister.

"Yeah. Then ET can come to our house," the normally sedate Kyla said excitedly.

Michaela thought it best not to mention yet that ET would be leaving soon. There was no time for explanation, no time to answer the inevitable questions from the girls. And, of course, there was their father to contend with. Even now, as the girls ran to the door and rang the bell, she was not looking forward to facing Jefferson again, and prepared herself defensively.

He opened the door with a smile for his daughters.

"So, how was the party?"

The girls talked over one another, so filled with information and observations that she was doubtful if their father understood anything they said. But he seemed reassured by their enthusiasm.

"Great, great," he murmured. "Did you thank Miss Landry?"

The girls were again effusive, even surprising Michaela by giving her a brief hug.

"Go on inside. It's late and you have to get to bed."

After a final good-night, the girls disappeared inside. Jefferson turned to her, his expression guarded.

Michaela backed away. "Good night," she said quickly to Jefferson. There wasn't anything left for them to say to one another and she didn't want to end the evening on a sour note. She retraced her steps back to the house.

"Good night…"

She heard faintly behind her as his door closed.

Michaela found Cooper in the kitchen loading the dishwasher. She smiled her thanks.

"This is getting to be a habit," she said ruefully.

"Doesn't bother me," he replied.

She went out into the yard and found it pretty much back in order. She swept the flagstone pathway of any spilled food and debris, rolled the grill back into the garage, stacked the lounge chairs. When she went back inside, Cooper was drying his hands on a dish towel. The dishwasher was humming through the prewash cycle, and Lady was waiting to be fed, sitting by her empty dish and giving them both indignant stares.

"Where's ET? He should have fed her by now," she said, pulling out a can of wet food as a treat for the cat, as well as filling her dish with her usual dry mix.

"He spilled a bottle of salad dressing on himself. Didn't see that the top wasn't screwed on. I sent him to clean up."

"Oh. Okay," Michaela murmured, briefly petting Lady's back before standing up.

Cooper, leaning against the counter, held out a hand to her. Michaela took it and let him pull her to his side. He released her hand and put his arm around her shoulder, kissing her cheek and hugging her gently.

"Thank you," he whispered against her skin.

She relaxed her body against him, a hand resting on his chest. "For what?"

"For coming to Memphis."

She chuckled. "It certainly has been an interesting summer."

"It's been a very good one for ET. An even better one for me."

Michaela felt a rush of emotion come over her. It was unexpected and sudden, but she didn't want Cooper to see how much his words meant to her. "Me, too."

He slowly turned her so they faced one another. He looped his arms around her lower back so they were still pressed together. Her hands moved restlessly on his chest, aware of the rough skin beneath his usual black T-shirt. Her fingertips were gentle in their caress. She shook her head, afraid to look into his eyes.

"What happens next? What are we going to do?" she murmured.

Cooper sighed, leaning forward so he could rub his shadowed cheek slowly against hers.

"The right thing. I love you, Michaela. But you have to go back home. You need to do that."

"Oh, Cooper, how did this happen?" she asked, her voice broken and confused. "We've only known each other two months. How can you be so sure?"

"How long is it supposed to take? You're the one who

told me I'm a true believer. Well, I believe in how I feel. I trust what I feel for you. I knew for sure when I thought I'd lost you because I forgot to trust my instincts instead of my ego. I was playing too many old tapes in my head."

He slid a hand up her back, and when she raised her head, Cooper leaned in to kiss her properly, capturing her mouth and covering it with a tantalizing slowness that was filled with eloquence…and desire. There was no point in being subtle. There was no more time for that and, by their mutual, unspoken agreement, there were no other options open to them for expressing themselves. They separated, and she rested her forehead against his shoulder.

"I love you, too. But I…I feel so strange. Like this is a fantasy and it's not really happening. I'm afraid I'll wake up in D.C. next week and all of this…how I'm feeling right now…will be gone."

"That's why you have to go. We both have to know in our hearts that what's happening between us is real. And we both have to believe it's what we want forever. I've waited a long time, Michaela. I'm sure."

He kissed her again, Michaela putting her arms around his shoulders, allowing herself the full luxury and delight of the moment. They didn't even break apart when footsteps rumbled down the stairs, heralding ET's arrival. He reached the kitchen, and still they did not separate.

"Oh, man," ET exclaimed, as if he'd just witnessed something phenomenal. "You was lip-locked with Miss Landry. You gonna marry her, right?"

Cooper gazed lovingly into her eyes, and Michaela didn't even consider doing anything less. He used his thumb to stroke near the corner of her mouth.

"We'll see," he growled, tenderness and hope infused in his response.

Chapter 12

Cooper checked the time on his dashboard clock as he lifted his foot gently from the brake and his van rolled forward to keep pace with the traffic. Unfortunately at the moment, it was practically a snail's pace. He knew Michaela was waiting for him to take her to the airport, and there was still time...if the traffic picked up speed, soon.

The slow crawl, however, allowed him to reflect on the fact that Michaela was flying back home today. The summer was over. Whether or not she fully realized it, she was taking both his heart and his expectations with her. This was one of the most vulnerable moments of his life.

Cooper also had time to review the conversation he'd had with his uncle about his feelings for Michaela. The reverend, as always, had been insightful and understanding.

"My boy, if you're waiting for me to disavow what I believe to be your feelings for Michaela, I can't. I can see what's been developing all summer. But most of all, Cooper, I can see the change in you. You checked your ego at the door when you welcomed the Lord in. You don't need to doubt when you have respect, self-worth…and love. You've earned all of that. Now, if that young woman is partly responsible, then she gets my vote."

"Michaela wondered if it was too soon, maybe happening too fast. Do you think maybe she's right?"

The reverend chuckled. "Well, there's soon, and then there's soon, as in some indeterminate time in the future. Why postpone joy? Why put off finding love tomorrow, if you know for sure you can have it today? Now, if I'm right about Michaela, you don't have to worry, son. She strikes me as the kind of woman who wouldn't do anything she doesn't believe in, no matter the consequences…."

Knowing what he did about Michaela's failed engagement, the reverend's words were incredibly reassuring. In any case, her ex's loss was now his gain. And he meant to take it.

The van inched forward another few yards. It was getting late, and he'd waited and hoped as long as he could. Cooper pulled out his cell phone and began dialing Michaela's number. He put the phone on speaker. But before the second ring traffic moved again, this time consistently picking up speed. He disconnected the call.

Cooper realized now it might have been a mistake to take Jackson Avenue, Route 14, to reach Chickasaw

Gardens. He'd just left St. Jude where he'd met with Marilyn Caldwell about a consultation for the daughter of a parishioner of the church. That had only taken twenty minutes. He'd already been that long on the road. He thought that if he could get to Scott Street and hang a right, he'd be in the clear, and still on time.

But traffic slowed again, and Cooper finally realized there was an accident ahead. Cars were being directed to the far left lane to go around the scene. As his van got closer he opted to stay in the right lane of blocked traffic, eventually pulling up behind a patrol car. Already on the scene was another squad car, an EMS truck and an ambulance. There was a tentlike tarpaulin next to two cars, both of which had been totaled in a collision.

For a moment he had a strong sense of déjà vu, recalling his own horrific accident. Cooper could see that at least one person was dead on the scene, the body discreetly covered by the tarpaulin. He could see EMS workers huddled around a possible second or third person, on the other side of the vehicles. Cooper put his van in Park and turned off the engine.

He called Michaela again.

"Cooper?" Her voice was anxious when she answered.

"It's me. I'm stuck in traffic. I'm about a mile or so away, but there's been an accident." He heard her gasp. "I'm all right. I'm not involved."

"How bad is it?"

"Very bad."

Out the windshield Cooper could see an officer approaching his van, already signaling for him to move on and get out of the way.

"Michaela, I've got to stay. I may be needed. There's one death that I can see, and…"

"I understand."

"Are you sure?"

"You're doing exactly what you're supposed to be doing."

He relaxed. He could almost see her smile.

"Thank you. But we still have to get you to the airport."

"I can take care of that. Don't worry about me."

"I wanted to be there. I wanted to say goodbye again. Hold you for just another minute…"

He lowered his window for the officer, pulling his church ID from his overhead visor and showing it. The officer nodded an okay before turning back.

"I have a great imagination. I'll pretend that you're with me."

"I have to go."

"Yes."

"I love you."

"Yes."

"Call me when you arrive home."

"Yes."

Cooper opened his glove compartment and took out a small black leather-bound book. He got out of the van and approached the cluster of police and emergency workers. He got close enough to see there was a second covered body. An older woman who had facial lacerations, torn clothing and bloody hands was sitting on the shoulder being checked out by a medic. Her ash-blond hair was in disarray, with debris and dirt from the crash sprinkled in it. She was dazed but her attention was on an unconscious man being worked over, who'd just been freed from the wreck of one of the cars.

Showing his ID as he came closer, Cooper knelt beside the woman, gently touching her shoulder.

"I'm Pastor Cooper Townsend. Can I do anything to help?"

The woman looked at him, her gray eyes watery and filled with fear. She blinked rapidly, grabbed at Cooper's arm, starting to cry.

"Please don't let my husband die. Please ask the Lord to save him."

Soothing her, Cooper spoke to her in a low, calming tone. He then began to say a prayer while the medics continued to try to stabilize the injured man. The woman prayed through her tears, her bloodied hands clasped tightly together, as she prayed along with him.

"'Yea, thou I walk through the valley of the shadow of death, I will fear no evil, for Thou art with me...'"

Michaela sat holding her cell phone, frowning. She wondered if Cooper was telling her the truth when he'd said he was not hurt. Another car accident. She couldn't help but think of the horrific one he'd told her about that had nearly taken his life.

She suddenly felt uneasy about leaving Memphis without seeing him again. But he had assured her that he was okay.

That only left her with the immediate problem of getting to the airport.

For a moment Michaela considered calling and canceling, and trying to get booked on a later flight, or even one the next day. But she knew that was only postponing the inevitable. She'd already spent a torturous night dealing with the aftermath of watching ET leave with a city social worker, as he was being transferred two days earlier to his new home. She'd cleaned the house she'd been living in for two months, which had become almost like her own, and brought closure to all the memories that had been created there.

Lady had wandered the house for a time in search of ET's presence, meowing unhappily. Michaela had welcomed the cat's company in the night, fully appreciating and understanding her loneliness. They comforted each other. And she'd had a disturbing dream about being back in D.C., and not ever hearing from Cooper again.

Michaela looked at the time again and considered her options. After a few minutes of debate, she went to the kitchen phone and made a call.

"Hi, Jefferson. It's Michaela."

"Yes. The girls gave me your note. Thanks for your kind words. Kimika and Kyla liked you a lot, too. You're leaving today. When?"

"Right now. Actually, that's why I'm calling. I have a problem and a big favor to ask. I need a ride to the airport. Can you help me out?"

Michaela was a little surprised when there was no immediate answer from him. She rushed on.

"Someone else was supposed to take me, but they're stuck in traffic. There's an accident."

There was still no response.

"I totally understand if you can't or…if you don't want to. Under the circumstances, I have a lot of nerve…"

"I'll be around to pick you up in ten minutes. Is that soon enough?"

She sighed. "Perfect. Thank you."

"When are the Underwoods coming back?"

"Tomorrow. They were supposed to be back two days ago, but didn't want to leave their new grandchild yet."

"Got it. You're all set?"

"Yes. I'm ready."

Michaela found the levels of conversation in the restaurant annoying. It was loud and uncomfortable and somehow, too public. How could anyone hear themselves think, let alone talk above all the chatter? She took a sip of her red wine and glanced around.

It was a very twenties and thirties professional crowd, gathered on a Friday night, as was the routine, to relax, catch up on gossip, check out one another and, hopefully hook up with someone if not, at the very least, score a phone number. Shortly after her broken engagement, Michaela had welcomed being back in circulation. Not to pair off with anyone, but just to be included in the socializing with her girlfriends, Jill and Vanessa. Those first few weeks, before she'd ultimately made the decision to accept her godparents' invitation to crash at their house in Memphis for the summer, had revived her and put her back in the loop with her friends and their goings-on. Now it seemed so artificial and frenetic. So desperate.

What was she doing here?

When her arm was jostled deliberately by Jill, causing wine to slosh over the rim of the glass, Michaela quickly reached for her napkin to wipe up the damage.

"Jill! Watch what you're doing."

"Look, look," Jill said under her breath. "Over there at the end of the bar. Do you see him?"

"You mean the one who's looking this way," Vanessa said sarcastically. "Not very smooth, is he? That play is so obvious."

"So he's not housebroken. He can be trained." Jill smirked. "Isn't he cute?"

"Not bad," Vanessa agreed, pretending to ignore the come-on from the man.

"Not interested," Michaela murmured, not even bothering to look.

Jill sucked her teeth. "What is your problem?"

"What are you talking about?" Michaela asked with raised brows and a bewildered expression. "All I said was I'm not interested. To be honest, I'm ready to leave. It's too noisy in here. I don't want to drink any more wine. I'd like to go somewhere quiet and have a nice dinner."

"Did you hear that?" Jill asked Vanessa. "Who is this woman we've been hanging out with? And what has she done with Michaela?"

"Leave her alone," Vanessa said. "Not every woman we know is on a perpetual manhunt. Besides, Michaela was almost married this past summer. If that had happened she would have been out of the game anyway."

"But it didn't, and look at her," Jill groused. "If I didn't know any better, I'd say she was still in love. If not with Spencer, then with someone. Maybe that guy she told me about when she was in Memphis."

"Oh, yeah. You did say something like that," Vanessa said. She chuckled. "As I recall, Jill, you were ready to get on the next plane down South to see if there were any more like him."

"I wish I'd never said anything," Michaela complained. "I didn't intend for that to become public information, Jill."

"Sorry." Jill shrugged, unrepentant.

Michaela sighed, regretting the loss of her sense of humor. But she'd felt off balance recently, ever since returning home to D.C. That had been almost three months ago.

The dream she'd had the night before leaving Memphis now seemed like a prophesy. Not because Cooper had forgotten about her or had not called, but because it had been too easy for her to fall back into the routine of the life she'd lived before the summer began. And what she'd experienced with him had become surreal.

On the other hand, Michaela was no longer sure exactly where she fit in.

The fall semester started at Howard, and she was immediately inundated with program changes, canceled classes, staff disputes and student problems that went beyond academic. She'd been swept back into the social swirl of her friends and the abundant cultural opportunities available in D.C. For a while Memphis seemed provincial. She barely had time to reflect on Memphis, or on the people she'd met during the summer. And, for a while, she tried not to. Except for the calls and letters from Eugene Terrance Dunne.

While she was relieved that he was apparently doing very well in his new home, Michaela was secretly heartbroken that he'd moved on so easily, away from her and to someone else. It made her feel childishly bereft, abandoned, and jealous of Judith Macklin.

It had felt good to be back. For about three weeks.

And then she began to feel lost.

It was then that Michaela had gotten her first call from Cooper. He had caught her off guard. Her defenses were down, her doubts weighing heavily. But the moment she heard his voice, the strong and centered pitch and cadence of his words, Michaela was instantly swept back to the beginning, to the first night they'd met and what she'd felt about him even then. But the conversation wasn't about him or her or them. He told her about his teams, and Miss Faye, and the progress on the house out east of the city. And he told her how well ET was adapting to being in his new home. What Cooper didn't say was that he still loved her.

Thereafter he called her once a week. She looked forward to the calls, became anxious if he was off a day or two. By October Michaela found herself calling Cooper. She needed to hear his voice, and the assurance and safety that talking with him provided. The conversation became less formulaic and more like the way they were when she was in Memphis.

She missed that.

Not being able to actually see him that last day had left a void of some kind that she was trying to fill.

By the beginning of November, Michaela was beginning to shake off her lethargy and the protective armor she'd embraced to deal with the distance between her and Cooper. The phone conversations got longer. The endearments crept back in, a poor substitute for being able to touch and gaze into each other's eyes, but a salve for Michaela's longing as she found her way back to her real feelings.

She missed him.

Overwhelmed suddenly with a flood of memories and an eerie sensation of being off-kilter, Michaela caught her breath and swallowed. She even had what seemed like a sudden bout of vertigo, as she was shaken with a fact she had avoided for months.

With a start, she realized Vanessa was talking to her.

"Have you heard from this guy?"

"His name is Cooper. Yes, I have," she answered, including the nights she'd dreamed about him.

"I love that name." Jill sighed. "Is he anything like the sound of his name?"

"Yes," Michaela said, slowly smiling to herself now, as if the thought was a revelation. "But even better. He's the ultimate good guy," she added cryptically.

"You haven't said anything about how he is in bed," Jill probed.

Michaela stiffened, playing with the stem of her glass. "And I'm not going to."

She could hardly forget the limitations imposed on her relationship with Cooper. It made what they'd had together that much more profound. Private.

And sacred.

Vanessa wanted to know what he looked like and Michaela found herself invoking an image of Cooper in her mind's eye that actually made her heart beat faster. That made her wish it was real. She described his walk and his voice. The subtle layer of facial hair that gave him an almost dangerous appearance. She even talked about the way he dressed. That he rode around Memphis on a motorcycle.

"The kids call him the Man in Black."

"What kids?" Vanessa asked, confused. "Did she tell us he had kids?"

"Dozens," Michaela said airily, but in no way forgetting the terrible loss of his own child.

Jill made a dismissive wave of her hand. "He's some kind of teacher."

"What do you talk about?"

"Memphis. What's going on there. People we know. My work here."

"Doesn't sound very exciting," Jill said.

Michaela looked around the crowded restaurant. There were clusters of men and women everywhere, in a Friday-night ritual that seemed tired to her. She'd begun to feel that way more and more lately. And now it was no fun at all.

What are they talking about? she wondered.

Michaela wasn't even sure what she was doing there, except that it had become a habit. One that she wanted to break for something better. Something more meaningful. And it finally, irrevocably dawned on her. She missed Cooper more than she could have imagined, having known him for only two months.

But it hadn't been just two months. For all she knew it might really have been a lifetime and they had only found each other during the summer.

Exciting?

Michaela silently considered that. Exciting was not the right word. Everything she and Cooper had talked about had been deep and meaningful. Their conversations had been about issues that were important, and people other than themselves.

"You know what? I was really happy while I was there."

"But you're happy to be home, right?" Jill asked. "It's not like you talk about this guy a lot. You just need some time to get back into the swing of things."

Michaela thought about that. She shook her head. "No, I don't need more time. I only need to be sure of what I want. Maybe that's what I'm supposed to find out…" she said almost to herself.

"What?" Vanessa questioned.

"Nothing," Michaela responded, shaking her head. A sudden awareness washed over her, giving her a clarity she'd been lacking all these months. Her heart felt like it skipped a beat as she fully realized what she'd been going through.

Separation anxiety.

Withdrawal pains.

She reached for her purse and found her wallet. Taking out several bills, Michaela put them on the table. "That should cover my glass of wine and a tip. I'm going home."

"Going home? Girl, what's wrong with you? We just got here."

She stood up and put on her black quilted coat, wound a green-and-blue-plaid scarf around her neck.

"I know. I'm sorry, but I just can't be here."

"Look, if you really want to have dinner, we'll go someplace else." Vanessa tried to compromise.

"Michaela, you know I was just teasing you," Jill said, contrite.

"This isn't about you guys or anything you said. It's about me," Michaela told them. "I didn't mean to spoil the evening. Stay and enjoy yourselves. Maybe one of you will get lucky tonight."

"What about you? Are you going to call me? When are we going to see you again?"

"I don't know," Michaela answered, waving as she headed for the door. "It all depends."

Jill and Vanessa exchanged puzzled looks. "On what?" they yelled after her.

But Michaela was already through the door, her arm raised to hail a taxi.

When she got back to her apartment, the first thing she did was to call Cooper. She got his answering machine. When it came time to leave a message she didn't know what she wanted to say, and hung up. He didn't call back that night. Or the next. By Sunday, as she went about preparing for another week of work, she wasn't sure what to think of the silence. Except that she didn't like it at all.

Michaela had the dream again that night. With a difference.

She was sitting on a bench on the campus of Howard. It was summer. There was a wave of students walking in both directions, briskly off to classes, or part-time work, or to get together with friends. And she sat alone…watching the world go by.

Suddenly she sensed a presence behind her. Strong enough to make her glance over her shoulder. There, standing still and quiet, dressed all in black, was Cooper. She felt a jolt in her chest, a surge of blood and air and hope. Was it really him? It had been so long.

She stood up in slow motion, unable, it seemed, to move faster, even though she was impatient. He was really there. And now that he was, an urgency compelled her to call his name. But no sound came out.

Frightened that he might not see her, she tried calling again. But she had no voice.

Without warning, he turned and began walking away. Her heartbeat jumped, felt lodged in her throat. She struggled to say the words that would call him back, that would make him hear her.

"Wait" formed on her lips and still there was no sound. She went into action, running after him, her feet leaden, her legs heavy and clumsy. "Wait…"

He did not stop, and did not turn around. He couldn't hear her. Or maybe he didn't want to. She tried harder, running to catch up, but he seemed to be getting farther away. He was getting smaller in the distance. He reached a corner and stopped, just long enough to look once more over his shoulder at her. Then he walked around the side of the building, and she lost sight of him. She ran faster.

Having reached the corner herself, she slowed down. If she looked he would be there, just around the side. She stepped forward and glanced over the edge of the building expecting to see him…

And then she woke up.

Suddenly, totally startled and breathless, Michaela bolted upright.

She listened to the quiet of the room, and heard the fall of snow against the windows of her bedroom. But she had broken out in a cold sweat.

Michaela collapsed back into the bedsheets. She took deep breaths trying to dispel the painful sense of loss at the disappointing turn of her dream. But it was just a dream.

She glanced at the digital clock. It was 3:37 a.m.

She closed her eyes and groaned. The middle of the night. She thought about her next move for only a matter of seconds. Not even bothering to turn on the light, she reached for the cordless phone and speed-dialed Cooper's number.

It rang once.

"Smith," he answered, his voice even deeper than usual because he'd been asleep.

The sound of his voice had an immediate effect although Michaela's heartbeat had yet to slow down.

"Hi," she said, barely a whisper.

"I was hoping it was you."

"And not another emergency?"

"Haven't had any lately. I wanted to hear your voice."

"I'm sorry to wake you up. It's so…late. Or, is it so early?"

"You called. That's all that matters."

She sighed. "I don't want you to be annoyed with me."

"I can't think of any reason why I'd ever be annoyed with you."

"You're being kind. I don't deserve it."

He was quiet for a second.

"Michaela? Are you all right?"

"Oh…I'm fine. I guess."

"Talk to me," he encouraged, his voice a comforting growl.

She felt on the verge of tears. His voice was so gentle. It blanketed her, and felt warm and protective. Michaela had the sudden suspicion that Cooper might know exactly why she called. But how could he? She hadn't known herself until the moment he answered. And now it was very clear. Finally.

"I had this dream."

"Nightmare?"

"No. But scary. And then I woke up and…and I knew I had to call you. Cooper, I love you. I had to tell you. I couldn't wait until the morning. I need for you to know right now."

"Thank you. I can't tell you how glad I am to hear that. I needed to hear you say it."

"I want to be with you. I don't even know what I'm doing here in D.C. anymore," she said, still sounding confused and anxious.

"You had to go back, so that I could get this call."

"I didn't even realize. I took too long."

"You took as long as you needed. Say it again."

She let her eyes drift closed, beginning to find peace and safety with Cooper on the end of the line.

"I love you. So much."

She heard him sigh.

"Then, a call in the middle of the night was worth waiting for."

The box was sitting outside her apartment door when she got home from Thanksgiving weekend with her parents in Silver Springs. Michaela giggled when she found it and saw it was from Cooper, with insured and confirmation of delivery stickers all over it. He'd playfully threatened to mail her dinner, turkey and all, when she said that she was not going to bring home any leftovers from her weekend.

"You have to have leftover turkey," he'd said. "All of it tastes better on the second and third day."

She'd laughed. "I'm usually sick of turkey by then."

"Thanksgiving is my favorite holiday in the year."

"Really? How come?"

"Because it's all about family, good friends, coming together to share a meal. Most of all, I can give thanks for all the good fortune in my life. Despite everything that's happened, life is good. I'm blessed."

"Me, too. I thank most sincerely the powers that be for leading me to Memphis last summer. And to you."

"Amen." Cooper chuckled.

Michaela struggled inside with her suitcase and the box. In truth, it felt too light to be an actual cooked turkey with all the trimmings. After putting away her coat, she took the box into the kitchen, placing it on the counter as she cut through the tape and peeled away the wrapping.

The box under the brown wrapping paper was itself wrapped in a silver metallic paper with little hearts all over it. It was tied in a red grosgrain ribbon and fashioned in a simple bow. Michaela sniffed at the box. There definitely wasn't a turkey, or any other kind of cooked food inside.

Curious now, she untied the ribbon and opened the paper, being careful not to tear it. She felt a sentimental desire to save it, because it was from Cooper. Everything from him had a special meaning to her.

But, in all honesty, she didn't have a clue what to make of the contents of the box. Inside, covered by tissue paper, was a motorcycle helmet. She lifted it from the box, bewildered. She quickly saw that it was not a new helmet. In fact, she recognized it as Cooper's helmet, the one he'd first given her to use when they'd ridden together on his bike.

She was totally mystified, turning the helmet this

way and that, looking for a note and trying to figure out why he would have sent it to her. After several moments, bemused, Michaela shrugged and went into her bedroom to unpack her weekend bags.

She was there for perhaps ten minutes when, suddenly, a shriek emitted from her room. Not of fright or horror, but a sound of surprise and profound understanding. Michaela raced back into the kitchen, her feet sliding on the tile floor. She snatched up the helmet and hugged it to her chest. She laughed and laughed.

And then, she started to cry.

Cooper sat staring out the office window, deep in thought. He was supposed to be working on the announcements for the Sunday service, but had only managed to get through half of the list. He also would be delivering the sermon on Sunday and had yet to come up with a theme or a selection of hymns to be sung that spoke to that theme. In another month it would be Christmas. Maybe it was a good time to speak about the birth of Christ, separating what would be the start of spiritual salvation from the secular celebration of gift-giving.

His uncle was traveling to Rome with a group of African-American church leaders for an audience with the pope. Reverend Wallace had been looking forward to the trip as an opportunity to meet with Catholic officials and discuss the common grounds between the two faiths, rather than the differences. Cooper had only rehearsed the message a few times alone, always sensitive to his lack of experience. A state that his uncle had frequently assured him was not as important as the growth of his faith.

When his cell phone rang, Cooper was distracted. He was also just finishing the foundation for a new house in North Memphis and was expecting a call from his crew foreman. He'd offered to do the work pro bono in conjunction with Habitat for Humanity. There were whole streets in several communities there that needed attention.

And he was also scheduled to hold tryouts for the senior basketball team, having lost two of the members who had moved to other cities.

But when Cooper looked at the number displayed on his LCD screen, he recognized it as Michaela's.

He'd been waiting for this call, too.

But he was almost afraid to answer. He suddenly realized that his future, his life…his happiness, rested almost completely on the outcome of this call.

It was fine for his uncle to say, put it in God's hands. But Cooper couldn't help a desire, a belief, that he would have as much input in the outcome of the call as the good Lord. Maybe even more because his life was, after all, here on earth.

His cell phone rang a second time.

With a deep breath, he swung around in the chair, away from the window and faced the desk. He found himself leaning on it, as if for support.

Cooper flipped the cell open.

"Smith," he answered in his public voice and customary manner.

"Yes!"

The one word was emotional and loud and emphatic in Michaela's voice.

He couldn't even say anything he was so relieved, so grateful.

"Yes," she repeated.

"Sweet Jesus," he blasphemed, his voice cracking.

"Do you hear me, Cooper Smith Townsend? My answer is yes. A thousand times, yes. I accept your proposal. I'll marry you. Yes…I'll be, most happily, your wife."

Epilogue

Cooper stood a little to the left of Reverend Wallace, more or less facing the gathered guests. Almost directly behind him was his mother. Widowed for three years, he could, nevertheless, interpret the warm smile she gave him. She was, of course, sorry his father hadn't lived long enough to see this moment. And no doubt she was thinking of the very tough and long road he'd traveled to get to this beautiful June day in the chapel on the St. Jude campus. Cooper reflected that his father would have been witnessing more than his son's marriage to the woman he'd chosen to be his wife, he would also have shared in Cooper's redemption.

That's how Cooper himself saw the moment. God's grace was shining upon him. He was humbly grateful.

Besides the presence of both his grandmothers, the rest of the groom's side of the chapel were close friends, including a wide array of professionals from both his present and former career as a licensed architect, and also including Miss Faye and Marilyn Caldwell, as well as some of the kids he coached and mentored.

The bride's side was fuller, which might have scared him a bit if he had not already had a chance to meet and spend time with Michaela's parents during a brief visit to D.C. in the spring. They'd insisted on him staying at their home in Silver Springs, in a comical and unspoken plan to keep him and Michaela apart and away from temptation.

He had met her sister, Barbara, Michaela's maid of honor, who was still called by her childhood nickname, Bindy, her husband and their three children. There was also Michaela's paternal grandparents, her Memphis godparents and several D.C. friends who'd made the trip.

A quartet of three women and one man from his church discreetly took their places about fifteen feet behind the reverend. The gathering immediately quieted down.

Cooper looked to his left, where Eugene Terrance Dunne stood as best man. He was wearing a rented tux, but one that had been fitted to his teen frame. His hair, once cornrowed, was growing out in dreadlocks. He was standing at relaxed attention, his arms straight down with his hands laying one atop the other. Cooper remembered Terrance telling him that was how all the pro players stood.

Cooper was impressed but also moved that Terrance was taking this so seriously. And he also knew that his mature attitude about his place in the wedding had more to do with Michaela than with himself.

He remembered that after she'd arrived from D.C. to stay with her godparents in Chickasaw Gardens until the wedding, one of her first requests was to see ET. It had been simple enough to arrange when Cooper said he'd take the three of them out to dinner. He smiled to himself at the memory because he'd already anticipated Michaela's reaction to seeing ET again, after nearly ten months.

She'd gasped, her eyes wide and bright with pleased surprise.

"ET! Look at you!" she'd exclaimed. "You've grown at least four inches. And you're so handsome."

"Yes, ma'am."

ET had tried hard to look cool, but had instead succeeded in looking bashful and tongue-tied.

He was four months away from turning sixteen. He looked healthy, and very much a typical teen.

Cooper recalled how Michaela had then looked at him, her gaze filled with dozens of questions, and his brief nod responding to all of them. After a rough start with sticking to his medication routine, ET was on a schedule that was working. He'd later told Michaela that ET's T cell count was 325, an excellent level for his condition. He'd gained a little weight. And his voice was changing.

But Cooper knew that there was a far more significant question that Michaela had not voiced about ET's obvious maturing. He had already had that talk with ET, as had Marilyn Caldwell's team at St. Jude. It would have to be repeated as often as necessary. About dating, and how to be safe—and careful.

Delighted as she was to see ET, Cooper was still aware that Michaela had been circumspect about showing her affection. She understood that he would still be cautious about who he gave his to. But that didn't stop her from giving him a quick hug. None of that had stopped ET from hugging her back.

The double doors at the back of the apse slowly opened, and the choir of four quietly began, a cappella, "The Lord's Prayer." Cooper, his eyes riveted to the entrance, waited for his first sight of Michaela since last seeing her, the morning before when they'd gone to Miss Faye's for breakfast, and had sat and talked about their future.

Almost as if by magic, a vision appeared beyond the doorway, approaching at a graceful cadence. He felt a constriction in his chest, overwhelming emotion, as Michaela stood at the door, pausing for a moment for the right note on which to walk down the aisle. The chapel was small; she didn't have far to walk. And he didn't have long to wait.

Cooper couldn't take his eyes from her. His gaze locked with hers, and they might just as well have been the only people left in the universe.

Her hair was swept back and up. The knot was adorned on one side with a gardenia, lush and full. There was no veil covering her hair or face. Michaela's dress was a simple, almost bare, strapless A-line in ecru silk taffeta, without any lace, beading, nets or other adornments. She wore a pair of small, pearl stud earrings and a single strand of Mikimoto pearls around her slender neck. Michaela's small bouquet was made up of more gardenias. She looked regal, even ethereal, and seemed to float toward him.

Cooper could hear and see nothing else for a brief second, suddenly locked in a bubble in which only he and Michaela existed. She took her place next to him and immediately reached to clasp his hand. He couldn't recall if that was part of the tradition. If not, then they were making their own. They stood grinning privately at each other until the choir had ended the hymn and Reverend Wallace began the service.

"We are gathered here today, in the eyes of God, to bear witness to the marriage of Michaela Tyese Landry, to Cooper Smith Townsend…"

Twenty minutes later, they were husband and wife.

Cooper turned to Michaela and she to him. He cupped her face in his hands and kissed her.

Michaela held Cooper's hand as he helped her out of the back of the town car and they entered the Peabody. The world-famous hotel was busy with guests and tourists, but everyone parted as they entered the lobby, making way for them to proceed in grand fashion. Some spontaneously broke out in applause.

The reception was in a function room on the second floor. She and Cooper had allowed time for their guests to arrive first and find their tables. They, in the meantime, had sat with Reverend Wallace privately to finish the formalities of the ceremony, and to receive his blessings.

Reverend Wallace examined the signed and witnessed certificate before slipping it into a heavy vellum envelope. He held it out to Michaela.

"I couldn't be happier for both of you. Guard this well. It seals your life together."

Cooper smoothly took the envelope and placed it into an inside pocket of his formal jacket.

Michaela pouted prettily at him and turned to the reverend. "Did you see that? Already he doesn't trust me not to lose it."

Cooper laid an arm along the back of Michaela's chair and leaned over to kiss her cheek. "Trust is not the issue. Now your hands are free to hold on to me."

As they stared into one another's eyes, his uncle cleared his throat. "So, Michaela. Did you ever find out what your name means?"

She looked sheepish. "I'm sorry. I forgot all about that. Is it important?"

"Let me just say I think it's significant." Reverend Wallace smiled at her, and then glanced at Cooper. "Don't you agree?"

Michaela, puzzled, glanced back and forth between the two men. "Tell me."

Cooper leaned in closer, his fingertips touching her nape and shoulders. "It means, 'who is like the Lord.'" His smile and the light in his gaze were overflowing with love. "Thank you, Lord."

As they walked into the room now, without the fanfare of music to herald their arrival, they were quickly noticed and everyone came to their feet, clapping and cheering.

Michaela beamed at Cooper. He raised her hand, the one with her wedding ring, and kissed it. He twirled her around twice and into his arms, leading her into the first dance. She laughed happily.

To Michaela it was just a big, dress-up, wonderful party. It was fun to be surrounded with her favorite people. She and Cooper got separated often, as they circulated around the room and were congratulated and toasted, and they danced. They laughed at the testimonies and were moved by the loving reception of their families.

The evening for Michaela was a whirlwind of music

and color and hugs and posing for pictures, of champagne, slow dances, best wishes and longing looks exchanged with Cooper. It was memorable. But she wanted to be alone with him.

"Where are you two going for your honeymoon?" Marilyn Caldwell asked.

Michaela had shrugged with a grin. "I don't know. Cooper said he wanted to plan it. It's a surprise, I guess. We're staying here tonight and leaving tomorrow afternoon for parts unknown."

In a pocket of silence she created for herself, Michaela looked at her wedding band with a mixture of awe and joy. Cooper had picked it out in secret, wanting to surprise her. And she had been. It was a narrow white-gold band completely encircled with diamonds all around it—an eternity band. Cooper was taking no chances. He had made his desires and intentions perfectly clear, and she meant with her whole heart to honor them.

She knew that their real life together would begin later, in another way, when they were alone. After the music had stopped, and the guests had all gone home. Michaela's anticipation was heightened as the evening wore on and, one by one, their guests left the celebration.

Finally, in a room on a high floor, where an extravagant arrangement of flowers and yet another bottle of champagne had been given as a courtesy by the hotel, they closed the door on the rest of the world. The bed had already been turned down for the night. Michaela turned silently to Cooper, hoping that the stars in her eyes would express what she didn't think she had enough words to say.

He gathered her gently into his arms and they held each other. Michaela could feel his strong heartbeat, feel his warm breath against her neck and shoulder. He slid a hand up her back to caress her neck. It was tender and titillating. With her eyes closed, she quickly felt the rush of blood through her veins, stimulating her senses.

With her hands placed flat against Cooper's chest, Michaela pulled back so that she could look into his face and his eyes. A slow, teasing smile curved her lips. In a soft whisper she began to sing as she swayed against him.

"'You'll never get to heaven if you break my heart, so be very careful not to make us part. You won't get to heaven if you-ou break my heart…no, no, no.'"

Cooper's rich laughter rumbled deep in his chest. As a response he kissed her, effectively quelling any doubts. There was also something in the gentle passion of their caress that, somehow, dispelled any urgent need to consummate their marriage. As if the ceremony itself was enough.

And after almost a year of building to this moment, there was no more need for conversation. Michaela knew that she and Cooper had the rest of their lives to fill in the blanks. So, smiling into his eyes and feeling herself content, she slowly began to undress him, and he stood willingly. Piece by piece, in silence, laying bare his body with his history permanently stamped with his burns.

Michaela never flinched, freely exploring with her hands out of curiosity…out of love.

Then she stood back and began to undress herself. It didn't take long for her to step out of her things. Cooper carefully removed the fragrant flower from her hair.

They stood before each other, open and at their most vulnerable, but as husband and wife.

There was no hesitation or shyness when they climbed into the king-size bed. They cuddled and curled together, the shock of their bare skin touching an odd relief, familiar and comforting.

They lay in the dark, closer than they'd ever been. Michaela loved the strength she felt in his limbs, loved the heat of his body and his telltale breathing.

"It's after midnight," Cooper murmured. "This is our first night together."

"The start of our first day," she added.

They were both silent as the fact of that sunk in…as if they didn't already know.

"I love you, Cooper."

He gathered her closer to him with a deep sigh, as if he had everything he ever wanted or needed.

That's how they fell to sleep.

Hours later, Michaela sighed and drifted into consciousness. She was aware of every touch point of their bodies, from his chest and stomach, to his hips and thighs. She pressed closer, lifting her face and sighing when Cooper's mouth captured hers. Their kiss was languid and deep and endless until they were both fully awake, and could see the predawn light through the curtains.

They had come full circle.

What had seemed effortless between them the summer before now became unbearable as their desire took over and demanded satisfaction. She was ready.

But Cooper refused to be rushed. He continued to kiss her with titillating thoroughness until her breathing was labored and she felt her body go soft with longing.

"Cooper," she whispered against his mouth.

"I know," he answered, his voice low.

Michaela undulated against him, feeling his body respond in kind.

His hands took the same liberties with Michaela that she had with him the night before. They held nothing back, finally free to love as God had designed.

On the bed they moved together, a sensual tangle of limbs and hands and lips. Michaela lay ready, wanting Cooper to finally possess her, to make it permanent and meld their bodies, as their spirits and souls had been in the church earlier the day before. She greedily wanted all of him, and she intended to leave her mark on his heart forever.

With her eyes closed and her breathing heavy, she let Cooper learn her body, find his way, fill her, claim her. It was an ancient dance, instinctive and natural. She wrapped herself around him, holding him, until they began a free fall together through space. And when they finally landed, Michaela experienced a profound sense of peace, love. It was far richer for having waited.

They held on to each other, silently kissed and kissed and embraced and fell to sleep again. Michaela turned into Cooper's arms, her head on his shoulder, their legs entwined, one thought filling her heart with peace and joy.

"'What God has joined let no man put asunder...'"

* * * * *

Dear Reader,

Thank you for taking the time to read my novel, *For All We Know,* a romance with a message. I hope you enjoyed the story of Michaela and Cooper, whose moral centers are part of the driving force of the book. The message in the story is that we need to protect and care for those in our communities least able to care for themselves...*our children.*

Besides the love story, the secondary subject of my book concerns a serious, life-threatening disease that is decimating African-American lives—HIV/AIDS. The statistics are both frightening and heartbreaking for something that is *totally* preventable. According to a recent article, seventy-eight percent of our teens are becoming infected annually with HIV. Sixty-eight percent of African-American women are becoming infected, and over seventy percent of children in treatment for HIV/AIDS at St. Jude Children's Research Hospital in Memphis are African-American. These numbers should be unacceptable to all of us.

I feel an imperative and a responsibility to get the word out, especially to Black women, and I hope my book will serve as a cautionary tale—as well as a story of hope—to take care of ourselves, our bodies...our children.

I hope you've enjoyed *For All We Know.* I hope you'll embrace its important message.

Regards,

Sandra Kitt

NOVELS OF LOVE & HOPE

SUPPORTING ST. JUDE CHILDREN'S RESEARCH HOSPITAL

No child should die in the dawn of life.
These powerful words represent the dream
of one man, Danny Thomas, the founder of
St. Jude Children's Research Hospital.

I ask you today to join me in keeping Danny's
dream alive by becoming a Partner in Hope.

Let's work together to make Danny's dream a
reality and support St. Jude's in the fight against
childhood cancers, sickle cell disease and
pediatric HIV/AIDS.

Please visit
www.novelsofhope.org
for more information.

ARABESQUE®

Thanks,

Sandra Kitt

KPSKI040908B

What Matters Most

ESSENCE BESTSELLING AUTHOR
GWYNNE FORSTER

Melanie Sparks's job at Dr. Jack Ferguson's
clinic is an opportunity to make her dream
of nursing a reality—but only if she can keep
her mind off trying to seduce the dreamy doc.
Jack's prominent family expects him to choose
a wealthy wife. But he soon realizes he's fallen
for the woman right in front of him…. Now he
just has to convince Melanie of that.

*Coming the first week of October
wherever books are sold.*

ARABESQUE®

www.kimanipress.com   KPSKI040908C

All work and no play…

SUITE
Temptation

Acclaimed Author
ANITA BUNKLEY

When Riana Cole kissed Andre Preaux goodbye to conquer
the San Antonio business world, Andre had given up without
a fight. Now, years later, they are reunited, and memories
of delicious passion come flooding back. Andre is
determined to get her back, but this time he's negotiating
for one thing only—her heart.

"Anita Bunkley's descriptive winter scenery, likable,
well-written characters and engaging story make
Suite Embrace very entertaining."
—*Romantic Times BOOKreviews*

Available the first week of September wherever books are sold.

KIMANI
ROMANCE

KPAB0800908

Essence Bestselling Author

GWYNNE FORSTER

BeyondDesire

Pregnant and single, Amanda Ross needs
a husband *fast* if she has any hope of keeping
her new promotion. Embittered divorcé
Marcus Hickson said he would never marry
again—but when Amanda offers to pay his
daughter's medical bills if he marries her, he
agrees to a "strictly business" arrangement. But
long days and nights under the same roof soon
ignite an affair of the heart...and a deception that
endangers everything they hold dear.

"Only a gifted writer such as Gwynne Forster can
coordinate these elements while literally making
words dance on the page."
—*Affaire de Coeur* on *BEYOND DESIRE*

*Coming the first week of September 2008,
wherever books are sold.*

ARABESQUE®

www.kimanipress.com

KPGFI090908